Jonathan Tropper is the author of the novels *Everything Changes*, *The Book of Joe* and *Plan B*. He lives with his wife, Elizabeth, and their children in Westchester, New York, where he teaches writing at Manhattanville College. *How to Talk to a Widower* has been optioned by Paramount Pictures, and *Everything Changes* and *The Book of Joe* are currently in development as feature films.

Jonathan can be contacted through his website at www.jonathantropper.com.

By Jonathan Tropper

The Book of Joe
Everything Changes
Plan B
How to Talk to a Widower

How to Talk to a Widower

Jonathan Tropper

An Orion paperback
First published in Great Britain in 2007
by Orion
This paperback edition published in 2007
by Orion Books Ltd,
Orion House, 5 Upper Saint Martin's Lane
London WC2H 9EA
An Hachette Livre UK company

A CIP catalogue record for this book is available from
the British Library.

Printed in Great Britain by Clays Ltd, St Ives plc

The Orion Publishing Group's policy is to use papers that are
natural, renewable and recyclable products and made from wood
grown in sustainable forests. The logging and manufacturing
processes are expected to conform to the environmental regulations
of the country of origin.

www.orionbooks.co.uk

For Alexa Rose,
who hangs with me
in the wee small hours
With love

Acknowledgments

Writing is a lonely profession, so thank you to all of the people who keep me company along the way:

Lizzie, of course, for all that you do and all that you are; Spencer and Emma, a whirling tag team of love and bedlam; my parents, for your unflagging support...Simon Lipskar, because you get me and you get me paid, and all the good people at Writers House...Kassie Evashevski, my guardian angel in the city of lost angels, and everyone at Brillstein-Grey...The irrepressible and unstoppable Phil Raskind and all of his troops at Endeavor...Danielle Perez, she of the soft tongue and sharp mind, Nita Taublib, Irwyn Applebaum, Patricia Ballantyne, and everyone else at Bantam Dell...Wendy, Mark, and Tobey...Sara and John...A thick chunk of this book was written in the library at Manhattanville College, so thanks to Jeff Bens for providing such a fantastic place in which to write and teach...Marc Moller, for taking the time to share his considerable expertise...Dr. Hal Klestzick and Dr. Abe Schreiber, for keeping me medically accurate...Maja Nikolic and Matt Caselli for getting it done overseas...Jon Wood, Genevieve Pegg, Timothy

Sonderhusken, Martine Koelemeijer, Elisabetta Migliavada...
David Adelsberg at Softsphinx, for designing my Web site...
My friends and family at Coda... All of the book clubs that have
invited me to sit in with them, and all of the readers who have
emailed me over the years. I hope you all like this one.

No animals were harmed in the writing of this book.

How to Talk to a Widower

1

RUSS IS STONED. YOU CAN SEE IT IN THE WHITES OF his eyes, which are actually more of a glazed pink under the flickering yellow porch light, in the dark discs of his dilated pupils, in the way his eyelids hang sluggishly at half-mast, and in the careless manner in which he leans nonchalantly against the pissed-off cop that is propping him up at my front door, like they're drinking buddies staggering out into the night after last call. It's just past midnight, and when the doorbell rang I was sprawled out in my usual position on the couch, half asleep but entirely drunk, torturing myself by tearing memories out of my mind at random like matches from a book, striking them one at a time and drowsily setting myself on fire.

"What happened?" I say.

"He got into a fight with some other kids down at the 7-Eleven," the cop says, holding on to the top of Russ's arm. And now I can see the lacerations and bruises on Russ's face, the angry sickle-shaped scratch across his neck. His black T-shirt has been stretched beyond repair and torn at the neck, and his ear is bleeding where one of his earrings was snagged.

"You okay?" I say to Russ.

"Fuck you, Doug."

It's been a while since I last saw him, and he's cultivated some facial hair, a rough little soul patch just beneath his bottom lip.

"You're not his father?" the cop says.

"No. I'm not." I rub my eyes with my fists, trying to gather my wits about me. The bourbon had been singing me its final lullaby, and in the freshly shattered stillness, everything still feels like it's underwater.

"He said you were his father."

"He kind of disowned me," Russ says bitterly.

"I'm his stepfather," I say. "I used to be, anyway."

"You used to be." The cop says this with the expression of someone who's tasted some bad Thai food, and gives me a hard look. He's a big guy—you'd have to be to hold up Russ, who at sixteen is already over six feet tall, broad and stocky. "You look young enough to be his brother."

"I was married to his mother," I say.

"And where is she?"

"She's gone."

"He means she's dead," Russ says contemptuously. He raises his hand and lowers it in a descending arc, whistling as it goes down, and then hissing through his teeth to generate the sound effect of an explosion. "Buh-bye."

"Shut up, Russ."

"Make me, Doug."

The cop tightens his thick fingers around Russ's arm. "Keep quiet, son."

"I'm not your son," Russ snarls, trying in vain to tear himself away from the cop's iron grip. "I'm not anybody's son."

The cop presses him easily up against the doorpost to quash his flailing arms and then turns back to me. "And the father?"

"I don't know." I turn back to Russ. "Where's Jim?"

Russ shrugs. "Down in Florida for a few days."

"What about Angie?"

"She's with him."

"They left you alone?"

"It was just for two nights. They'll be back tomorrow."

"Angie," the cop says.

"His father's wife."

The cop looks annoyed, like we're giving him a headache. I want to explain everything to him, show him that it's really not as screwed up as it all sounds, but then I remember that it is.

"So the kid doesn't live here?"

"He used to," I say. "I mean, this was his mother's house."

"Look," the cop says wearily. He's a middle-aged guy, with a graying caterpillar of a mustache and tired eyes. "Whatever he's been smoking, I didn't find any of it on him. My shift is just about over, and I have no desire to spend another hour processing the kid over a stupid parking-lot scuffle. I've got three boys of my own. He's being a hard-ass now, but he cried in the squad car and asked me to bring him here. So this is how it works. I can take him to the station and write him up for a handful of misdemeanors, or you can let him in and promise me that it will never happen again."

Russ just stares sullenly at me, like this is all my fault.

"It will never happen again," I say.

"Okay, then." The cop releases Russ, who whips his arm away violently and then bolts into the house and up the stairs to his room, shooting me a look of unrefined hatred that pierces the blubber of my drunken stupor like a harpoon.

"Thank you, Officer," I say to the cop. "He's really a good kid. He's just had a tough year."

"Just so you know," the cop says, scratching his chin thoughtfully. "This isn't the first time he's been in trouble."

"What kind of trouble?"

The cop shrugs. "The usual stuff. Fighting mostly. Some vandalism. And he's obviously no stranger to the weed. I don't know your deal here, but someone needs to start enforcing a curfew, and maybe get him some counseling. The kid is headed for trouble."

"I'll talk to his father," I say.

"Next time, he gets booked."

"I understand. Thanks again."

The cop gives me a last skeptical look, and I can see myself through his eyes, bedraggled, unshaven, bloodshot, and half crocked. I'd be skeptical too. "I'm sorry about your wife," he says.

"Yeah," I say, closing the door behind him. "You and me both."

Upstairs, Russ has crawled under the covers in the darkness of what used to be his room. Everything is just as he left it, because, as with just about every other room in the house, I haven't disturbed anything in the year since Hailey died. The house is like a freeze-framed picture of the life we once had, snapped in the instant before it was obliterated. I stand backlit in the hallway, my shadow falling on the bends and folds of his comforter as I try to come up with something to say to this strange, angry boy to whom I am supposed to somehow feel connected.

"I can hear you breathing," he says without lifting his face off the pillow.

"Sorry," I say, stepping into the room. "So, what was the fight about?"

"Nothing. These assholes just started talking shit to us."

"They go to your school?"

"Nah, they were older guys."

"I guess it's hard to put up too much of a fight when you're stoned."

"Right." He rolls over and lifts his head to sneer at me. "Do you really feel like you're the best person to give me a lecture on the evils of drugs, Captain Jack?"

I sigh.

"Yeah. I didn't think so," he says, rolling back onto his pillow and burrowing his face into his arms. "Look, it's been a long fucking night, so if you don't mind..."

"I lost her too, Russ," I say.

He makes a sound into his arms that might be a derisive snort or a smothered sob, I can't quite tell. "Just close the door on your way out," he whispers.

You never know when you're going to die, but maybe something in you does, some cellular consciousness that's aware of the cosmic countdown and starts making plans, because on the last night of her life, Hailey surprised me by wearing a blood red dress, cut low and tight in all the right spots. It was almost as if she knew what was coming, knew that this would be our last night together, and she was determined to keep herself from fading too quickly into the washed-out colors of memory.

I couldn't stop looking at her, my eyes dwelling for longer than usual on the familiar curves and contours of her body, still lithe and toned after one child and almost forty years, on the soft pockets of her exposed clavicles, the satiny white surface of her skin, and I wanted her in exactly the way you generally don't want someone you've been sleeping with for almost three years. I found myself considering the practical implications of sneaking away from the table to meet in the bathroom for a quickie, pictured us in the confines of the locked bathroom, chuckling at our audacity between deep kisses as I pressed her up against the wall, the red dress pulled up over her waist, her smooth bare legs wrapped around me, pulling me into her. That's what happens when you spend enough years living on your own with premium cable.

But even as the mental image aroused me to the point of discomfort beneath the table, I knew it wasn't going to happen. For one thing, there was no way for both of us to slip away inconspicuously. For another, I was twenty-eight and Hailey almost forty, and while I liked to think that our sex life was good, better than most probably, quickies in public restrooms were no longer part of our repertoire. Actually, they'd never really been part of it to begin with, since I'm somewhat germ phobic, and the thought of exchanging fluids in the presence of all that random bacteria would be more than I could handle.

On the drive home, my hand slid higher and higher up the

smooth vanilla expanse of her bare thigh, and by the time we'd pulled into the garage she was in my pants. I pulled up her dress in the darkness and bent her over the hood of the car, still hot and pinging from the drive, and then we were hot and pinging and we were teenagers again, except we were good at it, and we actually owned the car.

We must have been trailing afterglow like fairy dust when we came into the house a short while later, because Russ paused his video game, gave us a funny look, and then shook his head and told us to get a room. "No need," Hailey said, grabbing my hand and heading for the stairs. "We've already got one."

"Gross!" he said and, having rendered his judgment, went back to nonchalantly annihilating the undead on the widescreen. And Hailey and I went upstairs to break the laws of God and the state of New York, and we went at it deliriously, with a renewed passion, kissing and licking and drinking and devouring each other. Like there was no tomorrow.

We'd been married for just under two years. I had left the city and moved in with Hailey and Russ, into the small Colonial she'd lived in with her first husband, Jim, until she found out he was cheating on her and kicked him out. And I was still getting used to the transformation, to being a husband in suburbia instead of a prowling dick in the city, to being a stepfather to a sullen teenager and the youngest member of the Temple Israel softball team, to dinner parties and backyard barbecues and school plays. I was still getting used to all of that when she got on a plane to see a client in California and somewhere over Colorado the pilot somehow missed the sky. And sometimes that life we were only just starting seems as tenuous to me as a fading dream, and I have to convince myself that it was actually real. *I had a wife,* I say to myself, over and over again. *Her name was Hailey. Now she's gone. And so am I.*

But we're not going to talk about that right now, because to talk about it I'll have to think about it, and I've thought it to death over the last year. There are parts of my brain that are still tirelessly thinking about it, about her, an entire research and development department wholly dedicated to finding new ways to grieve and mourn and feel sorry for myself. And let me tell you, they're good at what they do down there. So I'll leave them to it.

2

MOST DAYS, WE GET RABBITS ON OUR LAWN. SMALL brown ones, with gray speckled backs and white tufts like frayed cotton around their hindquarters. Or, more accurately, most mornings *I* get rabbits on *my* lawn. There is no *we,* hasn't been *we* in over a year. Sometimes I forget, which is odd because usually it's all I can think about. It's my house. My lawn. My fucking rabbits.

It's supposed to be charming having rabbits on your lawn, a selling point, incontrovertible proof that you've made it out of the city and into the rarefied country air of suburban Westchester. We may be driving enough minivans and SUVs to singlehandedly melt the polar ice caps, may be retrofitting our stately eighty-year-old homes with enough fiber optic cable to garrote the planet, may be growing Home Depots, Wal-Marts, Stop & Shops, and strip malls like tumors on every available grassland, but we've got these rabbits, scurrying back and forth across the lawn like a goddamn Disney movie, so case closed. We are one with nature.

New Radford is pretty much what you'd expect from an upper-middle-class suburb. You've read the book, seen the movie. It's all here. The original masonry homes, Tudors and Colonials from the 1930s, housing expanding families and imploding marriages, German luxury cars positioned in driveways like magazine ads, bored-looking kids dressed in the faded palette of Abercrombie & Fitch congregating nefariously in parking lots, morning commuters loaded like cattle onto the Metro-North trains into Manhattan, minivans and midlife crises dotting the landscape like freckles. On every block, scores of immigrants in creaking pickup trucks with wooden sidewalls built up over the beds arrive every morning to landscape, keeping the lawns trim and fertile, the hedges along property lines tall and proud.

It's no doubt these lush lawns that are to blame for the burgeoning rabbit population. Once in a while I'll actually see one emerge from the hedges and scamper across the grass, but usually I find them already poised on their haunches in the middle of the yard, still as statues, their little nostrils vibrating almost imperceptibly, as if they're tapped into some minor electrical current running beneath the lawn. I find that that's usually the best time to throw things at them.

Bugs, Thumper, Roger, Peter, Velveteen. I name them after their storied counterparts and then I try my best to brain them. Because they remind me of where I am, marooned out here in this life I never planned. And then I get pissed at Hailey, and then I get sad about being pissed at her, and then I get pissed about being sad, and then, never one to be left out, my self-pity kicks in like a turbine engine, and it's like this endless, pathetic spin cycle where all the dirty laundry goes around and around and nothing ever gets clean. So I throw things at the rabbits. Small rocks mostly—I keep a stash stacked like a cowboy's desert grave on the front porch—although, in a pinch, I've been known to throw whatever is on hand: the odd unopened beer can or a gardening implement. I once threw an empty Bushmills bottle that landed neck down in the grass with enough force to stay planted for a few days, like a whiskey sapling.

Oh, calm down. It's not like I've managed to hit one of the little buggers yet. And they know it too, barely moving when my missiles hit the lawn three feet behind them or a yard to the left. Sometimes they'll cock an ear, other times they'll just look at me, daring me, mocking me, trash-talking with their beady rabbit eyes. *Is that all you got? Shit, my grandmother throws harder than that.*

Energizer Bunny, Playboy Bunny, Easter Bunny, Harvey, Silly-Rabbit-Trix-Are-For-Kids Rabbit, White-Rabbit-With-The-Pocket-Watch from *Alice in Wonderland*. I'm sitting on my front porch, stone in hand, taking aim at the one that's wandered onto the driveway, when my cell phone rings. It's my mother, calling to make sure I'm coming to a family dinner celebrating my little sister Debbie's upcoming wedding.

"You're coming for dinner," she says.

There's no way in hell I'm coming for dinner.

"I don't know," I say. The rabbit takes a tentative hop in my direction. Harvey. I draw a bead on him and throw my stone. It goes high and wide and Harvey doesn't even dignify it with a sideways glance.

"What's not to know? You're so busy all of a sudden?"

"I don't really feel like celebrating."

Debbie is marrying Mike Sandleman, a former friend of mine, whom she had the great fortune to meet in my house while I was sitting shiva, which was something I hadn't really intended to do. I've never been much of an affiliated Jew—Ben Smilchensky, who sat at the desk next to me at Beth Torah Hebrew School, used to bring Batman comics that we would slide between the pages of our Aleph-Bet letter books, and that was pretty much the beginning of the end for me. It seemed absurd to start being religious now, at the very moment that God had finally tipped his hand and revealed that he didn't actually exist. I knew because I was there, standing beside Russ at the cemetery, watching from miles above as Hailey's coffin was lowered on two handheld cloth belts. Even floating way up there, I could hear the creak and scrape of the coffin as it bumped against the hard rock sides of her freshly hewn grave, and then the sharp thuds of the flint-laden earth hitting the dry, hollow wood as they shoveled in the first few mounds of dirt. She was underground. My Hailey was underground, in a gaping wound of a grave in the Emunah Cemetery just past the reservoir, a half-mile from the Sprain Brook Parkway, where we used to drive in the autumn to see the leaves change colors. Hailey jokingly called it "foilage," and that became our own little word for it. And now she was underground and I knew I would always think of it as foilage and autumn would always hurt, and I'd probably have to move out west, someplace where they had fewer seasons.

So don't talk to me about God.

But my twin sister Claire insisted that the shiva ritual would be good for Russ, and I may not believe in God, but I believe in guilt and no one wants to dick around with eternity, even if it isn't there. So we sat shiva, and it was as bad as I'd anticipated, sitting there all day with Russ, asses sweating against the vinyl seats of the low mourner's chairs provided by the Hebrew Burial Society, nodding and pursing my lips at the endless parade of rubberneckers through our living room: friends, neighbors, and relatives offering lame conversational gambits from flimsy plastic catering chairs, before heading into the dining room to grab something from the buffet. Yes, there was a buffet: bagels, lox, salads, poached salmon, quiche, and gooey Hungarian pastries, all donated by friends of Hailey's from Temple Israel. Grief can be catered just like anything else.

And there was my kid sister Debbie, treating the shiva like a SoHo bar, dressed to the nines in short skirts and push-up bras that raised the rounded tops of her medium-sized breasts above the horizon of her V-neck sweaters like a couple of rising suns. At the best of times, no one wants to see their sister's breasts, but there was something particularly offensive about watching her wield them like cocked weapons in my house of mourning. And that's how it came to pass that she got busy in the den with my buddy Mike, so you'll forgive me if I'm not terribly invested in their happiness. If Hailey hadn't died they never would have met, and now their whole happy future together, their marriage, their kids, will all be the result of Hailey's death, and while I can rationally accept that this doesn't make them exactly complicit in her death, they're still reaping the benefits, and it just seems wrong to build your whole life on the cornerstone of someone else's cataclysm.

"It's not about celebrating," my mother says. "It's about spending time with your family."

"Yeah," I say, keeping my eye on Harvey. "I'm not really up for that, either."

"That's a terrible thing to say to your mother."

"That's why I went with the celebration line first."

"Ha," she says. She is one of those people who actually say "Ha" instead of laughing, like she speaks in comic-strip balloons. "If you can be a wiseass, you can come for dinner."

This is what passes for logic with my mother. "I don't think so."

She sighs, and the way she does it makes me picture the word "sigh" in faint print, hanging above her in another comic-strip balloon. "Doug," she says. "You can't be sad forever."

"I think maybe I can."

"Oh, Doug. It's been a year already. Don't you think it's time you got back out there?"

"That's right, Mom. It's only been a year."

"You never leave your house."

"I like it here."

There's no sense explaining the value of self-pity to someone like my mother. You either get it or you don't. Everyone deals differently. My mother, for instance, takes pills, little yellow ones that she transfers into a small, faded Advil bottle which she keeps in her purse at all times. I don't know what they are and she'll never tell, since to her, medication is like incest, a dark family secret that must be kept from the neighbors at any cost.

Claire named them Vil Pills, since the "Ad" had long ago been rubbed off the label from my mother's constant handling. Back in the day, Claire and I would nick a few Vil Pills from her bag and wash them down with wine to get high. If my mother ever noticed she was short a few pills, she never said anything. And with my father writing the prescriptions, which he could still do back then, she had an endless supply.

"There's no talking to you when you're like this," my mother says.

"And yet, you keep talking."

"So I'm concerned. Sue me."

"I'd settle for a restraining order."

"Ha ha. There's no authority on this planet higher than a mother's love."

"How's Dad?"

"He's having one of his better days, thank God."

"That's good."

"How's Russell?"

"He's okay. I haven't seen him in a few days." Not since the cops brought him to my door, stoned and bleeding and hating my guts.

"That poor boy. You can bring him if you like."

"Bring him where?"

"To dinner. What are we talking about?"

"I thought we'd moved on."

"It's *you* who needs to move on."

"Yeah. I'm going to move on right now, Mom. Good-bye."

"Debbie will be devastated if you don't come."

"Somehow, I think Debbie's perfect life will go on."

She knows better than to touch that one. "Just tell me you'll consider it."

"That would be lying."

"Since when do you have a problem lying to your mother?"

I sigh. "I'll consider it."

"That's all I ask," she lies back. She starts to say something else, but I can't hear her anymore because I've just fired my cell phone at Harvey, who has finally wandered out of the shadow of the giant ash tree on my front lawn. I miss the rabbit and hit the tree, and my cell phone explodes on impact, sending plastic shrapnel flying across the lawn. The rabbit looks at me like I'm an asshole. And my mother is probably still talking, even though no one can hear anymore.

3

MY MOTHER WARNED ME NOT TO MARRY HAILEY. She also told me when I was five years old that I would contract an incurable venereal disease from the toilet seats in public bathrooms, and that the exhaust from passing buses would turn my lungs black if I didn't hold my breath, and that fast food was generally made out of processed rat meat. So by the time I was twenty-six, which is how old I was when I told her I'd be marrying Hailey, there were credibility issues.

"You positively can't marry her," she told me over dinner, her thin eyebrows bowing under the weight of her conviction.

I had taken the train from Manhattan up to Forest Heights to see the folks and share the good news that their historically most useless child was actually going to be getting married. They weren't taking it well.

"It will be an unmitigated disaster," my mother said despondently, clutching her wineglass so tightly I worried it might shatter and cut her spa-softened hands.

"You barely know her."

"I know enough. She's too old." My mother had been a moderately acclaimed stage actress back in the day, nominated for a

Tony award for her portrayal of Adelaide in *Guys & Dolls,* and even though the last *Playbill* in her scrapbook was older than me, like most retired thespians, she had never actually stopped acting. She was always enunciating, always projecting, always selling it to the cheap seats, her eyes wide and expressive, her mouth forever poised to break into some concrete emotion to which she could finally commit.

"She's only thirty-seven."

"A thirty-seven-year-old divorcée. What every mother dreams of for her son!" Divorcées were only slightly higher than pedophiles on my mother's extensive checklist of defective people.

"Her husband was screwing around," I said, annoyed by my defensive tone.

"And why do you think that is?"

"Oh, Jesus, Mom, I don't know. Because he's a dick?"

"Doug!" my father said reflexively, waving his hand demonstratively across the dinner table, in case I'd missed it. "We're eating." This would be as much participation as we could expect from him, and you would think the chief urologist at a major New York City hospital could handle the word "dick" with his dinner.

"Sorry, Dad. I didn't mean to wake you over there."

"Don't speak to your father like that."

"Don't speak to me like this."

"Like what?"

"Like I'm a child. I'm twenty-six years old, for Christ's sake."

"There's no need to be vulgar."

"I thought the situation called for it."

My mother downed her Merlot like a whiskey shot, absently

holding her glass out for my father to refill. "Stan," she said wearily, "say something to him."

My father put down his fork and chewed thoughtfully on his London broil, thirty chews per swallow. When I was a kid, I would count them to myself to pass the time, placing silent wagers that this would be the night he only chewed twenty-nine times. I never won, and that's as good an illustration of my luck as anything else. Even betting against myself, I could always find a way to lose.

"You're not exactly known for your sound decision making, Douglas," my father said.

Okay. Here's what I've learned. You can live your life being nice to everyone, you can be a loving son, a moderately decent student, never do hard drugs or impregnate anyone's daughter, be an all-around good guy and live in harmony with all of God's creatures. But crash one stolen Mercedes in front of the police station when you're fifteen years old and they'll never let you forget it. My mother was scandalized, terrified about what the neighbors would think, although in this case she was somewhat justified since it was actually the neighbor's car, but that's why you pay for insurance, right? If you never file a claim, then they've beaten you.

"And you're not exactly famous for your emotional support," I responded to my father.

"I take issue with that, Doug."

Stanley Parker did not get pissed. He "took issue." He was an Ivy League–educated doctor, trim and fit at sixty-five, with lush silver hair and gold-rimmed spectacles, clinically aloof despite his deceptively warm Mentadent smile. I had no memory of ever being hugged by him. He did shake my hand heartily at my college graduation, though, and I still had the photo to prove it.

"Listen," I said, wishing I'd paid heed to my earlier instincts telling me to stay home and phone it in. But these were the same instincts that had led me to believe that taking the neighbor's Mercedes on a joyride would get me laid, and they hadn't been right then nor had they gotten any wiser in the intervening years, so I'd gotten into the habit of basically ignoring them. "I love Hailey and what we have works. She's beautiful, she's smart, she's a great mother, and she's heads above what I ever thought I could have found for myself."

My mother let out a horrified gasp and the wine in her glass sloshed over the rim, staining the tablecloth red. She should really stick to Chardonnay when I'm around. "She has a child?" she croaked, placing her hand against her chest, closing her eyes and taking labored breaths, like she'd just been stabbed.

I smiled. "Congratulations, Grandma."

"Sweet Jesus!" she wailed.

"Yeah," I said, getting up to leave. "I had a feeling you'd say that."

The last thing I heard as I fled the house was my mother angrily berating my father, like the whole thing was his fault. "Stanley," she cried, "it's going to be an absolute train wreck," inadvertently proving one of her favorite axioms that even a stopped clock is right twice a day.

4

How to Talk to a Widower
By Doug Parker

I lost something after Hailey died. I'm not sure what to call it, but it's the device that stops you from telling the truth when people ask you how you're doing, that vital valve that keeps your deeper, truer emotions under lock and key. I don't know exactly when I lost it, or how to get it back, but for now, when it comes to tact, civility, and discretion, I'm an accident waiting to happen, over and over again.

Socially, this makes me something of a liability.

I was standing at the prescription counter at CVS the other day, stocking up on more sleeping pills, when I ran into a friend of Hailey's. "Doug," she said, coming over and grabbing my forearm, the diamonds on her eternity band scratching at my skin like the teeth of a small animal. "I've been meaning to call. How are you doing?"

And I know the script, I've studied my lines. I'm supposed to say I'm doing fine, or okay, or some days are better than others, or as well as can be expected, and I swear, I opened my mouth to say something like that, but instead I held up the orange prescription bottle and said, "I take all these fucking pills, and I still can't fall asleep at night, so I take more pills and then I have nightmares that I can't wake up from because the fucking pills won't let me, and when I finally do wake up I'm even more tired than before, and it's not like I want to wake up, because when I do, I just think about Hailey and I want to go back to sleep again. How are you?"

And she looked nervously up and down the aisle, plotting her escape, and I felt bad for her, but I felt worse for me, so I just shook my head and waved to her like she was across the street instead of close enough for me to see the dark open pores in the skin under her eyes, and I left the store.

That sort of thing happens all the time now.

My sister Claire says I do it on purpose, that it's my way of keeping people at bay, and I guess there might be something to that, but I swear I don't mean to do it. It just bursts out of me without warning, like a sudden, violent sneeze.

A few weeks ago, a Jehovah's Witness or a Jew for Jesus or some other freak on happy pills selling God in a pamphlet showed up at my door, smiling like a cartoon, and said, "Have you let God into your life?"

"God can fuck himself."

He smiled beatifically at me, like I'd just compli- mented his crappy JCPenney suit. "I once felt the way you do, brother."

"You're not my brother," I hissed at him. "And you have never felt like this. If you'd ever felt like this, you would still feel like this, because it doesn't go away. And you definitely wouldn't be knocking on strangers' doors with that big, shit-eating grin on your face!"

"Hey!" he said, alarmed. "Let go of me."

And I realized that I had grabbed him by his skinny tie and pulled him into me, that we were nose to nose and I could see my spittle where it had landed on his chin, that he was barely out of his teens and he was scared. I let go and told him to go away, and he scam- pered down the steps like a kicked dog. I felt bad for him, but then he shouted "Fucking asshole!" and flipped me the bird, and normally that would have been funny, but it's been a while since anything has been funny. At least he would have a war story to tell the other God reps over coffee and donuts back at their holy headquarters.

And just the other day I was in Home Depot picking up some lightbulbs when I saw a couple around my age looking at paint chips. She was pretty and petite and he was wiry and balding and they were both wear- ing khakis and they were quietly in love. They were talking about the room they were painting, about the color of the carpet, the couches, and the wood of the armoire that housed the television, and the woman had brought one of the curtain ties with her to match, which is what Hailey would have done, and I watched them, showing each other chips, holding them against the curtain tie, and I pictured them back in their taupe room, sitting on their mushroom-colored couch watching television, tangled up in each other. And I was thinking that they could lose each other tomorrow, that one or both of them could be dead before the fresh paint on their walls had dried, and the woman looked at me with alarm, and I realized that I'd said it out loud. And the husband stepped forward like he was going to start something with me, although I guess, technically, I'd already started it, but then he just reached into his pocket and handed me a crumpled tissue and that's when I realized that I was crying.

But it's been a year now, and my family and friends seem to think that's the shelf life on grief, like all you need is one round through all of the seasons and then you're tapped like an empty keg, ready to start living again. Time to get back out there, they say. And so my mother calls me regularly, pimping out the latest girls she or her friends have come upon in their travels. But, honestly, what kind of bottom-feeder wants to go out with a depressed twenty-nine-year-old widower with no real career or goals to speak of? I picture strange, skinny women in shapeless peasant dresses, with large glasses and multiple cats that they talk to like children.

Or else they're sad, heavy women, nervously cheerful and self-deprecating, sweating through their foundation as they troll the bottom of the dating barrel in their ongoing quest for an orgasm that doesn't rely on double A batteries. Or they're divorcées, damaged, mistrusting man-haters looking for a new spittoon for their bile, or else drowning in fear and loneliness and ready to grab hold of the first man that might possibly share their bed and mortgage payments. And then there are the fetishists, vampires who feed on the blood of grief, who want to lick the tears off my face and absorb my immense sadness into their own swollen hearts, and while that might get me laid sooner than expected, I've become quite possessive of my grief, actually, and I'm not really up for sharing it.

So even if I was ready, which I'm not, I've still got to face the age-old problem of not being willing to belong to any of the clubs that would have me as a member.

5

THE SKY IS FUCKING WITH ME. IT'S ONE OF THOSE militantly perfect spring days, the kind that seems to be trying just a little too hard, the kind you want to smack in the face, and the sky is bluer than it has any right to be, really, an obnoxious, overbearing blue that implies that staying home is a crime against humanity. Like I've got anywhere to go. The neighborhood is alive with gardeners mowing lawns and trimming hedges, the mechanized hiss of twirling sprinklers and for those just joining us, it's a beautiful day and Hailey is dead and I have nothing to do, nowhere to be.

I'm picking the plastic shards of my cell phone out of the grass when a dark, battered Nissan with tinted windows pulls up to the curb. Angry, discordant hip-hop music and a thick cloud of stagnant cigarette smoke pour out through the open door as Russ climbs out. He's tall and beefy like his father, dressed in baggy shorts, flip-flops, a faded *Battlestar Galactica* T-shirt, and an iPod strapped to his arm. Hand slaps are executed and cheerful obscenities shouted over the music. A half-filled Slurpee cup comes flying out an open back window, spilling across the sidewalk like blood spatter at a crime scene. Russ smiles and hits the roof as the car speeds off, tires screeching as it rounds the corner. I listen for the crash, but none comes. Russ has fallen in with a bad crowd these days: self-mutilators with veiled eyes under pierced eyebrows, long, messy hair and fake IDs, kids who drive around aimlessly at night, seeking out opportunities for random vandalism, hanging out in empty parking lots, getting drunk on cheap beer, blasting obscure punk rock, and talking about all the assholes in their high school. I know I should try to do something about it, especially in light of the incident with the police a few days ago, but grief and self-pity are a draining occupation, and multitasking has never been my thing.

"Hey," Russ says, walking up the lawn, pulling his headphones off his ears to rest around his neck. His long messy hair, the same honey color as Hailey's, falls like a veil over his big dark eyes. It's been almost a week since his fight in the parking lot, and the cuts on his face and neck have faded to faint pink lines.

"Hey," I say.

"Sorry about the other night," he says. "I was a little fucked up."

"I thought you'd stick around the next morning."

"You were still sleeping at nine," he says with a shrug. "Is that your cell phone?"

"It was."

"Good shot. If you were aiming for the tree, I mean."

"I was aiming for a rabbit and hit the tree instead."

He nods sagely. "It happens."

I get up and head back to the porch, stuffing the guts of my demolished phone into my pocket. "Shouldn't you be in school?"

"So what, you're like my father now?"

"I'm just making conversation."

He looks at me and shakes his head. "And I'd love to answer you, I really would, but you gave up the right to ask those kinds of questions when you banished me to go live with Jim and Angie."

"I'm sorry about that, Russ, but Jim is your father. There wasn't very much I could do about it."

"So you say," he says. "He hates me. He'd be thrilled if you took me."

"You know that's not true."

"You know it is."

From the start, I knew Russ preferred me to his father. I also knew that this was primarily a function of the fact that I had the good sense to not get caught on tape with my pants around my ankles screwing an old girlfriend, and then all but abandon Hailey and him in favor of a shiny new family the way Jim did. So while Russ was hardly thrilled when I moved in three years ago, if nothing else, I had the advantage of being the lesser of two assholes. And my parents thought I'd never amount to anything.

It's a tricky enough business forming a friendship with a pissed-off teenager under the best of circumstances. Now try it when you're sleeping with his mother, when you are, quite literally, a motherfucker. Let me tell you, that requires a whole other skill set. When I first moved in, I knew I'd have to make an effort to bond with Russ so that Hailey could feel good about the whole arrangement. If she didn't, it wasn't like she was going to give her kid the boot. Last one hired, first one fired. And so I applied myself like a laid-back uncle, giving him lifts to school or the mall to meet his friends, taking him to the occasional weeknight movie, editing his term papers, and, more recently, taking him out for driving practice in my secondhand Saab. I was a lazy boy and I am a lazy man, and the beauty of the situation was that I wasn't really expected to be a parent to Russ, which, based on the limited wisdom I have to offer, was a win-win situation for all involved. Once we both figured out that neither wanted anything more from the other than easy cohabitation with no strings attached, we got along just fine.

But when Hailey died, what did he expect me to do, petition for custody? I know Jim is bad news, but I am too. I'm twenty-nine years old, for God's sake, and I'm sad and pissed and lazy, I'm drinking too much and at some point I'm going to work up the nerve to sell the house and blow this town, and I can't really do that if I've got Russ to worry about. He's better off this way, believe me. The kid will have a few million dollars in trust from the airline settlement, so he just needs to stick it out with Jim until he turns eighteen and he'll be home free.

"You should hear what goes on over there at Casa Jimbo," Russ says. "I knew he was a horny bastard, but, dude, it's like living on a porn set. The minute they get that little step-bastard to sleep they just start going at it, for hours. My room is right under theirs, and it's like they never stop. And Angie yells all this shit while they're fucking, like 'fuck me harder, fuck me harder,' and I'm sitting down there watching the ceiling shake and thinking that if he fucks her any harder the two of them will come right through the ceiling and land in my bed, and believe me, I have been traumatized enough and I do not need that kind of shit." He runs his fingers through his shaggy hair, pulling it off his face, and I see a splash of color on the side of his neck.

"What'd you get, a tattoo?" I say, trying not to sound alarmed.

"Yeah," he says, looking away.

"When did you do it?"

"Last week."

"Let me see it."

He pulls back his hair to reveal a blue tadpole-shaped squiggle trailing around the bend of his neck, surrounded by orange comic-book flames. And I know it shouldn't make me sad, I know that these days tattoos are just another accessory, like thumb rings and wrist cuffs. Oscar-winning actresses have Buddhist texts scribbled across their backs. Every girl in low-rise jeans has a floral design or a butterfly hovering over her ass crack. But still, the idea of something so permanent on this sad, angry sixteen-year-old brings a lump to my throat. That, and knowing how much it would have hurt Hailey to see it. Hailey, who was practically inconsolable the first time Russ shaved his peach-fuzz mustache. But still, it's not like he can take it back, so there's nothing to do but be supportive.

"Nice," I say weakly.

"What is it?" Russ challenges me.

"Flaming sperm?"

"Fuck you."

"It's a meteor."

"It's a comet," he says.

"What's the difference?"

"How the fuck should I know?"

"Okay, then. It's a comet."

He rubs it protectively. "It's Hailey's comet."

The tears come to my eyes so fast, there's just no way to stop them.

"I know the real one is spelled differently," Russ says, suddenly self-conscious. "But I just kind of liked the image, you know. Hailey's comet. And she was always on my back about how bad my spelling is, so it's kind of fitting, in a way."

And now I want to cry, and hug him, and go out and get my own tattoo, all at the same time. But doing any of that would require more of me than I have in stock these days, so instead I just look away and say, "That's cool, Russ. She would have liked it."

"She'd have yelled and cried and grounded me for a year."

"Maybe. But secretly, she would have loved it."

"No," Russ says, shaking his head. "She wouldn't have."

I think about it for a moment, and then nod slowly. "Yeah, I guess you're right. But I still think it's a nice tribute."

"I did it because I knew she would hate it."

I try to look wise, like the kind of guy who might actually know what he's talking about. "Well, even though you can't see it now, it's still a tribute to her."

"Doug?"

"Yeah."

"You are so full of shit."

I sigh. "Tell me something I don't know."

He snorts derisively and produces a bent joint, seemingly out of thin air, and then rummages around in his pockets for a lighter.

"Could you please not do that in front of me?" I say.

"Why not?"

"Because I'm your stepfather, and it's irresponsible."

"I wonder," he says. "Do you retain the title even though you didn't defend it? I mean, Mom's dead, and we're in a kind of gray area here, legally speaking. Now, if you were my legal guardian—"

"Fine," I say. "Fire it up. Just spare me the lecture."

He lights up, sucking so hard that I can hear the crinkling whisper of the immolating paper, and we sit there quietly in our little Hallmark moment, my stoner stepson and me. "You know," he says thoughtfully after a few minutes, "if you think about it, he's only my father because he happens to have fucked my mother."

"Right. You know, that's actually something I try really hard never to think about."

"All I'm saying is that by those standards, you're equally qualified. More so, actually, since he demonstrated poor moral character."

"Yeah," I say. "And I'm a paragon of virtue. That's why you're getting high right in front of me."

He shrugs. "So you're progressive."

"I'm an asshole."

"Preaching to the choir," he says emphatically, pointing to his head, and even though I know he's just busting my balls, it hurts anyway. What can I say? I've got sensitive balls.

He passes the joint in my direction, but I shake my head. "Pass."

"Bullshit," he says. "I stole this from your stash."

"Russ," I say softly, turning to stare right at him. "If you hate me so much, why do you come here so often? And why did you ask that cop to bring you here the other night?"

He looks up to meet my gaze, but by then I've looked away. I have not been able to sustain eye contact with anyone, strangers and loved ones alike, ever since Hailey died. I'm not sure what that's about, but there it is. Russ shakes his head at me, his face contorting angrily as he fights back the tears. "This was my home, man," he says. "You just got here, and . . ." His voice cracks and he says, "Shit," and turns away.

"Russ," I say.

"Forget it," he says. "I just came by to apologize for the other night. It won't happen again."

"I don't want to forget it." I reach out to him, but he hurls himself out of the porch swing, flicking the joint away in disgust. "What's going on with you, Russ?"

"Nothing. Life's a fucking dream. I gotta go."

"I wish you wouldn't."

"Yeah," he says, stepping off the porch. "Well, when was the last time one of us got what we wished for anyway?" He heads down the driveway, pulling on his headphones to drown out the world with the angry soundtrack of his life, and all I can do is what I always seem to do, watch him go.

I don't believe in heaven or God or an afterlife. I don't believe that Hailey's gone to a better place, that she's an angel watching over me from above. I believe her soul was obliterated in the same instant her body was, when her plane hit the mountain at three hundred miles per hour and crumpled like an empty soda can. But as I sit sprawled worthlessly on the porch, eyes closed, sucking the last few puffs out of Russ's discarded joint, I can feel Hailey so strongly that it momentarily stops the breath in my smoke-filled throat and makes the hairs stand up on the back of my neck. *Hey, babe,* I say to her in my mind. *Is that you I feel, or just the hole where you used to be?*

But then the moment is gone, and it's just me again, sitting on my porch rocker, lazily getting stoned in the middle of this stupidly beautiful day. I watch my sad, angry stepson growing smaller and smaller as he heads down the street and think of Hailey's comet, flaming against his skin, and wonder how badly it hurt to get it. I watch him until he disappears, and then I stare up unblinking into the ridiculously blue sky and I do too.

6

LANEY POTTER SHOWS UP AROUND NOON TO DROP off a meatloaf for my dinner. Hailey's friends set up a rotation in the weeks after the crash, and while I've long since convinced most of them that it's no longer necessary, Laney, who had Tuesdays, has yet to relinquish them. As soon as she arrives, she puts her meatloaf in the fridge and hugs me, kissing my cheek on her way in. She holds me tightly against the full length of her body, not at all the way a married woman should hug a single man, and she touches me a lot when she talks, asks me if I'm doing okay, and she would love it if I would just fall apart in front of her, so that she could hold me and comfort me. Laney is a rowdy redhead, big boned and curvy, with the bee-stung lips of a porn star, and a husband named Dave, a lawyer about fifteen years older than me. At thirty-four, she was the only other spouse in our circle from my generation, and she'd always been somewhat flirty with me, in a harmless, joking way, like we were in this together, but lately she's turned things up a few notches. Nothing that couldn't be explained away if it backfired, but there's a pointed invitation in these comprehensive hugs of hers.

"You don't look too good," she says, pulling back from her embrace, but not yet releasing me, her lower body still incidentally pressed up against mine.

"I've been looking at pictures and crying." It's not what I mean to say, but it's what comes out anyway. It's such a strange condition I have; I can't look anyone in the eye for more than a second or two, but ask me a simple question and I'll pour my heart out uncensored. When Laney rang the doorbell, I'd been lying on the living room floor going through a shoebox of pictures of Hailey and me—we hadn't gotten around to albums yet—waiting for the last bits of afternoon sunlight to stop pouring through the windows to illuminate the galaxy of floating spores, so that I could legally break out the Jack Daniel's.

"Poor Doug," Laney says, pulling me back into her embrace, and I can feel her hardened nipples, like two sand-smoothed pebbles against my chest, can smell her skin in the hollow of her neck, that earthy scent unique to redheads, and I actually find myself thinking about opening my mouth against her neck, running my tongue against her skin, and seeing what will happen. It's been a shitty, shitty day, and the idea of undressing the voluptuous and seemingly game Laney Potter, of losing myself in the folds of her soft dimpled flesh, is suddenly very appealing. I can tell that she'll be an energetic lover, that she'll be loud and wild and without boundaries of any kind, and when was the last time I had that kind of sex? I haven't gotten laid in a year, and maybe a little slap and tickle with Laney Potter would be just the thing to cheer me up.

But even as I feel myself growing hard against her, even as I feel her heartbeat accelerating in her chest and her breath against my ear becoming more pronounced, I know it would be a mistake. She'll start coming over every week, maybe even more than once a week, and before I know it we'll be in some twisted relationship, and then she'll start complaining to me about Dave and how she's thinking of leaving him, and so I'll have to start avoiding her, which won't be easy since I never leave the house, and all of this because in a moment of weakness I mistook my own immense loneliness for garden-variety horniness.

"I'm sorry," I say, stepping out of her embrace. "I'm a little out of it today."

"Can I do anything?" she says, her face ever so slightly flushed, her eyes flitting anxiously around the kitchen.

"I think I'll just have some dinner and go to bed."

"I hate to think of you all alone here when you're not feeling well. You want me to stay for a while?"

She's talking and I'm talking, but there are other conversations going on, between our carefully averted eyes, our nervously animated hands, and our throbbing groins, and that's just too many conversations for me to follow. It's like blasting the radio while you're watching television, vacuuming, and talking on the phone.

"No, I'm fine," I say, walking ahead of her toward the door. "Really. I just need to get some sleep."

"I can tuck you in," she says, and I can feel her eyes on my back.

"It's okay. Thanks."

At the door, she hugs me again, and this time I kiss her cheek, ridiculously proud of myself for having resisted the temptation.

I've never slept with a married woman, less out of principle than because it simply never came up, but something tells me that now would be a bad time to try it. Dave Potter, Laney's husband, is a lawyer in private practice and partners with Mike Sandleman, the man who will be marrying my sister Debbie in a few weeks. Did you follow that? The interconnectedness of everything? Your wife dies dramatically and your life becomes a goddamn soap opera.

Still, Laney has those ridiculously sexy lips, like two tapered pillows glossed to a slick sheen, and since I'm not going to sleep with her, I don't see the harm in letting the corner of my mouth accidentally graze them as I kiss her cheek. "Thanks for everything, Laney."

"I'm always here, Doug, for anything you need," she says meaningfully, looking into my eyes before she goes. "You know that, right?"

"I do."

Her smile is a naked confirmation that something is happening between us, that it's there for the taking. And I feel the smallest pang of regret as I watch her get into her car, can still feel the soft fullness of those lips on mine. I don't know why she's offering herself up to this possibility, could be that her marriage is lousy, could be that she's lonely, or bored, or that Dave is as dull in bed as he is out of it, but whatever the reason, I think the wisest course is to maintain the status quo. Because, ultimately, I would just have to break it off and she'd feel used and I'd feel bad, and while I don't know exactly how it would all play out, I'm pretty sure it would mean the end of Tuesday nights with Laney Potter. And in the final analysis, I think I would miss her meatloaf more than anything else.

Still, I'm bummed when she's gone. I want to touch someone, to kiss and lick and suck on them and hear them writhe and surge beneath me. I want to taste the tart sweetness of a woman's mouth, want to be naked and sweating and tangled up in the hot wetness of Laney Potter's heaving thighs.

"I'm horny," I complain to Claire over the phone. We talk every day.

"And you feel guilty about it."

"I guess."

"Don't."

"Okay. I'm glad we had this talk."

"I'm serious, Doug. It's perfectly natural. Everybody fucks."

"It seems kind of soon."

"To get married, maybe. To date, possibly. But to get laid? That's purely physiological. It's no different than taking a dump."

"Somehow, I've never connected the two."

"It's exactly the same thing. Something building up inside of you that needs release."

"It just doesn't seem right."

"Get over yourself, little brother. If some horny hausfrau is willing to make booty calls, then pick up the damn phone and get busy. You spent the better part of your life wishing you had a number to call for something like that. Well, now you do."

"It can't end well."

"It hasn't even started and you're already worried about the ending," Claire says exasperatedly. "Look at it this way. The first few times you have sex, it's going to suck. You're like a born-again virgin, carrying all this emotional baggage. You'll have trouble keeping it up, or you'll come too soon, or not at all, and you'll get all depressed afterwards. So you might as well get all that shit over with now, so that it's out of your system by the time you meet someone real."

"Thanks for the confidence booster."

Claire laughs. "It's what I do."

I sigh. "She's a married woman."

Claire sighs right back at me, mimicking my resigned tone. "You live in New Radford, little brother. That's pretty much the only kind you'll find there."

Claire is my twin sister and the voice inside my head, whether I like it or not. She was the first person I called when Hailey died. Well, that's not exactly true. I called my mother first, sort of. It was the middle of the night and the airline had just called to tell me about the crash, and I didn't even remember dialing the phone.

"Hello?" my mother said, her voice still thick and syrupy with slumber. "Hello?" I could hear the darkness in her bedroom, the heavy silence I had just shattered. "Who is this?"

I couldn't speak. To speak would be to grant entry to the angry mob of my reality now protesting at my embassy gates. "Hello?" she said one more time, and then she said, "Creep," and hung up on me.

Hailey was dead and my mother thought I was a creep. It's the little things you know you'll always remember.

Somewhere, in a field or a forest, the wreckage was still smoking, with luggage and body parts and charred, twisted sections of fuselage scattered all around. And somewhere, in the midst of that carnage, lay my Hailey, the same woman I had kissed good-bye only a few hours ago, the same cascading mane of blond hair, the same long legs she used to wrap around me, the same wide, knowing eyes, button nose, and thin sensuous lips I could never get enough of, they were all there, in some random place, as inanimate as the crushed and burned debris all around her. It just didn't seem possible. I understood it to be true, but I wasn't getting it.

The guy in the mirror looked like he might be getting it; his face was pale and drawn, and there was something pulsating behind his eyes, some glimmer of horror that had not yet radiated out to twist his expression. But I felt nothing. I ran a quick test on the guy in the mirror. I smiled at him. He flashed back the lopsided smile of the mentally deranged. Then I made us look horrified, and then sad, like I was practicing for some Method acting class, where a bunch of skinny dweebs sit around applauding each other's exaggerated expressions while some never-been Gloria Swanson type offers meaningless critiques between puffs on her cigarillo. Hailey was dead, and I was fucking around in the mirror. I'd always felt unworthy of her love, and if I ever needed validation of my unworthiness there it was, staring me right in the face.

"Hailey is dead," I said aloud, my voice filling the room like an audible fart at a dinner party. Normal people reacted violently to calls like this, didn't they? They screamed anguished denials and fell to the floor sobbing, or pounded the wall in a blood-red haze until they could no longer tell if the cracking sounds were coming from the dented wall or their broken fists. But all I could do was stand beside the bed, rubbing my neck and wondering what the hell to do. I supposed I was in shock, and that was, at least, a little bit comforting, because Hailey didn't deserve this pathetic excuse for a reaction.

My first instinct was to call someone. My first instinct was to call Hailey. I dialed her cell phone, not sure what I was hoping for. Her voice mail picked up instantly. *Hi, this is Hailey. Please leave me a message and I'll call you back as soon as I can. Thanks, bye.* She'd recorded the outgoing message in the kitchen one night, and in the background, faintly, I could hear Russ and me laughing at the television. I heard the message so many times over the last few years that I had long ago stopped actually hearing it. But now I heard her calm, confident voice, her distracted tone as she hurriedly recorded the message, the faded background noise of her family laughing. She couldn't be gone. She was right there on the phone, sounding every bit like herself. The dead didn't have voice mail. The phone beeped and I realized that it was now recording me. "Hey, babe," I said stupidly, but I couldn't get any more words out, so I hung up.

A terrible, selfish thought entered my mind unbidden, and then another and soon they were coming in droves, one after another, like when you hold the door for one old lady, and fifteen more people decide to walk through and you get stuck there on door duty when all you meant to do was accommodate one old lady.

How I will handle this?
Where will I live?
Will anyone ever love me again?

I pictured Hailey naked, coming through the bathroom doorway, smiling lustily at me as she walked over to the bed. Would there ever be another naked woman smiling at me like that? And even right then, at that terrible moment, I knew there would be other naked women, and I felt ashamed for knowing it. But still, would any of them look at me like she used to?

Also—and this was the worst one, not for the weak stomachs—I felt an undeniable twinge of relief at the knowledge that she would never have the chance to fall out of love with me, that she would love me forever. I felt like a bigger asshole than I'd ever been, and that was saying something.

Hailey is dead. I tried to comprehend it. *She's not coming back. I will never see her again.* None of it meant anything to me. They were just words, nothing more than unproven hypotheses. What was I supposed to do now? *Hailey is dead. Hailey is dead. Hailey is dead.* It seemed important that I grasp this concept in its entirety, so that I could function, do whatever needed to be done.

What needed to be done? I had no fucking idea, but I was highly aware of Russ, in his room down the hall. He was sleeping now, but he would wake up to a nightmare and never sleep the same again. He would never breathe, smile, eat, cry, think, cough, walk, blink, piss, or laugh the same way again, and he didn't even know it, and that seemed particularly cruel and unfair. I already suspected that I would have a harder time facing his grief than my own. I wanted to leave before he stirred, run away and never have to see his eyes fill with the horrible knowledge of his changed life.

What needed to be done?

Keep moving. Call someone. Someone would know what to do.

I picked up the phone again.

"Hello," grunted Stephen, Claire's husband.

"Can I talk to Claire?"

"Doug?" he said drowsily. "Christ! Do you know what time it is?"

"It's one forty-three. I need to talk to Claire."

"She's sleeping," he said firmly. Stephen had never liked me all that much. I'd made an impassioned plea to Claire not to marry him, spontaneously articulating a long, detailed list of all the reasons why he was wrong for her, and he'd taken offense, particularly because I had the admittedly bad sense to incorporate this diatribe into my toast at their wedding reception. In my defense, I was young and there was an open bar.

"It can't wait."

"Is everything okay?"

Hailey is dead. "I just need Claire."

There was a brief, muffled rustling and then Claire came on the phone, sounding all hoarse and confused. "Doug, what the fuck?" Claire's potty mouth was always legendary, and even now, married to one of the wealthiest scions in Connecticut, she clung to it like a precious keepsake from her childhood.

"Hailey's plane went down. She's dead." Finally, I'd said it, and something cold and hard clicked into place.

"What?"

"Hailey's dead. Her plane crashed."

"Oh, Jesus. Are you sure?"

"Yeah. The airline called."

"They know for a fact she was on the plane?"

"She was on it."

"Oh, shit," she said, starting to cry, and I wanted to tell her not to, but I still hadn't cried and I figured somebody should, so Claire cried for me and I listened to her do it.

"I'm coming over," she said.

"It's okay. You don't have to."

"Shut the fuck up. I'll be there in an hour."

"Okay."

"Should I call Mom and Dad?"

"No."

"Stupid-assed question. Sorry." Her breathing grew more labored over the phone as she moved around her room throwing on clothes, telling Stephen to just shut the fuck up. "Where's Russ?"

"Sleeping," I said. "Claire."

"Yeah."

"I don't know what to do."

"Just breathe. In and out. In and out."

"I'm thinking some pretty sick shit."

"You're in shock. Okay, I'm in my car."

Moments later, there was a loud, protracted crashing sound.

"Motherfucker!"

"What was that?"

"I just backed through the garage door."

"Jesus. You okay?"

"I'm fine," she said. "The whole damn door came down. I'll just drive over it."

"Drive carefully."

"Whatever. Listen—" But she forgot that she was on her cordless and not her cell phone, and as soon as she turned out of her driveway she was out of range and the line went dead.

7

THURSDAY AFTERNOON. LANEY'S ENDLESS HUG. SHE generally comes only on Tuesdays, but she tells me she was in the neighborhood.

"You live in the neighborhood," I point out stupidly.

"Exactly," she says, blushing, and it's two p.m. and I've already put away a few preliminary shots of Jack Daniel's, and she's wearing this tight sleeveless blouse and her cleavage is like a warm, inviting smile so I'm not going to quibble. Her breath is hot on my ear, her fingers spread out like a web across the back of my neck, burrowing into my hair, and my face is pressed against the lightly freckled skin of her shoulder. Something's happened with our legs, some trick of positioning, and they've become intertwined even as we stand there, so that I can feel the heat from her crotch through my jeans, and I'm sure she can feel the incipient commotion in my pants as well.

This is wrong, I think.

There is no God, I think.

Hailey, I think.

And then, *There is no Hailey*.

And that's when I pull back and kiss Laney smack-dab on those plump, berry-colored lips, grabbing fistfuls of her red hair just behind her neck, and her mouth has anticipated me, is already open, her tongue snaking easily over mine and through my teeth. The kiss goes on forever. It's many kisses, actually, packaged together like cereal at the price club, a continuous stream of clashing tongues and crushing lips, because if we stop there will be time to think, and no good will come from thinking. No good will come from screwing Laney, either, I know, but when did that ever stop anyone? After Tuesday's close call, Laney came dressed for the kill today, skin tight and low cut in a short skirt, her long Coppertone legs waxed and buffed to a low sheen, and she had me at "Hello."

Hands start flying furiously, like Hong Kong choreography, pressing, cupping, stroking, and squeezing at targets under our clothing. Her fingertips run swiftly up and down my back, sliding under my T-shirt to tear at my skin, and mine slide under her skirt to clutch at the curve of her naked ass. Doesn't anyone wear underwear anymore? Because I do and, frankly, it's about to become a problem. But she unfastens my belt buckle one-handed, her fingers encircling me tightly as my pants and boxers fall around my knees. She tries to mount me right there, backing me up against the fridge, fruit-shaped magnets and outdated calendars falling at our feet. But when has that ever really worked? Laney is my height in her heels, and we just can't find the right angle. I see her eyes dart over to the kitchen table, but I have to eat off that table. The truth is that while I like sex as much as the next guy who hasn't gotten laid in a year, I've learned that, contrary to what you see in the movies, floors bruise and rugs burn, and there's just no substitute for a good bed. Going up to my and Hailey's bedroom is out of the question, so I take Laney down to the guest room off the basement, where she shimmies out of her clothing and spreads her long, toned body invitingly across the comforter, gazing doe-eyed at me, her mouth open like a nested chick waiting for its mother's beak. "Hurry," she says, her voice thick with sex as I get momentarily stuck in my T-shirt. It's the only word either of us will say for the duration.

And it's beyond strange, to be kissing these lips that aren't Hailey's, to be tracing the alien landscape of these unfamiliar breasts, first with my fingers and then my tongue, to be hearing someone else's most private sounds, to be adjusting to the innate rhythm of someone else's rocking hips. I don't know what she likes, and I have no reason to look into her eyes, which must be why I'm avoiding them. Laney is voluptuous, and I mean that in a good way, not the way people will sometimes use it as a euphemism. But still, she's bigger than Hailey in every way, and at first there's something intimidating about her melon-sized breasts, her broad, powerful shoulders, her wider hips. When, after a while, she rolls over to straddle me, I actually experience a passing instant of claustrophobic panic as she lowers her body onto mine. But regardless of the peripherals, the hardware remains the same, and as soon as I slide into her, everything clicks into place. She keeps her open mouth locked on mine the whole time, her tongue darting in and out continuously as she moans to the beat of our rocking bodies, biting down on my lower lip so hard that I can briefly taste my own blood before she licks it away.

And I try not to think of Hailey, I really do, I try to lose my-self in the unmitigated exuberance of Laney's undulations, in how alive and uncomplicated she is in her lust, but even as she cries out loudly, I find myself floating above us, dispassionately observing it all, and trust me, the last thing you want to do is watch yourself having sex. I don't care how attractive you are, you'll still feel like an idiot when you see that stupid expression on your face, eyelids at half-mast, jaw set determinedly, ur-gently humping away like the fate of the civilized world hangs in the balance. Women close their eyes during sex, not to picture Brad Pitt, but just because they don't want to see your stupid-looking mug. The Brad Pitt thing is just a bonus.

When I was sixteen, Claire decided that my virginity was holding me back, so she convinced her friend Nora Barton to sleep with me. Nora was skinny and flat-chested, but willing to do me for "shits and giggles," which made her a perfect ten in my book. We did it in my bedroom, while she was supposedly sleeping over to study with Claire, and for the entire time, all six or seven minutes of it, I remember thinking, *So this is sex, I'm having sex,* over and over again, and wishing that I could stop thinking for just one minute and lose myself in the sensation of it all. And then it was over, and Nora tiptoed back to Claire's room so they could laugh themselves to sleep talking about me, and a half hour later I was sitting in bed mournfully handling my resurgent erection, wondering why I hadn't felt anything.

Hailey is dead, and I'm having sex. And maybe it's the strange-ness of the situation—I'm screwing the neighbor's wife in my basement—or maybe it's Hailey, whose naked body suddenly fills my eyes like tears, but it's Nora Barton all over again, and I could swear that I don't feel a thing, like my groin was injected with Novocain, even as I hear my own moans growing louder and more frequent.

Afterwards, we lie side by side and she runs two fingers up and down my slick back, kissing my face softly as I taste the light sweat on her neck. "Doug," she whispers tentatively, after a long, long while.

"Laney," I say, and the air around us grows heavy.

"Nothing," she says after a pause, which is perfect because, really, that's all there is to say. And because she said that, and only that, I feel a surge of warmth and gratitude toward her, so I kiss her. And because I kissed her, she kisses me back, those impossibly full lips absorbing my thinner ones, her teeth gripping, her tongue probing. And because of that, I move my fingers between her damp thighs, and she rolls onto me to run her tongue over my nipples, and in no time we're at it again. And because she's more comfortable now, she guides my lips down to exactly where she wants them to be and her moans are louder, her hips bucking with reckless abandon. And because of that, I am able to lose myself in her, in her flesh and smells and taste. And because of that, this time I actually feel it when I come. Because, because, because. Because Hailey is dead, I am fucking a married woman in the basement. Because I don't care anymore. Because I'm lonely and horny and drunk. Because, because, because.

Because I'm fucked anyway.

Laney leaves me with deep lingering kisses and meaningful glances that promise she will be back soon. "Today was magical," she whispers into my ear. "I wish I could come back later, make love all night, and wake up in your arms in the morning." But she can't. Because I need some time to absorb this, to reflect on it and torture myself about it, and because I get the creeps whenever anyone says "make love" instead of "have sex," or "fuck." Hailey never said "make love." It's just goofy.

And now Laney has to go home and start getting dinner ready for her husband and children, and I have to crawl back into this rumpled bed and be alone as the first tears come, burying my head in this pillow that smells of sex and still bears a few stray auburn hairs. The sobs come, heavier now, racking my body, slicing through me like hot blades. I never cheated on Hailey, never even thought about it, so the fact that I just had sex with someone else must mean she's really, truly gone. And I already knew she was gone, but now my body knows it too, and it's like finding out all over again. I'm sorry about Laney, not because it was wrong, but because I already know we'll do it again, and it's just one more step into a life without Hailey, one step further away from her. And so is every day and every night, and even this empty, sexed-out sleep, falling on me now like a cartoon anvil, driving all coherent thought from my mind.

8

LISTEN. I NEVER ASKED FOR ANY OF THIS.

I'm only twenty-nine years old, for God's sake. My story should be one of those urban romantic slacker-finds-true-love-and-grows-up comedies, not this random, senseless tragedy. Just over three years ago I was living in my little studio apartment in the West Village, going out to the bars with my friends, getting drunk and laid and fired from dead-end writing jobs with the same relative frequency. I never could have fathomed that I'd be widowed and living alone in New fucking Radford, in a house I didn't buy, mourning the dead wife that never should have been mine to begin with.

You know guys like me, there's one of me in every crowd, the laid-back wiseass who's never going to amount to very much. I used to imagine that I was like Rob Lowe in *Saint Elmo's Fire,* minus the saxophone, but as I got older I came to understand that Rob Lowe could pull it off only because he looked so much like Rob Lowe. I looked a little too much like Doug Parker, and last I heard, Demi Moore wasn't losing any sleep trying to figure out how to share a bathtub with me.

I was the kid about whom teachers always said he's a bright boy, if only he'd apply himself, the kid who could always be counted on to decimate classroom decorum with a well-timed one-liner, the one who always took the joke just a little too far. My parents heard this so consistently about me at parent-teacher conferences that they stopped going altogether after a while, choosing to accentuate the positive by focusing on the stellar achievements of my sisters. Claire was a notorious slut, but smart enough to get into Yale, where she slept around prodigiously, leaving her bed just long enough to earn an advanced degree in clinical psychology. Then she surprised us all by marrying the interminably boring Stephen Ives, heir to the Ives Lawn Manure fortune, and was now devoted to the business of being an obscenely wealthy housewife. You could almost hear the click of the switch when she powered down her brain and tossed her career, but as far as my folks were concerned, all was forgiven when she married the horseshit heir.

Debbie, three years younger than us, seemed to understand from an early age that all of my parents' hopes and dreams were pinned on her, and she didn't disappoint. She was a straight-A student, the kind who whiningly appealed every less-than-perfect test score to teachers who ultimately caved just to shut her up. She graduated Harvard Law School with honors and is already on the partnership track at a Manhattan firm whose name generates instant nods of approval among those in the know. She has a spacious office with a view of the Hudson River, her own secretary, and textured linen business cards with raised silver lettering. Somewhere along the way, though, she discarded her sense of humor, probably because there would never be a test on it, and now her laughs are rare and her smiles often rushed and vaguely pained, which is a shame because she was a beautiful girl and smiling had always suited her when she was younger. She's still beautiful, but now it's the kind of beauty that comes with a barbed wire fence around it.

Not cut out for the Ivies, I just barely scraped through the State University of New York with a bachelor's in English, leaving me perfectly qualified to do absolutely nothing that would earn me a living. As far as I knew, there were no essay portions at job interviews, and, that being the case, there hardly seemed any point in trying. So while my friends all splurged on pin-striped Brioni suits and joined investment banks and hedge funds, I bounced around a few PR agencies, writing inconsequential press releases and getting fired for a wide range of corporate delinquency. At one agency, I decided that I was going to re-create my work cubicle, item for item, in my apartment. Every day I would steal office supplies, from Post-it pads and pens to staplers, secreting them out of the office like Tim Robbins and his tunnel dirt in *The Shawshank Redemption*. I brought a gym bag to handle the larger stuff, like the telephone and fax machine. It was the actual cubicle walls that would prove to be my undoing. There was no way to sneak them out, so I waited until after hours and then acted like I was authorized to be taking a cubicle wall down in the elevator. The security guard in the lobby was unimpressed, and the next day I had to sit in a conference room with the head of HR and my flabbergasted boss, Stephanie, watching my criminal enterprise on the building's surveillance tapes.

"I can't believe that's you," Stephanie said, looking away from the surveillance video.

"The camera adds ten pounds," I pointed out.

"Doug," she said miserably, and I could see she now regretted even more having slept with me after a late client dinner a few weeks earlier. She'd worn her heels to bed and commanded me to slap her ass while she rode me like a cowgirl. In the morning she went through all five stages of grief before breakfast and then made me swear I'd never tell a soul. Then, since we were already there, we had sex again, to seal our pact.

"You know I'm going to have to fire you," she said.

I was actually kind of relieved, because my plan to steal the copy machine was proving to be a logistical nightmare.

I had to return everything, but not before I photographed the cubicle I had so painstakingly re-created in my living room. Then I wrote a funny little article about it, which I sold to *M Magazine,* and that's when I discovered magazine writing. I got myself an agent, a high-powered little blowhard named Kyle Evans, who sold my stuff and ultimately landed me a gig at *M,* where I wrote a fairly popular column called "How to Talk to a Movie Star," a loose, comic riff on anything remotely connected to the Hollywood zeitgeist. Plastic surgeries and eating disorders among young actresses, trends in the current crop of summer movies or the fall TV lineup, profiles on up-and-coming actors and directors, you get the picture. Occasionally, I was sent out to Los Angeles to profile somebody famous, and despite my high hopes, I never did manage to sleep with a movie star, although I think I came pretty close once or twice.

I was perfectly content with this easygoing life, making my own hours, hanging out with my buddies, falling in and out of love, and basically waiting for life to begin. Sure, I got lonely sometimes, sunny-Sunday-afternoon lonely, but until I met Hailey, I just never knew what I might be missing.

* * *

Fate. Destiny. God.

It's all a crock.

People want their lives to make sense, want to sit back like cosmic detectives and examine what's happened to them so far, identifying the key turning points that shaped them and retroactively imbuing these moments with a mystical aura, like the celestial forces of the universe are a team of writers on the serialized television show of your life, charged with concocting outrageously convoluted plotlines designed to achieve resolution by the end of the season. No one wants to believe that it's all completely random, that the direction of our lives is nothing more than a complex series of accidents, little nuclear mushroom clouds, and we're just living in the fallout.

As near as I can figure, these were the accidents that shaped my life. If Hailey had never married Jim, then he never would have cheated on her with his ex-girlfriend Angie. And if Jim hadn't forgotten about the nanny cam in the basement playroom, he never would have gotten caught when he did. Since it was Jim who had installed the nanny cam, most shrinks would see this as unassailable evidence that he wanted to get caught, but they just say that because there's no prevailing psychological term for a dumbass. And if Hailey had never divorced Jim, then years later she would not have ducked into what she thought was an unused office to have herself a quick, single-mother cry. It was actually only a mostly unused office. It was mine. And if I hadn't picked that day, of all days, to actually show up for work, I never would have found her there. If I'd met her at any other time, under any other circumstances, she never would have gone for me. Women of her caliber never did. And, knowing my own limitations, I never would have had the nerve to ask her out. But by then, the accidents had built up a momentum all their own, like a tornado whipping through the heartland, and we were sucked up into the twister like a couple of grazing cows.

I stepped into my tiny office at *M Magazine* that morning and there was Hailey, crying at my desk. "Oh," I said, which is what you say when you find a beautiful stranger crying at your desk.

She looked up at me through her tears, blew her nose into a twisted, crumbling tissue, and said, "Can you please come back in a few minutes?"

She was a VP in ad sales, and I was an articles editor and columnist, which meant our paths rarely crossed, but I knew who she was, had already nursed my little office crush on her and moved on. After all, she was beautiful, older, and an officer in the company. But now she was crying at my desk, and there's nothing like a weeping woman to bring out your inner white knight. So I stepped out of my office and closed the door, not only to give her privacy, but also to keep any other white knights from joining the fray, because I was not up for a joust. I took a quick walk and picked up two coffees. I don't drink coffee, but as an old girlfriend once said to me, sometimes you have to fake it for the greater good of mankind. When I returned, Hailey was reapplying her makeup. "Here," I said, placing the cup in front of her and leaning against the wall.

She smiled at me through the last of her tears, and she was

ragged and worried and ever so slightly damaged and that's what you need with a beautiful woman, some chink in her armor that gives you the guts to approach. Otherwise, you just circle like a scavenger, watching the other predators move in. "Thanks," she said, taking a long, grateful sip. "Who are you?"

"I'm Doug," I said. "This is my office."

"Hailey." We shook hands across the desk. Hers were small and soft, her fingernails bitten and unpolished. "I'm sorry about this. I'm just having a bad morning."

I waved my hand. "I just wish I'd known you were coming. I'd have brought donuts. And Kleenex."

She grinned. "I'm usually not like this."

"It's not your fault. I always have this effect on women."

The grin escalated into a full-on smile. It was a killer smile, a warm, piercing humdinger of a smile that I felt in my thighs. Women like this generally didn't smile at me like that. Usually they flashed polite, blinking smiles like hazard lights that said *Keep moving, nothing to see here.* But Hailey said, "I don't want to go to my office."

"So stay here," I said.

"I should let you get back to work."

"If you knew me, you'd know how ridiculous you just sounded."

She looked at me thoughtfully. She had long, honey-colored hair, skin like burnished ivory, and dark almond eyes that opened wide when she spoke and crinkled magnificently when she smiled. "Today is my birthday," she said.

"Happy birthday."

"Thanks."

"Birthdays can be rough."

"Tell me about it."

"How old are you?"

"Thirty-six. And divorced. And mother of an angry twelve-year-old."

"You're only as old as you feel."

"Well, then I'm fifty."

"You look outstanding for fifty."

She smiled. "It's just not what I thought it would be, you know?"

"Thirty-six?"

"Life."

"Ah, life," I said, just like somebody wiser than me might say it. "Don't get me started."

She flashed me a wry grin. "How old are you?"

"I'm twenty-five. But I feel twelve."

She snorted when she laughed, but I liked it anyway, and so I made her do it a few more times, and then she opened up and started to tell me about her divorce and her troubled son, and her bad luck with men. She was thirty-six, divorced, and a single mother. I was twenty-five and still waiting for something to happen to me. We were from two different universes, suddenly thrown together in the twilight zone of my office. It wasn't just that she was too old for me; it was that she was too pretty, too sad, too wise, and altogether too worldly for someone like me. But something had happened, some hiccup in the cosmos, and we could see behind each other's curtains, and we were talking and laughing, and she was smart and funny and vulnerable and just so goddamned beautiful, the kind of beautiful that was worth being shot down over.

"Listen," I said, after a little bit. "We can go on like this all day, but today is your birthday, and in my family, a birthday means one thing, and one thing only."

"And what's that?" she said.

"Great Adventure."

"What, the theme park?"

"So you're familiar with it."

"We're at work."

"I don't know about you, but I won't be missed."

"We can't just leave work and go to an amusement park."

"Normally I would agree. Or I'd pretend to agree so that I seemed responsible. But it's your birthday today. My hands are tied."

"I have a budget meeting at ten-thirty."

"Blow it off. I've never seen someone who needs to ride Nitro as badly as you do right now."

Hailey looked at me for almost a full minute, I mean, really looked at me, like she was studying a map. "I'm eleven years older than you."

"So if I were thirteen, then this would be weird."

She shook off her smile. "Just tell me why?"

"Because the more you talk, the more I like you. And because you're so beautiful that it actually hurts if I look at you for too long. And I'm sure you get asked out a lot, by older, smoother men than me, but they're asking you out because you're good-looking, and there's nothing wrong with that, I mean, you have to start somewhere, but you see, normally that would be exactly why I didn't ask you out, so the fact that I am now means that we've already passed all of that." I took a deep breath. "And because I think you would really like me, if you gave me a chance."

Her face turned red, and she didn't smile like I'd hoped she would, but she didn't look away. She did not look away. "Are you always this honest?"

I nodded. "Almost never."

"But that's honest too."

"I know. It's tricky."

"It's nothing personal, Doug. I've just had some bad luck with men."

"That's because you don't know the secret."

"What's the secret?"

"You have to train us when we're young."

And this time her smile was like a ray of sunlight, the kind that pierces the clouds on an angle and makes you think about heaven. And so we drove her car out to Great Adventure, and we rode Nitro and The Great American Scream Machine and The Batman Coaster and Kingda Ka, and I bought her a funnel cake and a sparkler and sang "Happy Birthday" to her on the Ferris wheel and she kissed me at the top. And sometimes that's all it takes, no epiphanies, no revelations, just funnel cake on a Ferris wheel and one crazy, miraculous day that should never have happened, but somehow did. It was fate, I thought. Destiny. But I only thought those things because I was in love and didn't know any better.

I didn't know about the accidents yet.

9

CLAIRE SHOWS UP IN HER PIMPED-OUT ESCALADE and her Gucci sunglasses and her three-hundred-dollar jeans. It's been a few hours since Laney left, and I've just woken up from a short postcoital nap to sit on the porch and eat Cap'n Crunch out of the box until my teeth are numb. Good sex, bad sex, right sex, wrong sex; I always wake up with the munchies. Claire barrels up the driveway, sending the rabbits scattering in a frenzied panic, and brakes much too hard, so that I hear the high whine of her grinding discs, but she somehow manages to avoid whiplash. She drives the way she lives, with equal parts zeal, impatience, and ineptitude.

"What the fuck, Doug!" she says, marching up onto the porch like she owns the place. I don't take it personally. That's just Claire. Even when we shared a womb, she was in charge. Two minutes older than me, she's walking proof that our DNA is much better executed in the female form, with her flowing mane of dark hair shined to a shampoo commercial gloss, flaw-less olive skin, eyes the color of the evening sky, and a crooked, knowing grin that, when called upon, can effortlessly transmute into a brilliant toothy smile. Our mother wanted her to be in movies, which naturally made it the last thing Claire would ever do. I've got the same hair, skin, and eyes, but on me they all seem randomly placed, like rubber features slapped onto Mr. Potato Head, never quite coming together to form a cohesive whole. Claire says she got the brains and the looks and I got the spare parts in case anything ever breaks down.

"I've been trying to reach you all day!" she shouts at me. "Why don't you answer your fucking phone?"

"I threw it at a tree."

She gives me a look. "Anyone I know?"

"Mom."

She nods. "Next time, just say you have another call and hang up. It works for me."

"I'll try to remember that."

"I tried the house phone too."

"Yeah. I never pick that up."

"No shit, Doug." She fixes me with a stern look. "But you can't go silent on me. Not after what happened."

"Oh, for God's sake. Will you let go of that already."

"You tried to kill yourself."

"I fell asleep in the tub."

"You ODed."

"They were sleeping pills. I just misunderstood the recommended dosage."

"Generally speaking, half a bottle is too much."

"Let it go, Claire. You're worse than Mom. You guys have created this whole myth of my attempted suicide. It wasn't like that. Trust me. I was there."

"Maybe you were there, but you didn't have to watch the cops kick down your front door and pull you out of the tub. You were too busy going into cardiac arrest."

"Enough, Claire."

"You were fucking blue!"

"It was an accident."

She looks away, shaking her head in frustration. The truth is I don't even remember that night. The booze and sleeping pills had scrambled my brain and I woke up in the hospital, strangely euphoric and unable to remember what month it was.

"We'll have to agree to disagree," Claire says, shaking it off. She can do that, change moods like taking off a hat.

"I'll get a new phone," I say, which is the closest thing to a concession I'm going to make on the subject.

"Way ahead of you, little brother." She reaches into her bag and tosses me a colorful box. "It's got a camera and plays movies and picks up your dry cleaning for all I know, and I'm not leaving until you activate it."

"Thanks."

"And no throwing this one. It cost like five hundred bucks."

"Deal."

Having tended to business, she bends over to kiss my cheek. "What's new and exciting in the grief racket?"

"Same old same old."

"Your last column made me cry."

"Sorry."

"No. It was great. Mom's got it on the fridge."

I smile. "Wow. I finally made it back to the fridge."

It was our mother's strict policy that only A-plus work was displayed on her stainless-steel Subzero refrigerator. Growing up, Claire's and Debbie's schoolwork was always plastered all over it, but once I'd moved beyond first-grade spelling tests, I never made it back up there again.

"I guess you get an A in being sad and lonely."

"Top of my class."

She gives me a fond smile and grabs me by the hair to look down at me. There are faint creases at the corners of her eyes that I never noticed before. You see the people you love the way they are in your head, but every once in a while you accidentally catch a glimpse of them in real time, and in those split seconds, as your brain scrambles to adjust to the new reality, small things inside you swerve off the road and drive over cliffs, spinning and screaming all the way down.

"We're getting older," I say.

"Fuck you. I am not." Her eyes narrow into slits. "Hey," she says. "You have the look of someone who's been freshly fucked."

"What?"

"My twin telepathy is telling me that you went ahead and bagged the meatloaf babe."

"We don't have twin telepathy."

"Of course we do, it's just subtle, like . . . flesh-colored nail polish."

I grin. "Like . . . central air."

"Like . . . a white wine buzz."

"Like . . . Mel Gibson's Australian accent in *Lethal Weapon*."

She laughs and then stoops to lower her face directly in front of mine, staring at me nose to nose until I look away. She's the lone person I can look in the eye these days, but even so, in twenty-nine years, I've never outstared her.

"Oh shit, you really did!" she shouts gleefully. "No wonder I couldn't get you on the phone. You were boning the horny hausfrau!"

"Keep it down, will you?" I say, looking around the street.

But Claire's enjoying this too much. "Dougie, you slut!"

I lean back on the porch swing, shaking my head. "What gave it away?"

"Elementary, little brother," she says, sitting down next to me. "There's lipstick on your ear, your T-shirt is on inside out, and you've got a world-class case of bed head."

"Come on," I say skeptically. "I always look like this."

"Well, then, I guess you'll have to reconsider the twin telepathy thing." She grabs some Cap'n Crunch from my box and starts shoveling it into her mouth. "You and the meatloaf babe," she says, starting to laugh. "That is just too funny."

"Hysterical."

Her laugh tapers off and she rests her head on my shoulder, which means she has something to tell me. Whenever she's stressing, that's what she does, and over the years, her head has carved out its own little spot there, like water dripping onto a rock for a hundred years. I always imagine that we must have floated that way in the uterus, and in times of stress it's our version of the fetal position. "Good for you," she says softly, rubbing the fleshy part of my hand between her thumb and forefinger. "I think it's a big step."

"It's adultery."

"You're not married."

"She is."

"With all of your problems, you're going to start worrying

about hers now?" She licks her finger and wipes something, probably some of Laney's lipstick, off my cheek.

"It's my problem too."

"Wrong. Your problem is that you stopped living when Hailey died. An emerging sex drive is the first positive sign we've seen in a long time. It's not a problem, it's cause for celebration, is what it is. I can't wait to tell Mom."

I laugh, but then quickly say, "You're joking, right?" If there's one thing you can be sure of with Claire, it's that you can never be too sure.

"We'll see how nice you are to me," she says with a shrug. "So how was it?"

"I don't know. I think I'm still in shock."

"Dougie, Dougie, Dougie. When will you learn to keep your brain out of your bone?" She sighs. "Sometimes I think I should have been the boy."

"Sometimes I think you are."

"Which actually provides a convenient segue to our next topic."

"Which is?"

"I'm pregnant."

That puts some lift in my eyelids. "That's great, Claire. Congratulations."

She nods against my shoulder. "Thanks."

Then she says nothing, but I can feel her muscles flexing like springs under her skin, her breath short and quick. We just sit there for a few minutes, staring into the yard. There's a gray rabbit nibbling on the grass in the shadow of the hedges. Out of range. "There's more," I say.

"Yup."

I think about it for a minute. "Stephen."

She looks up at me, smiling even as a lone tear emerges from the corner of her eye and slides across the bridge of her nose. "And you said we don't have telepathy."

Then she stands up, shaking it off, and heads for the front door. "Do you have anything to eat in here? I'm starving."

I get up to follow her in, but then, out of the corner of my eye, I notice that the gray rabbit has wandered within striking distance of the porch. "Hello, Bugs," I say under my breath, keeping one eye on him as I reach for the rock pile. My throw goes too high, sailing a foot over Bugs's head, and bouncing soundlessly across the lawn in front of him. The rabbit looks up at me, and something in his dumb, unthreatened expression enrages me, so I make a show of charging noisily down the steps. That gets him moving, and he zips away to the side of the lawn, stopping at the hedges to flash me a pitying look. I'm all out of rocks, so I run at him, waving my arms and screaming like a banshee until he flees into the underbrush. When I turn back to the porch, Claire is giving me a strange look from the doorway.

"I just like to keep them on their toes," I say sheepishly, coming up the stairs.

"Little brother," she says, throwing her arm over my shoulders as we head into the house. "You really need to get out more."

"So what happened?"

"It's a long story."

"You said you have time."

"I can't talk on an empty stomach."

I follow her into the kitchen. "Did you cheat on him?"

"Nice. Adultery loves company, is that it?"

"Did he?"

"I wish."

"So what happened?"

"Why are all the magnets on the floor?" she says, heading over to the fridge. "Oh! Shit. I don't want to know."

"Claire, for Christ's sake! Just tell me what happened already."

She opens the fridge and bends down, noisily sliding jars around, lifting up Tupperware lids to smell things. "Jesus," she says, her voice echoing inside the mostly empty fridge. "Do you ever actually eat?"

"I order in."

She slams the fridge closed. "I can't wait. Let's go out."

"First tell me what happened."

She looks at me, and then sort of collapses gently against the fridge. "Nothing happened. Nothing ever happens. And nothing ever will happen. And that," she says, sinking down to the floor and cradling her head in her hands, "is what happened."

I sit down on the floor beside her. "Have you considered counseling?"

She gives me a look. "I don't need some sterile Freudian with a bow tie and a dirty mind to tell me I should never have married Stephen. You've been telling me that for years. I seem to recall you actually making your case somewhat emphatically at my wedding."

"I was drunk."

"You were jealous."

"Maybe. A little."

"But you were right, of course. And I knew it. Even walking down the aisle, I remember wondering what would happen to the video, to the wedding pictures, when it was all over. How sick is that? The surprise here is not that I'm leaving. It's how long I actually stayed. I always meant to leave him, I just never got around to it."

"Why not?"

She frowns and raises her hands in concession. "You get rich, you get comfortable, you develop all these equations and pie charts to prove to yourself that you're actually happier than you think you are." She shrugs. "I fell asleep at my post."

"So why now?"

"Well, after Hailey died, I started seeing everything differently. I mean, you were a mess—you still are, by the way—and I would think of you sitting out here alone, all grief stricken and disconnected from everyone, and this is going to sound horrible, but instead of feeling sorry for you, I was actually envious of you. You were miserable and alone and I was fucking jealous. Because there's something beautiful in grief, isn't there? It's like mourning is your chrysalis and when the time comes you'll be reborn as this beautiful butterfly. And then I had to ask myself, when you start feeling envious of your fucked-up, bereaved brother, what does that say about you?"

"That you're deeply disturbed?"

"That you're even more fucked up and heartbroken than he is, you just don't know it."

"And now you do?"

"Now I do."

"Listen, Claire, I know that losing your wife in a plane crash and drinking yourself to sleep every night may seem somewhat glamorous, but just between you and me, it's really not all it's cracked up to be."

She gives me a shove. "You know what I mean."

"I'm not sure I do yet. Get to the part where you get knocked up."

She laughs softly and leans the back of her head against the fridge. "The irony of the whole thing is that we barely even have sex anymore. It's nothing less than a miracle that I haven't cheated on that man, a horny chick like me. It was just this one night, this anomaly, where he had no late meetings, and no calls to make, and there was nothing on TV, and I guess we were both bored, so we had sex. It was that or cleaning out my closet. And it was nothing special, believe me. I mean, I forgot about it as soon as it was over. But then, a few weeks later I was late, so I took a test and imagine my surprise..."

"You're sure the test was right?"

"I took five tests."

"Okay."

"So I'm sitting there in the bathroom, washing the pee off my hands, and it just hits me that I'm going to be a mother and now this is all I'll ever be. Mrs. Stephen Ives, just another rich, bored housewife, a sad cliché. And I don't want to be Laney Potter, screwing other men just to feel alive again for a few hours."

"Thanks for that."

"No offense."

"None taken."

"I thought maybe I could stay here for a while."

"Sure. The guest room's yours."

The fridge vibrates gently against our spines as we sit on my kitchen floor, talking quietly while twilight falls like a curtain over the windows. I can hear the sounds of kids in front yards, urgently attending to childhood affairs, shouting and laughing, young and untouched and thinking they'll always be that way. When we were kids, whenever I was sad, Claire would put on this white chef's hat and concoct ridiculous ice cream sundaes that we would then force ourselves to finish. Banana splits with chocolate syrup, Jell-O and gummy bears, hot fudge sundaes floating in root beer, quadruple-scoop ice cream cones with marshmallow fluff between each scoop. Half the fun was watching her dart madly around the kitchen, randomly selecting ingredients as she narrated the process in her best Julia Child voice.

"Remember the funny sundaes?" I say.

Claire rests her head on my shoulder, turning her face into my neck, and quietly starts to cry.

10

How to Talk to a Widower
By Doug Parker

Because of this newfound tendency I've developed of unleashing rapid-fire bursts of raw, unadulterated pain—my emotional Tourette's—and because I can't stand to be the object of anyone's pity other than my own, I pretty much stay home these days.

The only downside to this system is that the house is a minefield and I never know when I'm going to step on a latent memory of Hailey and get my legs blown off. Even after all this time, she's still everywhere. On her night table still rests the last book she was reading, some chick lit thing with a lipstick pink cover about overweight, smart-assed women and the men who cheat on them, and when I pick it up, I see that she doodled on the last page she read, a bug-eyed cartoon man with a handlebar mustache and evil eyebrows, and it makes me smile, but even as I do, I can feel the tears start to come.

I had a wife. Her name was Hailey. Now she's gone. And so am I.

Or in the bathroom, her red bra still hangs on the doorknob. She'd no doubt meant to toss it in the hamper but never got around to it. That's something I taught her, to let simple household tasks percolate for a little bit, to do no chore before its time.

I move through our bedroom like a ghost, careful not to disturb the haphazard evidence of her existence; the book, the bra, the hairbrush still filled with knots of her blond hair, her perfume and cosmetics scattered across the sink top, the water ring from a sweating glass of water she'd put down on her dresser, the silk blouse laid out across the chair next to her bed that she'd decided at the last minute not to pack for her trip, the frayed stuffed elephant named Bazooka that she kept wedged between her pillow and the headboard ever since she was a little girl. For a while after she died, I didn't even change the sheets because they still smelled of her. Then they stopped smelling of her and, after a few more weeks, they just smelled like ass. And that's as good a metaphor for grief as any of the thousands of others that occur to me on a daily basis. You cling desperately to every single memory, and in doing so the memories themselves grow stale and turn, like the sheets on my bed.

Still, it hurt when I changed the linens, was just one more way of moving Hailey into the past tense, one more step across the inevitable divide, and I can't bring myself to straighten up, because every little thing I remove or clean up is one more trace of her that I will immutably erase. I want to put up stanchions and red velvet ropes, like they do in historical mansions to keep the tourists from screwing with the past, because, given the chance, that's what we'd all do.

Like on my seventh-grade class trip to Philadelphia, on a dare, I scooted quietly up some roped-off stairs in Benjamin Franklin's house. I figured I would cement my place in history by taking a leak in old Ben's toilet. I got caught and hustled from the building, and was sentenced to spend the rest of the afternoon on the bus. The driver was cool, though. He bought me McDonald's and let me look through the extensive and well-preserved *Playboy* collection he kept in a cardboard box under his seat, forever linking in my mind the Liberty Bell and the puckered lips and conical, airbrushed breasts of April's playmate of the month. Her name was Janelle and she liked rock climbing, water sports, and men who weren't afraid to sweat. The point being, there are some things that should just stay roped off.

But as bad as the house is, I rarely leave it. Because the pain is my last link to her, so as much as it hurts, I wrap it around myself like a blanket, like a teenaged girl cutting jagged lines on her inner thigh with a razor blade, inflicting the hurt on myself just because I need to feel something. I'm not ready for time to heal this wound, but I also know I'm powerless to stop it. And knowing that makes me fight harder than ever to hold on to the pain and anchor myself in this tragedy while it's still freshly tragic. So every so often I pull at my scabs like a dog, desperately trying to draw some fresh blood from my open wound, but even as I do it, I know the day will come when I pull off that scab and there's no blood underneath it, just the soft pink expanse of virgin skin. And when that finally happens, when time has inevitably had its way with me, then I'll know she's gone for good.

And I know that at some point in the future there will be someone else. She'll be smart and beautiful and damaged in her own way, and we'll understand each other and we'll fall in love, and I'll feel guilty for being happy, so I'll do little things to sabotage us whenever things start getting too good. And she'll be patient with me, and then, when she's taken as much abuse as she can stand, there will be loud venting fights and then, presumably, a tearful ultimatum and after that we'll turn a corner. I'll still feel guilty, but I'll get over it in stages, and with each one of those stages, Hailey will fade further and further into the distant past, until she's nothing more than a footnote in the story of my life. And one day, an older version of me will tell his children how he'd been married once, before he ever met their mother, but that his wife had died, and Hailey will be not a person to them but a small, intangible, biographical blip, a sad thing that happened to their father on the way to happily ever after. And worse, maybe that's how I'll see it too.

And I don't need you to tell me that this will happen, that it's inevitable. I'm not fooling myself. But just because something is true, it doesn't mean I'm ready to face it today. Sometimes the only truth people can handle is the one they woke up with that morning. And this morning, like every morning, I woke up with my pain. So do me a favor and don't fuck with it.

11

From: *Kyle.Evans@EvansLitAgents.com*
To: *Doug.Parker@mmag.com*
Date: Wednesday, September 13, 2006
Subject: How to Talk to a Widower

You're a star! According to the folks at M, your last column broke the record for reader mail, the very record previously set by your column last month. I've forwarded yet another sack-load of mail for you to not open. The magazine has been forwarding calls from newswires and talk shows who want to interview you. I'm in the process of negotiating both US and overseas syndication deals. Some people from NBC called, they want you for a segment on the "Today" show. If I get my way it will be Matt Lauer who does the interview. He just comes off as more serious, less of a talking head. And Oprah's people have been sniffing around (!!!). More importantly, I've been talking to publishing people and there is significant interest at a few major houses. I smell a memoir! You just need to write up the proposal. This is what we've been waiting for! We need to talk. I tried you myself a number of times and left you something like thirty voice mails. What gives? E-mailing is so uncivilized.

—K

From:	*Doug.Parker@mmag.com*
To:	*Kyle.Evans@EvansLitAgents.com*
Date:	Wednesday, September 13, 2006
Subject:	No Thanks

Sorry about the phone, Kyle. Technical difficulties. Not really interested in meeting Matt Lauer or Oprah. I'm glad the column worked out, but like I told you before, I'm not interested in becoming the poster boy for young widowers.

—D

From:	*Kyle.Evans@EvansLitAgents.com*
To:	*Doug.Parker@mmag.com*
Date:	Wednesday, September 13, 2006
Subject:	Don't Be an Idiot!!!

How many times have you bitched to me about having to write the same senseless, masturbatory tripe about narcissistic, vacuous movie stars? *She was awkward and gangly in high school. He just wants to act and doesn't buy into the whole celebrity thing.* Nobody cares! You're finally writing about something real, and it's striking a chord around the country. You've tapped into something significant here, and you owe it to yourself to see it through. Also, the word has come down from Bernie over at M that the magazine will negotiate exclusive subsidiary rights for excerpts. They'll pay you to promote your book! Come on, Doug, it's the brass fucking ring! This is the best thing that ever happened to you!

—K

From: *Doug.Parker@mmag.com*
To: *Kyle.Evans@EvansLitAgents.com*
Date: Wednesday, September 13, 2006
Subject: Fuck Off Kyle

I know you pride yourself on being an asshole, but you can't seriously mean that the death of my wife is the best thing that ever happened to me? Even you, as horrible and self-absorbed as you are, can't be that callous and obtuse.

—D

From: *Kyle.Evans@EvansLitAgents.com*
To: *Doug.Parker@mmag.com*
Date: Wednesday, September 13, 2006
Subject: Chill the Fuck Out!

First of all, this is America, and I can be as callous and obtuse as I want to. Secondly, I wasn't referring to Hailey's death, but to your writing about it. When you started submitting the Widower column, no one at M

was thrilled about the change, but I beat the shit out of
Bernie to run with it, mostly because I figured the sooner
you worked through your grief, the sooner you could go
back to jerking off young starlets. Turns out, it made
you a better writer and now your stuff is resonating with
their readers. That's 300,000 or so potential book buyers
already lined up, and that makes you a publisher's wet
dream. Now everyone knows who you are. You want
to cling to some misguided notion that you're somehow
profiting from Hailey's death, you go ahead and do
that, but let's call it what it really is: Fear of Success.
And, my friend, you had that long before you lost your
wife.

—K

P.S. No charge for the free therapy.

From: *Doug.Parker@mmag.com*

To: *Kyle.Evans@EvansLitAgents.com*

Date: Wednesday, September 13, 2006

Subject: Maybe So, But . . .

Right or not, the point is moot anyway. For those of us
keeping score, I just passed the one-year mark. How long
can one legally write about this stuff anyway? At some
point you have to move on, at least outwardly, right?
And that means no more dwelling on my grief, which, in
my case, means no more writing about it. So bring on
the movie stars . . .

—D

From: *Kyle.Evans@EvansLitAgents.com*

To: *Doug.Parker@mmag.com*

Date: Wednesday, September 13, 2006

Subject: Funny You Should Say That . . .

Actually, that's perfect, because I was thinking that we expand it a bit, and you start writing about getting back out there, you know? I mean, there's some beautiful, heartbreaking material there. All the stuff you're going to be going through after so many years. Your first date, your first lay, your first girlfriend . . . It's like being born again. You'll write it with the same wit and pathos, and I will land you a nice two-book deal with a major publisher. Come on, Doug, you know this could be brilliant!

—K

From: *Doug.Parker@mmag.com*

To: *Kyle.Evans@EvansLitAgents.com*

Date: Wednesday, September 13, 2006

Subject: You Are a Sad, Sorry Excuse for a Human Being

Sorry, Kyle. Next month my last Widower column runs and then I'm back to Hollywood.

—D

From: *Kyle.Evans@EvansLitAgents.com*

To: *Doug.Parker@mmag.com*

Date: Wednesday, September 13, 2006

Subject: You've Got Another Thing Coming

Apparently, you haven't been reading the magazine. In your absence, they've given the Hollywood beat to Krause. So if you're going to keep a column, you're going to have to come up with something else to write about. You've been out of it for a year, what did you think they would do?

—K

From:	*Doug.Parker@mmag.com*
To:	*Kyle.Evans@EvansLitAgents.com*
Date:	Wednesday, September 13, 2006
Subject:	Krause Is an Idiot

He is.

—D

From:	*Kyle.Evans@EvansLitAgents.com*
To:	*Doug.Parker@mmag.com*
Date:	Wednesday, September 13, 2006
Subject:	It's an Idiot's Job

Now, are we going to do this or not? We need to strike while the iron is hot.

—K

From:	*Doug.Parker@mmag.com*
To:	*Kyle.Evans@EvansLitAgents.com*
Date:	Wednesday, September 13, 2006
Subject:	Not

—D

From: *Kyle.Evans@EvansLitAgents.com*

To: *Doug.Parker@mmag.com*

Date: Wednesday, September 13, 2006

Subject: You're Killing Me!

Fine. I'll give you a few weeks to think about it.

—K

12

DRIVING NORTH THROUGH NEW RADFORD, YOU CAN actually feel the real estate values rising like floodwaters around you. The quarter-acre plots become half acres and then acres, with increasingly larger houses set farther and farther back from the street, the minivans and Japanese sedans give way to upscale SUVs and German luxury cars, and the streets become wider, and lined with taller trees. And then you pass through a white-bricked gateway into the village of Forest Heights, and everything jumps another few income levels, and it's between these bulging tax brackets that you'll find the massive red-bricked center-hall Colonial of Stan and Eva Parker. I had been fiercely determined not to come to this dinner, but in the two days that Claire has been living with me, the old behavior patterns have already reasserted themselves and she has effortlessly assumed command.

Claire turns into the driveway like it's just another street, maintaining her speed until the last possible instant, braking just inches from the rear fender of my mother's Audi. In the backseat, Russ, who has come along because anything is better than spending another evening at home with Jim and Angie, lets out a strangled breath and says "Fuck." Russ is an accomplished linguist when it comes to swearing, and he can make the word mean anything he wants. In this case it's a fuck of relief that Claire hasn't killed us and the harrowing drive is over.

"You have a problem with my driving, you can take the bus home," Claire teases him, reaching back to muss his hair.

"Like buses even come to this neighborhood," Russ says, batting away her hand, his tone a complex adolescent amalgam of envy and contempt.

"How do you think the help gets here?" Claire says.

"Look," Russ says, pointing out his window. "Isn't that your dad?"

My father is out in the front yard, backlit like an apparition by the late afternoon sun, wearing nothing except sky blue boxer shorts and white Nikes with black socks, throwing a baseball against the side of the house and catching it in an old, weathered mitt of mine. He performs the exaggerated windup of a major league pitcher, his flab shimmying around him like Jell-O as he follows through on the release, his silver hair plastered against his forehead with sweat. Rudy, his nurse, is hovering in the foreground with a bathrobe in his hands, desperately trying to get him to come inside and get dressed.

"Please, Dr. Parker," he whines. "This is so not funny."

"Hey, Dad."

His face lights up when he sees me, and he comes lumbering over with a big grin while Rudy, who looks poised to have a breakdown, chases after him, plaintively holding out the bathrobe in front of him. "Dr. Parker, please! Just put on the robe!" Rudy's about my age, skinny, bald, perennially agitated, and no match for my bullish father, who outweighs him by a good seventy pounds and nudges him out of the way like an elephant swatting flies with his tail.

My father drops the mitt in the grass and pulls me into a tight hug, exactly like he never did before the stroke. He smells of grass and sweat, and his back is rough and hairy against my hands. "Doug," he says, squeezing the breath out of me. "What are you doing here?" This has become his standard greeting, a genuine query brilliantly disguised as a salutation, because he so often has no idea what's going on, or even what year it is. Sometimes he appears to be on target, and other times he thinks I'm a kid again, coming home from school. Two years ago, my mother discovered him on the shower floor in a wet crumpled heap. He was in a coma for three days, from which he emerged vibrant and healthy but with his mind somehow folded in on itself and the impulse control of an eight-year-old boy. The doctors called it a CVA, which turned out to be an acronym for cerebrovascular accident, which turned out to be a fancy way of saying that there was nothing they could do about it. There are days when he's lucid and days when he's lost, but even on the good days, he's never quite sure about the details. He's a man constantly in search of context.

On the plus side, he hugs me all the time now. I guess it took having his brain fried for him to start loving me. In my more twisted moments, I actually consider it a fair trade, but then again, I'm not the one parading grandly around his front lawn in his boxers with the fly open.

He steps back, keeping his hands on my shoulders. I wonder how old he thinks I am today. "Where's Hailey?" he says.

That narrows it down a bit. I turn away so he won't see the searing pain that momentarily melts my features. In the world he woke up in today, he loves me and Hailey's still alive, and it's like I'm standing outside in the rain, peering through the window and wishing I could come in from the cold and warm my chilled bones at the fire of his dementia. "She'll be along soon," I say.

"Hi, Daddy," Claire quickly interrupts, stepping in to give him a hug.

"Hey, sugar, what are you doing here?"

"Just coming to see Debbie," Claire says. "She's getting married, you know."

His expression falters and he frowns, his forehead becoming deeply furrowed as he tries to chase down a specific memory, but it loses him in the chaotic thought riot going on in his brain. "Mazel tov," he says mournfully, staring down at his feet.

"He really needs to come inside and get cleaned up," Rudy says.

My father shakes it off. "Who's this?" he says, sizing up Russ, who's been standing off to the side awkwardly.

"It's Russ," I say. "You remember Russ, Hailey's son?"

"Of course I do," he says, stepping forward to give Russ a hug. You can see the fight-or-flight debate played out in Russ's stricken expression as he stands stiffly in my father's sweaty embrace, but he keeps his cool and even pats my dad's back with his fist, ghetto style.

"Hey, Dr. Parker."

My father steps back and sizes him up. "You're all grown-up now. You play ball, Russ?"

"Sometimes."

He tosses him the ball. "You'll be the pitcher."

Russ grins and picks the mitt up off the ground. "Batter up," he says.

"I think that's a really, really bad idea," Rudy says.

"Duly noted, Rudy," my father says jovially, jogging over to pick up the baseball bat leaning against the wall.

"Dr. Parker. We have to get ready for dinner. You haven't even showered yet."

"Buzz off, Rudy," my dad says, twirling the bat and squatting down into a batter's stance.

"Yeah, Rudy," Claire says, grinning. "Buzz off."

My dad looks at her. "Can you call balls and strikes?"

Claire steps up to him and kisses his shoulder. "I was born for it," she says.

My mother is at her post in the kitchen, perched on a high stool at the center island, halfway through what I can only hope is her first bottle of red wine, arguing over wedding details with Debbie and barking the occasional order at Portia, the maid, who is fussing over a London broil. The counter is laid out like a photo shoot for *Bon Appétit,* with picture-perfect salads, side dishes, a glazed Cornish hen, breaded veal, and the London broil, which Portia is wrestling into a silver serving platter. My parents may behave like they were abandoned in Greenwich and raised by WASPs, but when it comes to preparing meals, we are once again the chosen people.

"Douglas," my mother says, setting her wineglass down on

the marble top of the island. "Darling." She leans forward to kiss the air somewhere in the vicinity of my face, taking care not to disturb the multiple coats of lipstick that cover her lips like paint sealant.

"Hey, Pooh," I say, kissing Debbie's cheek. She's immaculate as usual, dressed for dinner in a short black skirt and powder blue sweater, her hair pinned up off her face. She is severely beautiful, like a polished sculpture, and I wish she would wear her hair down sometimes and look a little less tucked in, a little less like someone who has forgotten to exhale, someone inches away from taking offense at something.

"You came," she says.

"Why wouldn't I?"

"Because you hate me?"

" 'Hate' is such a strong word."

She smirks. "Go to hell."

"Language, Deborah," my mother says sternly. "You're getting married, for heaven's sake. Try to at least sound like a lady."

"You look skinny," I say. Debbie's always been an aspiring anorexic, cheered on enthusiastically by our mother.

"I have to fit into that gown."

"She looks perfect!" my mother snaps at me. "For heaven's sake, Portia, garnish the brisket, don't bury it alive." She turns to me. "So how are you, Douglas?"

"Same old same old."

"I was worried when I couldn't reach you."

"I'm fine."

She gives me her best you-can't-fool-me look over the rim of her wineglass. Whenever I picture my mother it's always this image, large knowing eyes floating disembodied over the rim of a wineglass. "Did you bring Russell?"

"He's outside, playing ball with Dad." She nods and looks away. "How is Dad?" I say.

Her expression darkens and she waves her hand. "Every day's an adventure. He's discovered sex again."

"Mom!"

"He wants it all the time now. It's a wonder I can even walk."

"Jesus Christ!" Debbie says.

"Language," my mother says absently, snapping her fingers twice at her. "The other day, your father chased me around the house for a half hour before Rudy could calm him down."

"How's Rudy working out?" I say.

"I give it another two weeks." She pours herself some more wine, even though her glass is still half full. She sighs, a deep, dramatic, Oscar-clip sigh. "I love the man, I really do. But he's going to kill me."

"Speaking of which," Debbie says, turning to me. "I've been thinking. How would you feel about giving me away?"

"We tried for years, Pooh. No one wanted you."

"Be serious," she says.

"Dad should do it."

"Dad's insane, or maybe you haven't noticed."

"He's just occasionally befuddled. He'll be fine."

"I can't take that chance."

"It is what it is, Deb. If he's a little bit off, people will understand."

"This from the man who hasn't left his house in a year," Debbie says, shaking her head in disgust.

"What's your point, Debbie?"

"Nothing, Doug. I have no point."

My mother puts down her wineglass, nervously anticipating an explosion, but Claire walks in just in time. "Hey, Ma," she says, kissing her cheek and stealing the wineglass in the same motion.

"Where's Stephen?" my mother says.

"He had to go out of town on business."

"That's a shame."

"He'll get over it." Claire takes a long swallow of wine, which she shouldn't do in her condition, so I give her a look to remind her, and she raises her eyebrows defiantly to tell me to back off. "Hey, Pooh," she says.

"I wish you both would stop calling me that," Debbie says softly.

"Yeah," Claire says, nodding her head sympathetically. "That's probably not going to happen. Am I right, Doug?"

"It's funny, because I'd just been thinking that it was time to stop calling you that, but then you made that bitchy comment about me not leaving the house..."

"So it's unanimous," Claire says brightly. "How's the wedding shaping up?"

"She doesn't want Dad to give her away."

"Why the fuck not?"

"Claire!" my mother says, snapping her fingers at her. She can swear like a sailor when the moment demands it, but she hates hearing her children swear because it makes her feel old.

"Jesus!" Debbie says. "Have you met Dad? He's the one running around half naked in the front yard."

"He's your father."

"Oh, fuck off, Claire!"

If my mother snaps any faster, her fingers will start a fire.

My sisters and I start going at it, at high speed and in three-part harmony, and when my mother's snaps have fallen hopelessly behind, she silences us by slamming her fist down on the counter hard enough to rattle the hanging light fixtures. "You were an ugly baby, Deborah," she says.

"Excuse me?"

"It's true," my mother says, leaning back and closing her eyes. "You looked like a troll. A swarthy little troll. I was embarrassed to take you out with me. But your father, he loved you. He thought you were the most beautiful thing on God's green earth. He couldn't wait for you to wake up so he could pull you out of your crib and sing to you. He showed you off to everyone like you were the crown jewels. It didn't matter what you looked like. You were his beautiful little baby."

We all look at my mother. She's never told us this before, but it's very possible, likely even, that she's making it up on the spot. She's never been above some creative ad-libbing if it will enhance her performance. She opens her eyes and fixes Debbie with a steely glare. "He may be impaired, but he's still the same man who looked at that ugly child and saw his beautiful daughter, and he will be the one to give you away."

Debbie looks at her, flushed with exasperation. "You're all delusional," she says.

"We're your family, sweetheart. Deal with it."

"This isn't a family, it's a freak show!"

"Come on, Pooh," I say softly. "It's Dad. What's the worst that can happen?"

And that's when the baseball comes crashing through the kitchen window. Portia shrieks and throws herself to the ground; Claire drops her wineglass, which shatters on the imported tiles of the kitchen floor as the window erupts into a spray of glass over the food on the counter. Outside, Rudy can be heard shrieking, hysterically, and moments later, my father's sweating face appears at the broken window. "Everyone okay in there?" he says, panting lightly.

"Fine, Dad," Claire says, shaken.

Portia gets back to her feet, quietly invoking the Virgin Mary in Spanish as she brushes herself off.

Russ appears in the window next to my father, looking nervous and guilty. "Fuck," he says.

My father's eyes come to rest on the baseball, nesting perfectly in the center of the wild rice salad, and then he looks up at me. "Little help, Doug?"

I retrieve the ball from the salad, flick off a few clinging bits of rice, and toss it through the window frame. He catches it in the mitt and smiles at me. "The boy can hit," he says delightedly, and then disappears back into the yard.

It seems to me that in a normal family, this would be the part where the bride bursts into tears over the ruined celebration, and the mother of the bride swoops in to comfort her and reassure her that everything will be okay. But I could be wrong. I don't know very much about normal families. I just extrapolate from what I've seen on television.

"God almighty," my mother says, exhaling loudly and taking a swig of wine right from the bottle. "That man won't rest until he kills me." Then she reaches into the oversized designer purse perched on the stool beside her and ransacks it until her fist finally emerges clutching her trusty bottle of Vil Pills. "Forget it," she says to Portia, who is examining the spread to see what can be salvaged. "Throw it all out." She pops a yellow pill and washes it down with another swig from the bottle. "We are not serving food with glass shards in it. This isn't prison."

Debbie, meanwhile, is suddenly all business. She whips out her cell phone like a six-shooter and turns her back on us. "Mike, hey, it's me…no, just a typical day at the asylum. Listen, change of plans. My dad kind of trashed the dinner…Yeah. No, he was playing baseball, don't ask…Yeah. You may want to prepare them for that…Mike, now would be the absolute perfect time for you to *not* bring that up, okay? We're going to improvise. Just get us reservations at the Surf Club. Yeah. Seven-thirty. Call me once you have it confirmed…Okay…Me too. I'll be waiting for your call."

She snaps her cell phone shut with authority and turns back to face us. "Problem solved," she says with a strained, self-satisfied smile.

"And that's why they pay you the big bucks," Claire says.

"I got food poisoning the last time I ate at the Surf Club," my mother says.

"Mom," Debbie says, her voice low and menacing, like a distant thunderhead.

My mother shrugs. "I'm just saying. I didn't leave the bathroom all night. It was coming out of me like Niagara Falls from both ends."

"Jesus Christ, Mom!" I say.

"Sometimes at the same time," she says, lost in her reverie.

"We should have just eloped," Debbie says miserably, collapsing into a chair. "We should have just gone to Vegas and been married by an Elvis."

"Don't worry, Pooh," I say. "At this rate, everyone will have all the weird out of their system by your wedding day."

Debbie gives me a dark look. "Everyone," she says, "is just warming up."

Right then, I almost feel bad for her. But then I revert back to thinking that it serves her right for scoping men at my shiva, and I can feel the festering resentment grab hold of me once more. "I'll go help Dad get ready," I say, suddenly needing to be away from my little sister.

"I'll help you help him," Claire says, pinching Debbie's cheek on the way out. "Is it any wonder we're so fucked up?" she mutters under her breath to me.

"Don't anyone order the fish," my mother calls after us. "Word to the wise."

13

THE CRYSTAL CHANDELIER THAT HANGS IN THE cavernous dining room at the Surf Club is dimmed for ambience, emitting just enough wattage to make the diamond wedding bands and gold watches of the patrons twinkle like stars in the evening sky. The faces of the diners are bathed in the soft amber glow of their table candles, making everyone look like they have great tans, and the low din of hushed conversations is accompanied by the musical clinking of silverware on bone china, and a jazz combo playing off to one side. We're twenty minutes late for our reservation, because Dad got absorbed in a *Seinfeld* rerun while he was getting dressed, and could not be convinced to put his shoes on until it was over.

Mr. and Mrs. Sandleman, Mike's parents, who have driven in from West Hartford for the occasion, are waiting with him at the bar, and everyone stands around awkwardly while Debbie introduces Russ and me to them. I'm the only one in the family they haven't met, since I missed the engagement party a few months back, having had a prior commitment to get drunk and seethe with resentment that night. "This is my older brother, Doug," Debbie says. "You know, the one whose wife died in a plane crash and who's now a hopeless mess who can't stop feeling sorry for himself long enough to pull his shit together?"

Okay, she doesn't say it exactly like that, but that's clearly what she's implying.

"Pleasure to meet you," Mr. Sandleman says. His hand is damp and cold from holding his drinking glass. He is short and squat, with thick glasses and a bushy mustache that make him look like a political cartoon.

Mrs. Sandleman gives me a hug. She is soft and fleshy and smells like air freshener. "We read your column online every month," she says. "It's really very moving."

"Well written," Mr. Sandleman declares. At least, I assume he does. You can't actually see his lips move behind his mustache.

"Nice to meet you both," I say, unable to look directly at them because of the pity oozing like sludge out of their eyes. Pity, I've learned, is like a fart. You can tolerate your own, but you simply can't stand anyone else's.

"This is Russ," I say. "The son of my dead wife, who seems determined to fuck up his own young life at any cost, and whom I seem powerless to help." Or something like that.

"Hey," Russ says.

"Doug," Mike says, awkwardly shaking my hand and slapping my back. We haven't spoken since I skipped the engagement party. He's been letting Debbie do all the negotiating. Big mistake. "Thanks for coming. It really means a lot to us."

"Don't mention it," I say.

"Listen. I know the timing of all this sucked. And believe me—"

"I mean it, Mike," I cut him off, sharper than I'd intended. "Seriously. Do not mention it."

He looks like he's about to say something else, but something in my expression that I'm not even aware of manages to shut him up. I glance into the mirror behind the bar to note the exact look so that I can store it away for future use, but the maître d' has stepped in front of me to lead us to our table, and all I can see are my eyes, which don't look particularly threatening.

Once we're all seated in the dining room, my father undergoes a miraculous transformation. Sitting at the head of the table, he is completely in command, looking handsome and elegant in his pin-striped suit, his thick silver hair brushed back, staring down through his gold-rimmed reading glasses at the wine list. He speaks to the sommelier authoritatively, questions him on vintages, and then orders two wines for the table, folding his glasses and sliding them into his breast pocket, and you'd never know this was the same guy who was shagging flies half naked in his front yard an hour ago. "Sweetheart," he says to my mother, raising her hand to his lips. "You look as beautiful as the day I met you."

"You're just saying that because it's true," my mother retorts, but she's smiling. Before the stroke, Stan never engaged in public displays of emotion, and after a lifetime of his consistently stolid demeanor, it's still somewhat disconcerting to hear the unbridled affection in his voice.

"We made love for the first time in her parents' basement,"

he announces, turning to face Mrs. Sandleman, who turns red and seems unsure of what to do with this particular nugget of information.

Russ snorts into his water glass. Claire picks up a butter knife and mimes hara-kiri.

"Okay, Stan," my mother says, squeezing his arm.

He turns to look at her. "You were wearing a white silk blouse, and no bra, and we had one of your father's Sinatra records playing."

My mother smiles and takes his hand. *"In the Wee Small Hours,"* she says, nodding.

"That's the time you miss her most of all," he sings hoarsely, kissing her hand again.

"He loves Sinatra," my mother says to the Sandlemans, blushing profusely.

"Subject change, please," Debbie says.

My father nods. "So," he says, addressing Mr. Sandleman. "Phil, is it?"

"Howard."

"Howard, then. Tell me again what business you're in?"

"Commercial real estate."

"Ah."

Phil was my father's younger brother who was killed in Vietnam, and whenever my father reaches for a name, Phil seems to be his default response.

When the wine arrives, my father tastes it and nods his approval to the sommelier. After all of the glasses have been filled, he lifts his glass and says, "I'd like to propose a toast to the happy couple." We all raise our wineglasses except for Claire, who raises her eyebrows at me instead, before demonstratively grabbing a glass of water.

"Debbie," my father says, turning to face her. "You're my little girl, and no matter how far you go, and how much you grow, that will never change. And now, as your wedding day approaches, I just want you to know how proud your mom and I are of you, not because of all you've accomplished so far, but because of the kind of person that you are. I can still see you in your little pink whale pajamas, curled up on my lap and singing to me about the itsy bitsy spider. I remember it like it was yesterday..." His voice trails off and his eyes are suddenly brimming with tears. "Sometimes when I wake up in the morning, I still expect to see that little girl come running into our bedroom, dragging that stuffed frog you had, and take a running jump up into the bed to cuddle with me." He grabs a cloth napkin from the table and wipes the tears off his face, looking around at everyone. "I'm still in here," he says fiercely, apropos of nothing.

And now I can see that Claire and Debbie are both crying, and I can feel the hot wetness building up in my own eyes.

"Stan," my mother says softly, staring at him through her tears.

"It's okay, Evie," he says, clutching her hand in his free one as he clears his throat. "I guess what I'm trying to say is, no matter how old we all get, you three will always be my children, and Debbie, you will always be my baby girl." He raises his glass higher. "To Debbie and Phil."

"Mike!" Debbie snaps at him, and I want to throw my plate like a discus and cleanly sever her head.

"Right," my father says. "To Debbie and Mike."

* * *

The dinner goes on, the way these things do. Debbie talks to Claire and Mrs. Sandleman about the flowers and the band, my mother drinks steadily and charms Mr. Sandleman with war stories from the theater that we've all heard a million times before, and Russ excuses himself for a minute, is gone for fifteen, and comes back with his eyes glazed over. "You had to get high right now?" I whisper to him. "It was so important?"

"It was a biological imperative, dude. It is fucking intense in here."

"It's just dinner with the family."

"Come on, man. It's like there's a hunk of C4 strapped to the table and we're all just waiting to see when it will detonate. I can't believe you dragged me here."

"You invited yourself along, remember?"

"You should have blown me off, like you always do."

"I do not blow you off."

"Bullshit."

"I was pretty clear about how awful this would be. You said you wanted to see Debbie."

He nods, and looks across the table at my little sister. "I know you can't see this, because she's your sister and all, but she is beyond hot."

"She's your aunt."

"Step-aunt, and maybe not even that. It's not like you adopted me. Remember? The gray area? Your colossal failure to step up?"

"Jesus, Russ. Will you give it a rest already?"

"Don't worry, my friend. I'm too stoned to hassle you right

now." He lets out a long, heartfelt sigh, still staring at Debbie. "If I had any kind of balls, I would tell her how I feel."

"You understand she's getting married, right?"

He looks at Mike, who is tracing patterns in some spilled salt with the point of his steak knife, and shakes his head sadly. "What a waste."

So Russ stares at Debbie while I watch my father, who chews quietly on his steak, smiling happily as he surveys his family. It's haunting to see him like this, so regal and polished, so...there. It's like seeing a long-dead relative, and I can feel the sadness like lead in my belly. We were never very close, but ever since he had the stroke he likes me a lot more, and that makes me miss him in a way I don't fully understand, because how can you miss something you never really had?

I'm so caught up in staring at my father that I don't hear Mike, who is seated directly across from me, the first two times he calls my name. "Doug!" he finally shouts, and everyone else falls silent.

"What?" I say, annoyed.

"I was telling you that I want you to be a groomsman."

"What?"

"I want you to be in my wedding party."

I don't mean to laugh at him. It just happens. "You can't be serious."

"Come on, Doug," he says, looking nervously around the table. "You can't stay pissed forever, so why not bury it right here. We were good friends, and now we're going to be family." He extends his hand across the table to me and offers a wide grin. "So, what do you say?" Out of the corner of my eye, I can see Debbie watching this unfold out of the corner of hers, and I realize that it's all been choreographed, a public demonstration of goodwill designed to quell my resistance.

I leave his hand where it is. "I say no."

Mike pulls his hand back, looking hurt, and Debbie throws down her silverware. "What the hell is wrong with you?" she snaps at me.

"Nothing."

"If you were going to be such a bastard, why did you even come?"

"Claire made me. She didn't want to come alone."

She sighs and changes tack. "Okay. You're sad. You're still grieving. I understand that. I can only imagine how you feel. But don't you think that for just one day you can put it aside, just stop thinking about yourself and be happy for me?"

"Like you put aside your feelings for Mike to be sad for me when my wife died?"

"That's not fair, Doug."

"You're right about that."

"Take it easy," Claire says, looking over at me.

"I can't help where I met Mike. It was just . . . fate. Everything happens for a reason."

"You narcissistic little bitch," I say, and Debbie's head snaps back like she was slapped.

"Doug!" Claire says, but it's too late. If she wanted me to be nice, she shouldn't have brought me here.

"You really believe that, don't you?" I shout at Debbie, who is staring at me, her mouth open in wordless shock. "That Hailey dying was part of this grand, divine scheme so that Mike could bone you upstairs while I was sitting shiva?"

"Douglas!" my mother hisses across the table at me, and I realize that the entire restaurant has fallen silent.

"That's not what I meant," Debbie says, her voice shaking.

"You mean it's not what you meant to say out loud."

"Maybe you two should step outside," Mike says.

"Maybe you should shut the fuck up."

"Language, Douglas!" my mother says, snapping her fingers across the table at me.

"You are being such an asshole," Debbie sobs.

"And you're a self-absorbed little twat."

"Okay! So here's some news," Claire announces gaily. "I'm pregnant. And I've left Stephen." Everyone turns to stare at her. She sits in her seat, twiddling her thumbs on the table. "Don't everyone congratulate me all at once."

My mother grabs my father's forearm and looks at Claire. "Could you say that again, please?" she says, holding her other hand against her chest.

"Which part?"

"All of it."

"I'm pregnant and I'm getting divorced."

"Kaboom," Russ says loudly, and I guess it's the marijuana kicking in, but he suddenly starts to laugh, and then the laughing gets louder, and pretty soon he's hysterical, shaking back and forth, his mouth open wide, tears streaming down his face. "Russ," I say, nudging him under the table, "cut it out!" But that just makes him laugh harder, banging his hands deliriously on the table. "Kaboom!" he shouts again at the top of his lungs, waving his arms wildly over his head as he collapses into another loud paroxysm of laughter. For a minute, we all sit there in stunned silence, helplessly watching Russ, waiting for him to stop, and then my father starts laughing along with him, loud and hearty, and then, after another few seconds, so does Claire, and then me, and it spreads across the table like a wave, until we're all laughing uncontrollably, while Mike and his parents sit there staring at us, wondering what the hell could be so goddamn funny. And if I could speak I would tell them nothing, there's nothing even remotely funny, it's sadder than anything you could imagine, and then I would say welcome to the family.

By the time dessert comes, things have returned to some semblance of normalcy, which is to say that my mother is popping her Vil Pills like candy, Mr. Sandleman is talking my father's ear off about the federal interest rates, Russ is silently and methodically buttering and eating every leftover roll and breadstick in the breadbasket, and Mike is quietly and conspicuously groping Debbie under the table.

"It always has to be about you, doesn't it, Claire?" Debbie says bitterly. "I should have known you'd come up with something tonight."

"That's right, Pooh. I'm screwing up my life just to steal your thunder."

"No. You're screwing up your life because that's what you do. You're just announcing it here because God forbid anyone should go ten minutes without paying attention to you."

"Everything happens for a reason, right?"

"Go to hell, Claire."

"Language, Deborah," my mother says absently. She tries to snap but can't seem to get her fingers to cooperate. She washed down her pills with some white wine, and she's ensconced in a narcotic haze, feeling no pain.

"Do you know if it's a boy or a girl?" Mrs. Sandleman says to Claire in a bold conversational gambit.

"Excuse me?" Claire says.

"The baby."

Claire shakes her head. "No idea."

"That's right," Debbie says glumly. "Everyone pay attention to Claire. God only knows what she'll do next if we don't. A sex-change operation, maybe."

"Take it easy, baby."

"Shut up, Mike."

"Sinatra!" my father exclaims, jumping to his feet. And indeed, the band has started to play an old Sinatra tune. "Dance with me," he says, extending his hand to my mother.

"Oh, no," she says, pushing his hand away. "I don't think I can even walk straight right now."

"Debbie?" he says, looking down at her.

"Not now, Dad."

"Please?"

"No one's dancing, Dad."

"Wrong," he says. He steps past the two tables behind us and starts dancing by himself along the large bank of windows overlooking the Long Island Sound, spinning and stepping in time to the music. The sun is setting and the last pink crayon slashes of light color the sky behind him.

"Oh Jesus," Debbie says, pushing back her chair and getting to her feet. She runs over to my father and tries to pull him back to the table, but he pulls her into his embrace and begins dancing with her, humming along to the music as he goes. She struggles at first, but then she stops fighting it and her body goes limp as she settles into him, wrapping her arms around his neck and resting her head on his shoulder. And then she starts to cry, not quietly, but deep, anguished sobs that rack her body, and he just holds her, absorbing her small convulsions, rubbing her neck, and pressing his lips against her scalp. They stay that way for a long time, long after the song has changed, rocking gently back and forth as outside the sky goes dark and the Long Island Sound slowly disappears.

Mom vanishes after dinner, and I find her down on the beach, shoes off, standing on the rocky breakwater and looking out into the dark ocean, her black dress flapping and clinging to her, her hair released from its bobby pins to blow freely in the wind. I'm not saying my mother necessarily picks these poses purely for dramatic effect, but outside of the movies, no one really stands like that, just looking off to the horizon, thinking deep thoughts until someone joins them for a meaningful discussion. In real life we do our deep thinking in stolen moments, while we're eating, or driving, or shitting, or waiting on line. But because that's not as easily conveyed on film, some unheralded director invented the stare-out-at-the-horizon technique to signify deep thinking. My mother, who long ago lost sight of the line between real behavior and the depiction of it, is also high on Vil Pills and alcohol, which means her relationship to reality is probably even more compromised than usual.

"We used to come to this beach all the time when you were little," she says without taking her eyes off the blackness of the Sound. "Do you remember?"

"Sure."

She sighs. "I used to love coming here. The three of you loved to be in the water. It was practically the only thing you could agree on. And I would just sit on my blanket watching your little bobbing heads, and know that, at least for the time being, I was doing my job, and you were all happy. But then you started bringing your Walkman, and you would just lie on the blanket plugged into your headphones, lost in your own troubles, and Claire grew boobs and discovered bikinis and would run off with all those horrible boys, and that would leave Deborah with no one, so she'd bug you until you made her cry or you walked away, and then I'd end up yelling at her, and it was at that point that I stopped loving the beach."

I just stand quietly, an actor in the wings, waiting for my cue.

"You're being kind of hard on your sister, don't you think?" she says.

"Not really, no," I say, stepping up onto the breakwater to join her.

She nods, the floodlights from the restaurant casting her features in a blue glow. "Mike is a good man. Oh, sure, he's a little dim-witted for a lawyer, and we're going to have to have his hand surgically removed from your sister's ass, but he loves her and, more important, she loves him. I can see it in her eyes."

"She owns him."

"Oh, get off your high horse, would you? It's no less real. She loves with dominance, you grieve with hostility. Different strokes for different folks."

"Point taken."

"But that's not my point. This is." She turns to fix me with a stern look. "Cut her some slack. This is her time. With any luck, she's only going to get married once. So don't rain on her parade. It's not her you're really mad at anyway."

"No? Who is it I'm mad at?"

"At Hailey, of course," she says, looking back out to the ocean. "So am I, by the way, pissed as all get-out at her, for leaving you like this. But that's old news, and I don't want to talk about it anymore."

"Neither do I." The water slaps angrily at the rocks below us, splashing the air, and I can feel the tiny droplets of cold mist settling on my face like wet pinpricks.

"Whatever Debbie's heinous crime against you was, it was committed in the name of love, and you, of all people, should appreciate that."

"Self-love," I say.

"Oh, come on, Douglas. Is there any other kind?"

"Listen, Mom."

"No, you listen. Listen to your mother. I may be a flake, and I may be three sheets to the wind, but I've been around a bit longer than you, and I know a thing or two that you don't. I know Deborah can be a tight-assed bitch, but that's genetic and there's nothing she can do about it. But what you should understand is that it was no picnic for her, growing up with you and Claire. On your good days, the two of you were simply exclusive, and on your bad days you were downright cruel."

"Oh, come on. We weren't that bad."

She raises a thin, plucked-within-an-inch-of-its-life eyebrow at me. "You were terrible. You still are. She is one of three, but she's always been on the outside, looking in at the two of you, with your private jokes and your secret looks. She'd have given her right arm to be a part of it. She still would. Maybe it's my fault, for not making you include her more. All she's ever wanted was for you and Claire to love her."

It's rare for someone to say something to you, just a few words, really, and actually make you see yourself from a completely different vantage point. But my mother is still capable of occasionally turning in a revelatory performance. "I never really thought about it like that," I say, feeling like an asshole.

"Of course you didn't. You and Claire are always too wrapped up in your own dramas to notice anyone else. And that's genetic too," she says, flashing me a sad little grin. "Unbridled narcissism is practically your birthright."

In the distance, I can hear Russ's voice calling me from the parking lot. "They're looking for us," I say.

She nods and takes my hand as I help her off the breakwater, then carries her shoes as we walk across the sand toward the parking lot. I can see my father and Claire spinning around like Fred and Ginger in the glow of the sodium lights. "Dad was something else tonight, huh?"

My mother nods, and loops her arm through mine. "Here's

what will happen. When we get home he'll want to make love repeatedly, and then he'll lie in bed holding me, telling me stories about you all when you were kids, or about when we were first dating, and I'll stay up as long as I can, holding on to him, not wanting to miss a minute of it, wishing we could stay like that forever, but eventually I'll fall asleep while he's still talking. And when I wake up tomorrow morning, he'll be urinating in the flowerbeds, or playing ball in his underwear, or building a tower of glass on the living room floor with my grandmother's crystal, or God knows what. And I'll hide under my covers crying and wondering when and if I'll see him again." She turns to face me, her eyes wide and knowing, and puts a cold hand on my cheek. "You lost your wife, Douglas. My heart breaks for you, it really does. But I lose my husband every day, all over again. And I don't even get to mourn."

"Jesus, Mom," I say, my voice cracking, but she's already walking again. It's a favorite technique of hers. She likes to stick and move. Stick and move.

"Come on, Douglas," she says brightly, pulling me forward. "Life's a bitch, there's no doubt about it. But on the bright side, at least one of us is going to get laid tonight."

In the parking lot my father comes over to my mother and throws his suit jacket and then his arm over her trembling shoulders. They say good night to the Sandlemans, who are still looking a little shell-shocked from the whole horror show and probably can't wait to get into their car and start talking about us. Once they're gone, the rest of us hug and shake hands as we say our good-byes, and to an outside observer, someone who doesn't know us any better, we probably look exactly like a regular family.

14

How to Talk to a Widower
By Doug Parker

There are three things that people will say without fail when confronted with you, three things that you wish like hell they wouldn't say, inane platitudes guaranteed to make your bowels clench and the blood in your ears pound with rage. And even though by now you're braced for them, when you hear them you still find yourself struggling to quell the overpowering urge to bark obscenities and hurl large, breakable objects, to haul off and punch the well-wishers in their sympathetically creased faces, to feel the crack of bone under your fist, see the hot crimson spray of blood erupt like a geyser from their nostrils.

"I'm sorry."

I know it's the universal default, but the problem is, one's first knee-jerk response when someone says "I'm sorry" is to say "It's okay." We are programmed from kindergarten, from the first time the inevitable snot-nosed kid knocks over our blocks, to forgive. And it's not okay, it's as far from okay as it can really get, but there you are, tricked by a sociolinguistic tic into affirming that it is. Not only that, but now you've switched roles, and you're comforting instead of being comforted, which is fine, you're sick of people fruitlessly trying to comfort you, you're a man and you like to take your comfort in private; drinking too much and screaming at the television, punching brick walls, or crying in the shower, where your tears can be obliterated as soon as they emerge. But under no circumstances should you have to stand there and comfort someone else. You've just lost your wife, I think it's safe to say you've got your own problems. So after that happens a few times, you train yourself to simply say thank you, and then you just feel ridiculous. Thank you for being sorry. What the hell does that even mean? It's yet one more evidentiary exhibit of meaninglessness in what has become an almost completely meaningless existence.

"How are you doing?"

Once again, your first impulse is a betrayal. Because your mouth wants to say "fine," and they're expecting you to say "fine," hoping to God you'll say "fine," maybe with a sad, weary shrug, but "fine" nonetheless. They have expressed their rote concern, and "fine" is their receipt for tax purposes. But you're not fine, you're a fucking mess, often drunk before lunch and talking to yourself, weeping over photos, losing hours at a time staring into space, torturing yourself with an infinite array of if-only scenarios, feeling lost or devastated or angry or guilty or some potent cocktail blend of all of those at any given moment. You want to move on, but to do that you have to let her go; and you don't want to let her go, so you don't move on. Or maybe you do, just a little bit, and then you feel the grief of losing her all over again, and the guilt of trying to stop feeling that grief, and then you get pissed because you feel guilty when you shouldn't, and then you feel guilty for being pissed about your dead wife. Does that sound like "fine" to you? And to say it is to somehow discredit everything you're going through, and, in some way, it feels like a slight to your dead wife, the mark of an inferior love, for you to be fine. But no one wants to hear the ugly truth, and even if they did, you don't really feel comfortable sharing your grief like that, so once again you just say "fine," and breathe deeply until the impulse to commit a gory, ritualistic homicide has passed.

"Is there anything I can do?"

Yes, now that you mention it. Go back in time and stop my wife from getting on that goddamn plane. That would be a big help, actually. I'd be eternally grateful. Short of that, what could you have possibly thought you were going to offer that would solve my problems here? Cook me dinner? I lost my wife, not my micro-wave.

And whatever you do, do *not* attempt to empathize.

Don't whip out your own tragedy like a secret fraternity handshake. This misery wants no company. I don't want to hear about your father's car crash, your mother's heart attack, your sister's slow death from leukemia. My sorrow trumps all others, and I don't want to be mucking about in your grief any more than I want you mucking about in mine.

I know you mean well, but that doesn't make it any easier to listen to you. If you want to demonstrate your friendship and support, here's what you do: Leave it alone. Don't address it directly. I know you think praising my wife or sharing a warm remembrance will somehow ease my pain, but you'll just have to take my word for it that it won't. If you can't look the other way, then a simple greeting is really all that I can stand right now. If you feel you absolutely must acknowledge my tragedy, then you can do one of those somber nods, with the pursed lips and the raised eyebrows, and I'll let it slide. But beyond that, keep it light. Ask me the time, and I'll check my watch. Invite me along to a movie. I'll say no, but you'll have offered and we'll have shared a simple exchange that didn't make me want to flay the skin off your face. And maybe, if I have enough of those simple exchanges, just basic human contact that asks nothing of me, maybe I'll start being able to start maintaining eye contact once again, start engaging the world at my own pace.

And then, who knows? Maybe one day you'll catch

me at just the right moment and I'll actually agree to go to the movies with you, because it will get me out of the house and I'll know that for two hours I won't have to make conversation. Then, when it's over, we can talk about the movie. You won't have made anything better, you won't have helped me come to terms with my loss, but the sooner you give up on that dream, the better off we'll both be. Healing is a deeply private process and, honestly, you're not welcome to be a part of it. But you will have given me a short furlough from the dark, sorry prison of my mind, and that gift, precious in its own right, is really the best you can hope to offer.

And it should go without saying that if you bring me to a romantic comedy, I will shoot you dead before turning the gun on myself.

15

_____

From: _Kyle.Evans@EvansLitAgents.com_
To: _Doug.Parker@mmag.com_
Date: Wednesday, September 27, 2006
Subject: It's On

Talked to Simon & Schuster, Doubleday, and Riverhead.
They're all interested. I can start entertaining offers as
soon as you get me a formal proposal. We might even be
talking auction! Come on, Doug, let's do this! What the
hell else have you got to do?

—K

From: _Doug.Parker@mmag.com_
To: _Kyle.Evans@EvansLitAgents.com_
Date: Wednesday, September 27, 2006
Subject: No Thanks

Sorry, Kyle. I'm just not up for it.

—D

From: *Kyle.Evans@EvansLitAgents.com*

To: *Doug.Parker@mmag.com*

Date: Wednesday, September 27, 2006

Subject: Play the Hand You've Been Dealt

For fuck's sake, Doug! An auction! Remember all those years of shopping around one proposal after another? You would have given your left nut for this kind of opportunity!

—K

From: *Doug.Parker@mmag.com*

To: *Kyle.Evans@EvansLitAgents.com*

Date: Wednesday, September 27, 2006

Subject: That Was Then

This is now. Please leave me alone.

—D

From: *Kyle.Evans@EvansLitAgents.com*

To: *Doug.Parker@mmag.com*

Date: Wednesday, September 27, 2006

Subject: Strategy

Okay, you're playing hard to get. I like it. But just remember, you can only do it for so long. We need to make a deal soon.

—K

From:	*System Administrator*
To:	*Kyle.Evans@EvansLitAgents.com*
Date:	Wednesday, September 27, 2006
Subject:	Undeliverable

Your e-mail did not reach the intended recipient. Your
e-mail address [Kyle.Evans@EvansLitAgents.com] has
been listed as a blocked address by this recipient.

16

CLAIRE WAKES ME UP FROM A SWEET DREAM IN the later part of the morning. It was nothing too intricate, just Hailey and me driving somewhere, colored leaves rushing past us in an orange blur, listening to the radio. It's always autumn in my dreams. She was talking to me, and even though I heard her in the dream, I can't recall a single word or the tone of her voice. I lie in bed, feeling the emptiness take hold, the now familiar weight in my belly, the darkness hanging in the back of my mind. There's always this moment, when I first wake up, these precious seconds where I feel like me, the me before this one, and then lucidity sets in and the desolation pours into me, dark and viscous, like crude oil. I close my eyes and try to will myself back to sleep, back to Hailey, but the consciousness is electric, spreading through my body at the speed of light, and there will be no turning it off.

"Come on," Claire says. "Open your eyes."

I roll over to find her sitting Indian style at the foot of my bed, just like old times. Her designer sweat suit is a bright emerald green that actually hurts my eyes. "What time is it?" I say.

"Ten thirty-three. I made you some breakfast, but then I ate it. Sorry."

"It's okay," I say. "I'm not big on breakfast."

"It's the most important meal of the day," she says brightly.

I close my eyes and groan. "Can you come back later?"

"No. Wake up!" She pulls off my comforter.

"That's it," I say. "I think we need to lay down some house rules."

"Right. Because rules actually mean something to me."

I sit up groggily against the headboard. "What do you want, Claire?"

"Well, first off, I want you to put your soldier back into the fort."

"What? Oh. You're the one who pulled off the blanket," I say, straightening my boxers.

"Good point," she says, tossing it back to me. "Now, are you ready?"

"For what?"

She flashes a wide, talk show host smile. "For the rest of your life!" She looks at me expectantly.

"What are you babbling about?"

"Okay, Doug. Here's the way I see things," she says, pointedly patting her stomach. "Over the next little while, I am going to be creating an entirely new human being in here. Not only that, but I am going to do it with almost no conscious effort, right? So if I can build a completely new life in nine months with my eyes closed, I figure that we can rebuild your life in the same amount of time by focusing on it."

I look up at her. "It's as simple as that."

Her eyes are wide and unyielding. "As simple as you want it to be."

"I don't know what I want."

She nods. "And that's the beauty of having a twin who knows you better than you know yourself. I can know for you. If you needed a kidney or a liver transplant, I'd be your best bet, because inside we're the same. I'm just applying the same principle. I'm going to give you some of my heart to use until yours starts beating again."

"So what is it that you're proposing, exactly?"

"That you trust me completely, and agree to do whatever I say."

"Naturally."

"I'm serious, Doug. You're so busy mourning Hailey, you don't have time to think about anything else. But rationally, you know you have to start living again. So do the smart thing: delegate someone you trust to get the job done."

"What are you going to do, start setting me up on blind dates?"

She leans forward on her knees so she can get in my face. "I'm going to make you do anything that I think the old you would want to do."

"But I'm not him anymore."

"You're not anybody anymore."

We stare at each other for a long moment. She wins, as usual. "What would I have to do?" I say.

"Two things," she says. "And the first one is the hardest."

"What's that?"

She pulls herself forward to sit on my legs, effectively pinning me to the bed, and places her hands on my shoulders, her face just inches from mine. "You need to tell me that you want this."

"That I want what?"

"That you want to start living again, that you're willing to start being sad less often, that you're ready to move on, and you just need some help getting started. That you're willing to at least allow for the possibility of happiness."

"Of course I want that."

"So say it."

"Why?"

"Because you need to hear it."

"Claire." I start to look away and she grabs my chin and forces me to look right at her.

"Just shut up and do it."

"Okay," I say. "I want to start living again. I want to be happy again, at least sometimes. I don't honestly know if I'm ready to move on, but I know I want to be. And—" My voice catches in my throat, but I force my way through it. "And I don't know how to do it."

She brushes her pinky gently across my face to capture a solo tear I wasn't even aware of, and then kisses the tip of her dampened finger. "Okay," she says with a playful grin. "Good enough."

"What's the second thing?"

"Sorry?"

"You said there were two things I had to do."

"Oh right," she says. "That. That's actually pretty easy."

"Well?"

"Just say yes."

"To what?"

"To everything."

"To everything."

"That's right," she says, pulling herself off the bed. "Everything. You've spent the last year saying no to everyone and everything that came your way, and what do you have to show for it?"

"I didn't say no to Laney Potter."

"And it got you laid. Imagine if you said yes more often."

"I don't know if I could handle all the excitement."

"Well, we're going to find out. New rule: Just say yes."

"I thought rules didn't mean anything to you."

"They do when they're my rules. Now stop equivocating and just agree with me."

"Should I really trust my life to someone who is in the process of fucking up her own so spectacularly?"

"Make no mistake!" she says hotly. "I am unfucking my life. And while, to the untrained eye, the processes might look somewhat similar, I assure you the endgame is entirely different."

"Somehow, I don't think Stephen is going to see it that way."

She shrugs. "What can I tell you? You want to make an omelet, you have to break a few eggs. Now stop changing the subject, we can talk about me later. Are you in or not?"

I think about my father at dinner last night, smiling and lucid, so happy to be surrounded by his miserable, fucked-up children. I think of Debbie, weeping on his shoulder, and my mother's eyes following him as he danced. And then I think of

Hailey, kissing me slowly on the Ferris wheel as dusk settled like a warm blanket around us. "I'm in," I say.

"Okay," Claire says with a wicked smile. "It's on."

"So what happens now?"

"Now you get dressed and get your scrawny ass over to Radford Township High."

"What the hell for?"

"They called about an hour ago. Russ got into a fight. He's been suspended."

"Oh shit. Why didn't you tell me sooner?"

"It was on my agenda. I prioritized."

"Well, why don't they just call Jim?"

"Okay," Claire says, annoyed. "We're going to try this again. The school called you because Russ has been suspended. They would like you to come and get him. Are you going?" She fixes me with a stern look.

"Yes," I say.

She leans down and kisses my cheek. "Right answer," she says, heading for the door. "Now, was that so hard?"

17

RUSS GINGERLY PULLS OFF THE WET, BLOODSTAINED
paper towel wrapped around his right hand to reveal his torn
and bleeding knuckles. His left eye is half shut and a penumbra
of prune-colored swelling is spreading from the corner of his
eye socket down into his cheekbone. A smattering of minor
nicks and lacerations covers the left side of his face.

"Impressive," I say. "What did the other guy look like?"

"Like a big guy with his knees on my chest pounding the shit
out of me."

I nod. "You want to tell me about it?"

"It was just a stupid fight, Doug. No need to get all Dr. Phil
on me."

We're sitting on two of four attached chairs that line the hall
outside the guidance counselor's office. "So, what, I'm supposed
to go in and talk to your guidance counselor now?"

He nods indifferently. "She's waiting for you."

"I'm kind of relieved, actually. I thought I'd have to talk to
the principal."

"Dead mother gets you an express ticket to the school
shrink."

"I see." A group of three cute girls sashays past us in short, short, hip-hugging skirts and tight, midriff-baring T-shirts, talking and laughing a mile a minute. We turn as one to watch them head down the hall. "I did not have girls like that when I went to high school," I say.

"Neither do I," Russ says glumly, staring at the floor. I look at him, bruised and battered, still wordlessly grieving, but, unlike me, forced out into the world every day, to long for unattainable girls and do battle in the unforgiving halls of high school, with no one to come home to when the day is done, and I suddenly feel like a selfish, self-pitying prick.

"We don't talk very much, do we?" I say.

He looks up at me. "No. We don't."

"That's probably my fault."

"Probably." He shrugs, and holds his bloody hand up to the light, studying his shredded skin closely. "Jimbo and Angie are moving to Florida."

"What?"

He nods miserably. "They dropped the bomb last night. It's the Sunshine State, you know."

"Shit, Russ. That sucks. When?"

"After Christmas."

I don't know how to process this news. "What the hell is in Florida?"

"I don't know, some job or something. I kind of stopped hearing everything after the word 'Florida.'"

"Are you going to go?"

"What choice do I have?" he says, glaring at me. "It's not like I have anywhere else to live, right?"

I sigh, and put my head in my hands. "It's just not that simple, Russ."

"It is from where I'm sitting."

"Listen," I say, feeling completely out of my depth. "He's your father, and your sole legal guardian. I'm in no position to tell him what to do."

"Well, then. That makes two of us."

There's an important conversation to be had here, questions to be asked, assurances to be made, but I'll be damned if I can figure out how to do it. "Let me just go in and pay your bail or whatever, and then we'll go get some lunch and talk this through, okay?"

"There's nothing else to say."

"Then we'll eat in silence," I say, getting to my feet. "Don't worry, I'm used to it."

"Doug," he says as I'm opening the office door.

"Yeah."

"Could you please just talk to him?" His uninjured eye is wide, red, and earnest, and right at that moment I feel an overwhelming surge of affection for this sad, fucked-up kid, and the sudden tremor in my chest tells me that there are parts of my heart still able to be broken.

"Okay," I say, thinking resignedly, as I always do with regard to talking to Jim, that no good will ever come of it.

Russ's guidance counselor, Ms. Hayes, is younger than I expected, with straight black hair and milk-bath skin. "Mr. Parker," she says, shaking my hand. "Thanks for coming. I'm

Brooke Hayes." Her hair bounces as she sits back down, and I can see whole constellations of earrings, hoops and studs and bands, hiding under it, definitely not standard issue for high school guidance faculty.

"You're the guidance counselor?" I say.

"I get that a lot," she says. Her voice has the laid-back, slightly raspy quality of a rock singer, like she's just speaking between the measures and is about to break into a ballad of lost love.

"You look kind of young, that's all."

Her smile spreads like a brushfire across the open meadow of her face. "Well, thanks, I guess. But I'm fully licensed, I assure you. You look kind of young to be Russ's stepfather too. What are you, thirty?"

"Twenty-nine."

"Twenty-seven," she says. "I guess they figured the kids would relate to me."

"Do they?"

"Sometimes." She folds one knee under her, and beckons to the chair in front of me.

"So," I say, sitting down. "What's the deal here?"

"The deal is that Russ took on half the football team this morning and, as you can see, he got his ass kicked."

"They ganged up on him?" I say, feeling a hot band of rage tighten in my belly.

"According to witnesses, one of the guys made a remark and Russ just went off on him. The other kids were just trying to pull him off."

"Wow. What'd the guy say?"

"No one's talking."

"Was anyone badly hurt?"

She shakes her head. "Just the usual. But unfortunately for Russ, the high school enforces a zero-tolerance policy on violence. It's a mandatory three-day suspension."

"Ms. Hayes."

"Call me Brooke, please. And I'll call you Doug, okay? I mean, for God's sake, we're both under thirty, right?"

"Right," I say, somewhat disconcerted by her easy, casual manner. "Brooke. You realize that I'm not Russ's legal guardian. That he lives with his father."

"Yeah," she says slowly, biting down on her lip thoughtfully as she sizes me up. "I had Jim in here the last time Russ got into a fight."

"It's happened before?"

She gives me a curious look. "It's pretty much a regularly scheduled event these days," she says. "Anyway, Jim gave me a fairly incoherent speech about kids needing to fight their own battles, and how he didn't raise his son to back down from bullies."

"He didn't raise him, period," I say.

She nods, peering intently at me. "Then he asked me when I got off."

"Jesus."

"Yeah. So this time I figured it might make sense to try another avenue. Russ speaks very highly of you."

"He does?"

She grins and holds up her hands. "Okay, I might be reading between the lines there. I mean, you have to do that with a kid like Russ. He doesn't say very much. But from what little he has said, I can tell that he likes you. Also, I hope you'll forgive me for saying it, I read your column in *M,* and . . ." Her voice trails off. "Okay. Never mind that part. It's not relevant."

"What?" I say.

"I don't want to overstep my bounds."

"You don't strike me as someone who is very big on boundaries, Brooke."

"Sensitive and intuitive," she says with an approving smile. "Okay. What I was going to say is that, in addition to sounding smart and sad, you strike me as a deeply angry person."

"Angry," I repeat. "Who am I angry at?"

"Take your pick. Angry at the world for letting what happened to you happen, or at God, if that's your thing. Or maybe at your wife for having the nerve to die, or at yourself for not stopping her."

"You're psychoanalyzing me based on my column?"

"The very fact that you're writing that column is proof enough. You're lashing out, trying to hold the world accountable. It's perfectly natural to feel that way."

"I'm so relieved. Now, can we actually talk about Russ?"

"But I am talking about Russ," she says, ignoring my hostile tone. "When we are in the anger stages of grief, we will often subconsciously push away anything or anyone that we associate with the person we lost. And the tragedy is that the two of you are going through the same thing. He's as sad and angry and confused and alone as you are, plus he's a teenager, which means that on his best days his life is a shit storm. He needs someone to talk to, to help him through this, and there's no one better equipped to understand him than you."

"You're saying that I'm pushing Russ away?" I say, pissed. "You don't know a goddamn thing about me."

"You're right," she says, leaning forward in her chair. "I just know that he's not going to get the help he needs from his father, and he won't open up to me. He's a good kid, you know that. A little introverted, but very bright and compassionate. And when a kid like that starts acting out and getting into fights, generally speaking, he's trying to get someone's attention, and you can be damn well sure it's not Jim's."

Through the window behind her I can see a group of kids hanging out on cars in the parking lot, laughing, flirting, chasing, grabbing, kissing, and groping, and I would give anything to be any one of them, even if just for a few minutes, to feel the unspoiled future splayed out in front of me again as far as the eye can see.

"Doug," she says after a bit, and I realize that I zoned out for a little while there.

"What?"

"You're angry."

"So you've been telling me."

"No, I mean right now. At me."

"No," I say softly. "You're probably right. I screwed up. I haven't been there for him. I wanted to be, I just wasn't."

"It's not your fault," she says. "You were grieving. And it's not like it's too late. Just reach out to him. Let him know you're there for him."

"They're moving to Florida."

Her eyes grow wide and her jaw drops, her lips forming a perfect little O of surprise. "What?"

"It's the Sunshine State," I say dumbly.

"I meet with Russ every week. He never said anything."

"He just found out."

"Well, that explains today's fight, I guess," Brooke says, leaning back in her chair, deflated. "Jesus Christ, Doug! No one under eighty moves to Florida. Isn't that like a federal statute or something?"

"Well, they are," I say.

"If you asked me how to go about irreversibly screwing up that boy, you know what I would tell you to do?"

"What?"

"Take him away from his friends and his hometown and the memories of his mother, and send him to a new state with that father of his."

"Somehow, I knew you were going to say that."

"What are you going to do about it?"

"I don't think there's anything I can do about it."

"And somehow, I knew you were going to say that."

"Yeah," I say sadly, standing up to leave. "I'm predictable like that."

"Well," she says, standing up. "Maybe you'll surprise yourself one of these days."

"Maybe."

"Doug," she says hesitantly as she comes around the desk. "You didn't invent grief. My shrink once told me that."

"Really? Your shrink told you about me?"

Her laugh comes from her belly, loud, musical, and completely unrestrained. "The point is, people become possessive of their grief, almost proud of it. They want to believe it's like no one else's. But it is. It's exactly like everybody else's. Grief is like a shark. It's been around forever, and in that time there's been just about no evolution. You know why?"

"Why?"

"Because it's perfect just the way it is." She smiles compassionately, and I can see there's a faint dusting of glitter in her eye shadow, which strikes me as sweet, a glimpse of the little girl who still lives there, the one who believes in fairies and princesses.

"Why did he say that to you?"

"Excuse me?"

"Why were you grieving?"

She grins. "Now what kind of professional would I be if I discussed my personal life with you?"

"I guess you have some boundaries after all."

"When they suit me," she says, meeting my gaze. "Maybe I'll tell you under different circumstances. When I wouldn't be compromising myself professionally."

There are only a handful of ways to interpret or misinterpret that last remark, but I've been out of the game for way too long to try, no matter how loudly the Claire in my head is calling me chickenshit. "Okay," I say, extending my hand. "Thanks for the talk, or session, or whatever this was."

"You're welcome."

The doorknob sticks when I turn it. "You have to pull it up," she says, and as she squeezes past me to open it, I catch a whiff of her, a pleasant blend of blow-dried citrus shampoo, spearmint gum, and cigarettes that makes me suddenly homesick for something I can't quite pinpoint. Not that I'm trying to smell her or anything.

18

RUSS LOOKS UP WHEN I STEP BACK OUT INTO THE hallway. "So?" he says.

"So," I say, sitting down next to him.

"How'd it go?"

"Not really what I expected."

"I know. It's almost worth being a fuckup, getting sent to her office every week."

"You're not a fuckup. You're the brightest kid I know."

"I'm the only kid you know."

"So you're it by default. You still hold the title."

"Whatever," he says with a shrug. "Am I suspended?"

"Yes."

"Excellent," he says. "Paid vacation."

"But who's paying?"

He pulls his hair off his face and runs his fingers over his swollen eye. "Look at my face, dude. It's already paid for." He stands up and lifts his hands over his head to stretch his back. "Let's get out of here."

"Where to, exactly?"

"I don't know, but I'm driving."

* * *

Outside the sky has filled with thick ash-colored thunderheads, and as Russ adjusts the driver's seat and mirrors, the first droplets of rain start to fall onto the windshield.

"Check your mirrors before you pull out."

"I did."

"You didn't signal."

"Nobody signals."

"You'll fail your road test if you don't signal. Two hands on the wheel, please."

"I drive better with one."

"Well, I ride better with two. Look out!"

A van swerves around our protruding hood, honking angrily. Russ casually flips the bird out the window. "I saw him," Russ says.

"Of course you did."

"Should I get on the highway?"

"Sure, but stop at this red light first."

He stomps on the brakes and we skid to a stop, bouncing hard against our seat belts.

"She's pretty cute, isn't she?" Russ says.

"Who?"

"Ms. Hayes."

"If you like that look."

"Everybody likes that look."

"I guess I was too busy hearing about how you got your ass kicked to pay attention. What was that fight about anyway?"

"He made a crack about my tattoo."

"What did he say?"

"I didn't actually hear the whole thing."

"But you hit him anyway."

"He had it coming."

The light turns green and Russ accelerates a bit too hard, jerking me back lightly against my seat. "Easy." The rain is starting to come down harder, beating noisily against the windshield. Russ flips on the wipers and turns onto the entrance ramp of the Sprain Brook Parkway. "Have you driven in the rain before?" I say.

"Don't worry about it," Russ says, merging onto the highway and gunning the engine.

"Watch your speed."

"You watch it. I'm watching the road." He moves into the left lane and levels off at sixty.

"Where are we headed?"

"You'll see."

Ahead of us in the center lane is a tractor trailer, its wheels churning out a furious spray of water. Russ speeds up, trying to pass, but the truck keeps inching over into our lane. "Move it!" Russ says, beating down on his horn.

"Just slow down," I say. "You can't pass him here."

"The hell I can't."

Up ahead the highway turns, and as we enter the curve, Russ accelerates into it, inching up alongside the trailer, which shimmies noisily much too close to my window, obscuring our windshield with the thick blanket of mist coming off its immense wheels. "Russ!" I shout at him.

"Shut up!" he yells.

I can feel our tires sliding on the rain-slicked blacktop as the force of our turn pushes us within inches of the trailer, its mud flaps cracking like bullwhips, and our screams are drowned out by the bellowing horn of the truck as we slide toward the trailer's undercarriage. And then, a second before impact, Russ floors it and we zip out ahead of the truck, who yanks on his horn and machine-guns us with his high beams.

"Jesus Christ, Russ!" I say, still braced for the collision.

"That was pretty bad," he admits, eyes wide. "But at least we know for sure that you don't want to die anymore."

"Very funny."

He signals right and moves across the lanes toward an exit.

"Where are we going?" I say, but I already know.

Russ looks at me and smiles. "To tell Mom the good news."

I've learned that visiting the cemetery just doesn't work for me. I'm simply too caught up in the morbid physicality of it all. In the weeks after Hailey's death I tried to get used to it. I would come and sit on the lawn beside her grave and make halting attempts at one-sided conversation, but I just couldn't make myself believe there was anyone listening, and even if I could, talking to the grave never made any sense to me. If there's an afterlife, and they can hear you, shouldn't they be able to hear you from anywhere? What's the theory here, that talking to the dead requires range, like a cell phone, and if you go too far the call gets dropped? I know that if I were a spirit, the last place you'd find me haunting would be my grave, watching my body rot. I don't like looking in the mirror on my best days.

And so, without fail I would end up looking into the grass,

picturing her coffin six feet below, its lacquered surface, once buffed to shine like a Cadillac, now caked with dirt and grime. And that would lead to trying to visualize the contents of the coffin, so instead of communing with Hailey's memory, I'd find myself picturing the gruesome remains of what was once my wife. I don't know what we buried, but between the impact of the plane and the subsequent immolation, it couldn't have been more than a few pieces of her, splinters of bone and charred flesh and hair, all fused together in some grisly collage, some horror movie prop resembling nothing remotely human. If there's one thing I've learned from this whole experience, it's that cremation is the way to go. It's clean, efficient, and, most important, leaves nothing to the imagination. We could turn all the cemeteries into forests and playgrounds.

Russ and I stand solemnly in the rain, surrounded by white and gray tombstones that rise out of the earth like jagged teeth as far as the eye can see. We peer doggedly at the etchings on Hailey's as if looking for edits or amendments that might have been made since we last were here.

"I can't believe it's been over a year already," Russ says.

"I know."

"Sometimes it feels like a week, and other times it seems like so long ago, like I can't even remember what life was like when she was here."

"Do you come out here a lot?" I say.

"When I can get a lift."

"You've never asked me."

Russ nods, his hair slick and matted with rain. "I didn't want to bring you down."

"That would be a neat trick, considering where I am these days."

"Do you ever talk to her?"

"I hear her in my head all day."

He turns to me. "But do you talk to her?"

I brush the rain-soaked hair out of my eyes. "Not really," I say. "No."

"Well, I hope you won't mind if I do."

"Of course not."

Russ steps forward, brushes some leafy debris off the small, square-trimmed hedges at the foot of the grave, and then kneels, leaning his head against the stone, eyes closed. He does this without a trace of his usual self-consciousness, and I know that hearing him speak to her will be more than I can bear, so I step back a few paces and turn around. A funeral procession has just arrived on the other side of the cemetery, and I watch the small parade of red and black umbrellas bouncing almost jauntily among the graves, following the pallbearers as they make their way across the geometric landscape of glistening tombstones.

I had a wife. Her name was Hailey. Now she's gone. And so am I.

I watch the funeral for a little while longer, until I hear a rasping sound behind me, and turn to find Russ weeping violently against Hailey's tombstone, his face twisted into a mask of anguish, rocking back and forth like he's in the grip of unseen gale-force winds. "Russ," I say, stepping over to him. "It's okay." But of course it isn't, and he knows it, and he presses his fingertips desperately against the stone, desperate to feel something more than just the cold, wet granite. I bend down, unsure of how to approach him, but as soon as I touch his shoulder he collapses into me, pulling me down to my knees in the soaked grass, burrowing his face into the crook of my elbow, clutching my arm as he lets out a long, shuddering cry. And as my body shakes along with his, I look down to where his wet hair is falling away from his neck, and I can see the tattoo of Hailey's comet glistening on his drenched skin, staring right up at me like an accusation, and I decide that, afterlife or not, it's high time I had a talk with Jim.

19

THE PUBES IN THE WASTEBASKET HAD BEEN THE
first clue.

Hailey stood naked in her bathroom that morning, poised to
step into the shower, when a ball of fur in the wastebasket
caught her eye. She let out a small, startled cry, thinking it was a
mouse, but even as she did, she saw that the mound of hair, resting in the basket on some discarded soap packaging, was not
moving. She peered down into the wastebasket, still half asleep,
trying to comprehend what she was seeing. At first she thought
it was a Furby, one of those toy creatures that had been all the
rage a few Christmases ago. Maybe Russ's had broken and he'd
thrown it out. She crouched down to get a better look, and only
then did she see that the strange pile was actually a mound of
pubic hair. More specifically, it was Jim's pubic hair. It made for
a perplexing picture, Jim standing naked over the wastebasket,
shaving his pubic region. She stared at the dark, kinky mass,
which, she now observed, had reddish highlights. She'd been
married to Jim for almost ten years, and had never noticed that
his pubic hair had red highlights. Was this a spousal failing on
her part? Did other wives notice things like that? She stood

back up, frowning slightly. Why was Jim, after all this time, suddenly shaving his pubic hair? The options played out before her like a standardized test.

    A. He had too much and it irritated him.
    B. He had somehow contracted crabs or lice.
    C. He wanted his penis to seem bigger.
    D. None of the above.

She felt a knot forming in her stomach. Since she was fairly certain that A was not the correct answer—Jim was not a terribly hirsute person—and since B, C, and D all seemed to point to the same highly troubling scenario, she stepped out of the bathroom to grab her cordless and call her friend Sally.

"Oh God!" Sally said, panting on her StairMaster.

"What do you mean, oh God?"

"He's having an affair."

"I don't think so," Hailey said.

"Is Jim small down there?"

"Excuse me?"

"I'll apologize later," Sally said. "You didn't call me for polite conversation."

"No," Hailey said, after a moment. "He's pretty normal sized."

"So why does a happily married man suddenly feel the need to look bigger?"

"I don't know."

"Well, either he's doing porno, and I think we can rule that out, or he's looking to impress someone, and, honey, he doesn't need to impress you anymore. Oprah did this whole thing on cheating spouses, and a conspicuous change in grooming habits is definitely a red flag."

Hailey frowned into the phone. There was no reasoning with Sally once Oprah had been invoked. "There could be a million other reasons."

"That's true," Sally said, her voice clenched from her exertions. "But, Hailey?"

"What?"

Sally paused. "Nothing."

"What?" Hailey demanded. Over the phone she could hear the stair machine stop as Sally stepped off, breathing heavily.

"I don't know," Sally said. "It's just that he's done it before."

"Oh, for Christ's sake, that was before we were even married."

"I'm just saying."

"Well, don't," Hailey said hotly, her eyes filling with tears. "That was an isolated incident, an old girlfriend he hadn't quite gotten over, and we worked through it. We've been married for almost ten years, and I think he deserves the benefit of the doubt."

"He's probably counting on it."

"You are being such a bitch!" Hailey shouted at her.

Sally sighed. "Listen, honey, if you were looking for someone to just reassure you that everything was fine, you should have called Laney, and she would have talked you down. But you called me, and you know that's not my thing. But I'm not the person you should be calling, either. So why don't you ask yourself why you didn't just call Jim to ask him?"

So Hailey had called Jim and Jim told her that he'd been suffering from some bad jock itch, and that was that. Except that he'd never mentioned it before. And Jim always complained about the slightest ailment, a hangnail, a pulled muscle, allergies. And there were no fungus creams or powders lying around their cluttered bathroom. She sat down on the toilet seat cover, the cordless clutched in her fist like a weapon, and that's where she remained all morning, naked and shivering, staring at the brown hairs in the wastebasket for a very long time.

All this Hailey reported to me after the first time we had sex, an event which came off much better than advertised, what with her self-consciousness about her thirty-six-year-old body and my not inconsiderable performance anxiety. I was supposed to be the young stallion, after all, fit and virile and ready to fuck her sideways into tomorrow. That was exactly the kind of pressure that could play with your head if you let it, that could lead to the "it-happens-to-everyone-sometimes/not-to-me-it-doesn't" conversation.

We'd been dating intensely for over a month by then, and it had already taken on a life of its own: long, confessional phone calls fading into whispers as the hour grew late, roses and flowers and cute e-mails at work, making out for hours at a time in her car before she drove home. On days that we'd be going out, Hailey drove to work instead of taking the Metro-North, ostensibly because she didn't want to take the train so late, but the car, parked at the fire hydrant in front of my building, became the perfect venue for our extended good nights, so much more comfortable than groping at each other in my stairwell, which was poorly insulated and smelled of feet and spoiled milk. I couldn't recall the last time I'd spent so much time just kissing someone. It always seemed to me that any kissing that didn't advance to naked foreplay after the first ten minutes simply grew stale from lack of direction. But Hailey and I could go at it for hours, until our lips were swollen and chapped, tongues numb, jaws locked, and afterwards I'd climb back up to my apartment to ice my aching balls, with the taste of her delightfully lodged in the back of my parched throat, her scent inhaled so powerfully that it penetrated my brain behind my eyes in lavender cloudbursts. It seemed juvenile, really, a man my age barely getting to second base, but there was something undeniably exciting about it too. And while we knew that sex was inevitable, was the driving force behind the whole process, the fact that I was dating a single mother made me feel particularly responsible about introducing sex into the relationship before I knew I was committed. Also, she was a beautiful woman who'd been with the kind of men who routinely score beautiful women and, frankly, I was scared I wouldn't measure up.

But innate horniness will always prevail, and soon enough we ended up naked and sweaty in my bed, venting a month's worth of pent-up desire in a wild, unprecedented session that left no sexual stone unturned. When it was finally over, we lay motionless and panting beside each other on my wrecked sheets as the sweat cooled and dried on our skin, like two wounded soldiers left behind on the battlefield. "Oh my God," Hailey gasped softly, her eyes wide and incredulous in the dim light of my darkened bedroom.

"Who knew?" I agreed.

"Well, I had my suspicions," she said, turning her head to lick the sweat off my neck. I reached over for her and she rolled easily into me, throwing her thigh over mine, her head resting on my chest. "We fit perfectly," she said, and as I kissed her scalp, I felt the tears inexplicably come to my eyes. I knew from having been on the other end that crying after sex can send a bad message, so I closed my eyes and hoped Hailey wouldn't look up. She seemed to know, but instead of questioning me, she pressed her lips against my chest, her fingers splayed out over the line of hair bisecting my stomach. After a minute she said, "You okay?"

"I'm just a little more in love than I thought," I said, surprising us both. First tears, now love. I could practically feel the testosterone evaporating through my pores.

She nodded, and kissed my chest again in a way that made me shake. "Don't let it freak you out."

"I won't if you don't."

She looked up at me and grinned. "After what Jim put me through, it would take a lot to freak me out."

"You want to tell me about it?"

She slid up to rest her head in the crook of my neck. "Our story begins with the pubes in the wastebasket," she intoned softly, like Alistair Cooke.

"As such stories so often do," I said, and she shoved me playfully, and we both laughed. And it was good.

20

WHEN DOGS MEET, THEY SNIFF EACH OTHER'S ASSES. When women meet, they check each other out to determine who is prettier. When men meet, the paramount question is who would kick whose ass in a fight, and when Jim came by to check me out shortly after I moved in with Hailey, that wasn't really an issue up for debate. Jim was big, the kind of big that made me feel small and off balance. Somehow, in describing him, Hailey had failed to mention the sheer bulk of him, the superhero chin, the thick, corded neck of a Greco-Roman wrestler, the imposing, bearish frame, and large sausage fingers that closed over mine like a clamp when we shook hands. Thick raised veins snaked up his forearm like rural back roads on a map, all converging on the Wal-Mart of his bulging bicep. My first instinct was to match might with might, but to do that you have to actually have some might of your own, so instead I let my hand fall limp, taking the high road, refusing to be engaged in Jim's macho bullshit, but then I thought I might be coming off like a wuss, so I tried to consolidate my hand in such a way that, while not squeezing back, it would still feel solid and unyielding to Jim's force. Basically, I fucked up the handshake. It would never be mentioned, but I knew it, and Jim knew it, and that was all that mattered. I would soon learn that the unsaid things were all that mattered in dealing with your wife's ex-husband.

"How are you doing?" Jim said, nodding smugly as he looked me up and down, mostly down. *I can wipe the floor with you, you little prick.*

"Pretty good," I said. *You might have won the handshake, but I'm sleeping with your ex-wife. Do the math, big guy.*

"So, you all moved in?" *To my goddamn house?*

"Pretty much." *You snooze, you lose.*

"Well, maybe now you can fix it up a little." *You look like you wouldn't know a power tool if I shoved one up your scrawny ass.*

"I'm not really the handy type." *Maybe if you paid your child support every once in a while, Hailey would be able to afford some basic repairs. Fucking deadbeat.*

"Must be some adjustment, having to live with a kid like this." *My kid, motherfucker. So you just watch yourself.*

"Oh, I don't mind." *A small price to pay for sleeping with your ex-wife. Did I mention that I'm sleeping with your ex-wife? I am. Frequently. Repeatedly. Constantly. Everything else is just what I do when I'm not having sex with her.*

"He's a great kid." *Stay the fuck away from him.*

"I know." *No thanks to you, you pube-shaving freak.*

"So, I hear you're a writer?" *Fag.* "What sorts of stuff?"

"Magazine writing, mostly." *Like you even read.*

"Oh." *Broke fag.*

We stared across the gulf at each other, smiling like macho idiots. If we had antlers they'd be locked; if we were in high school, he would be tripping me in the cafeteria and stepping on my head.

Two long-haired girls in tight, low-riding jeans and bared midriffs walk past us, and Jim momentarily cranes his neck to watch them from behind as they walk toward the back of the bar. The place is crowded, but Jim has managed to snag a table off to one side, taking the seat up against the wall so that he can watch the passing parade of ass while we talk. I'd offered on the phone to come see him in his office, but he was already finished for the day, and told me to meet him here at Clover, which I'm sensing now is a regular after-work hangout of his. I don't know if he thought it would make for a friendlier meeting, or he just likes to look at the college girls who seem to make up about eighty percent of the bar's clientele, but I figured a little lubrication could only help, which is why I got here early and laid down a primary coat of two Jack and Cokes at the bar before he showed up. And now here I am, floating on my minor buzz and sharing a pitcher with Jim, who ogles the girls while drumming his fingers on the table to Gwen Stefani on the juke-box. I haven't seen Jim in some time, and I'm at that early, sharp stage of drunkenness, where all of your senses are heightened and you see everything in high definition, so I find myself doing a quick visual reconnaissance. He's dressed in khakis and a short-sleeve polo shirt that strains equally against his large bi-ceps and his impressive gut, which kind of cancel each other out. His hair, once dark and thick, is starting to gray on the sides and show more forehead, and the flesh under his eyes is gray and puckered like an orange peel. His once ruddy complexion has become soft and doughy, the incipient jowls just beginning to soften his square, superhero jaw. Still, he manages to look healthy and handsome, like a retired football player just beginning to go to pot.

Jim looks away from the girls and sizes me up thoughtfully, a salesman mentally choosing the right pitch. "You and I have never really hit it off," he says.

"I guess not."

"And if you think about it, there was really only one reason for that."

Because you're a colossal asshole? "How do you figure?"

Jim nods and takes a sip of his beer. "Hailey," he says. "It was a sticky situation. She was your wife and my ex. I don't doubt that she gave you an earful about me, and you would have been biased before you ever met me."

"If it makes you feel any better," I say, "I probably wouldn't have liked you very much anyway."

Jim studies my face, trying to calibrate his own level of antagonism against mine, and then chuckles lightly. "Nice." *Little shit.*

This is what inevitably happens when Jim and I are forced to approximate cordiality. Jim hates me because he takes it personally that Hailey loved me, even though that happened after they were through, and I take it personally that Jim cheated on Hailey, even though it happened long before I was in the picture. The chronology should nullify or at least temper our instinctive hostility, but we have penises, Jim and I, and so rationality is not really an option. These are the roles we've been assigned, and it's not clear why we're powerless to change this dynamic, but what is clear is that Jim is dying to hit me. In a perfect world, Jim would stand up, hurl the table between us out of the way, and reach for my throat. He is bigger and stronger than me, and has no doubt been in more fights, but I'm fearless and quick as greased lightning, and I'll dodge his clumsy swings, will dart in and out, sticking the jab repeatedly as the crowd gathers, will bloody him slowly, with great precision, until his eyes start to close and his gums drip with blood, until he's dazed to the point that I can step in, arms up, shoulders rolling in a natural boxer's rhythm, to land the uppercut that will lay him out for good. Then I'll apologize to the pretty bartender, who will look at me with newfound respect and hand me a towel filled with ice, and I'll sit on the stool, calmly icing my bloody knuckles while they prop Jim up and slap his face until he regains consciousness. "How many fingers am I holding up?" the off-duty paramedic will ask him. "Thursday," Jim will say, his eyes rolling up into his head. But this is not a perfect world, and if you need any further proof you'll find exhibits A and B conveniently located right here at this sticky table varnished with generations of spilt beer, so Jim and I are forced to internalize our natural antagonism, to sit on our hands while the juggernaut of our aggression spins furiously inside of us, stirring things up that have nowhere to go.

"Russ sleep at your place last night?" he says resignedly.

"Yeah."

"I figured as much." He downs a shot of whiskey and chases it with some beer. "I could dead-bolt that kid into his room, and he'd still find a way to get out of the house." He seems more amused than sad about this fact, so I just keep quiet. "He tell you about Boca?"

"He mentioned it," I say, sipping at my beer.

"He's not too happy about it."

"No, he's not."

Jim nods his head somberly. "Angie's brother's got a hurricane shutter business down there. After what happened in New Orleans, they can't expand fast enough."

"What do you know about hurricane shutters?"

He shrugs. "How hard can it be?"

He's probably right. Jim is used to making his living off the misfortune of others. He's an ambulance chaser, a bottom-feeder whose legal practice consists primarily of processing personal injury claims for Radford's large immigrant population. He has carved out a niche for himself over the years by passing his cards to the multitude of day laborers that enter New Radford each day: nannies, cleaning ladies, landscapers, and contractors. He has contacts in all the local emergency rooms, and will usually show up with Lucia, his on-call translator, while the patients are still in triage. He works on contingency, settles with the insurance companies, and on those rare occasions that the case seems headed for court, he dishes to more qualified lawyers for a percentage. Jim doesn't do court. In the ecosystem of the legal community, Jim Klein is pond scum. Cashing in on potential misfortune instead of actual misfortune will actually be a step up for him.

"I think it will be pretty hard for Russ," I say.

"Frankly, I think in the long run it will be good for him."

A pretty girl in short shorts and a tank top, with great

legs and impossibly luminous skin, smiles apologetically as she squeezes past our table and we both turn to watch her move away from us. Then Jim turns back to me, catches me looking, winks, and says, "Man, you could eat that ass with a spoon." But I will not let him draw me into any ass-banter. Okay, I looked too, I'll admit it, and yes, she did have an exceptional ass, truly first-rate, but unlike Jim, I'm not married and I'm actually within the outer limits of the girl's age range, which means I'm supposed to notice her, but if I respond to Jim, who is actually licking his lips, I'll be a dirty old man by association, so instead I say, "You think, after all the change Russ has been through this past year, that moving him to a new town, a new school, away from everyone he's ever known, will be good for him?"

Jim frowns and holds his beer mug up to the light like he's searching for clues, before taking another sip. "He's hanging out with some bad kids. The school shrink says he's been skipping school, and his grades are in the toilet."

"He can fall in with a bad crowd in any high school."

"Exactly," Jim says, turning to watch another gaggle of girls as they pass. "So what's the difference?"

"He's hurting, Jim. He's still grieving and he needs to come to terms. You move him to Florida, he'll just have that much more to be angry about. Can't you and Angie just wait a little while? He'll be off to college in a few years and then you can go."

"We've already put it off for Russ. We were all set to go last year. Everything was in place. But then Hailey died..."

"What a terrible inconvenience for you." I grip my mug tightly, wishing I was the kind of guy who would just smash it into Jim's face. He'd probably beat me to death and then sue my corpse. Goddamn lawyers.

Jim raises his massive hands apologetically. "Okay, that came out wrong. My point is just that with Hailey dying and my taking custody of Russ...this has all been a pretty big change for Angie and me to absorb."

"What about losing your mother in a plane crash? Where does that fall out on the scale of changes to absorb?"

Jim lowers his head to take a long swallow of beer, and when he raises it again there's a dab of beer foam on the point of his nose. "Don't get all high and mighty on me, Doug. Hailey's been poisoning that kid against me for years and you know it. You think it's easy, taking a kid who's been raised to hate you, and bringing him into a home with your wife and son? I already fucked up one marriage, and let me tell you, I'm not going to fuck up another one."

"So Russ doesn't matter."

"Of course he matters. But Angie and our little boy matter too." He takes another long sip. "I'm not the bad guy here."

"No. You're a fucking hero."

Jim's beer mug comes crashing down on the table, his hand closed into a white-knuckled fist on the handle, his face turning a deep, angry crimson hot enough to melt away the veneer of civility he'd worn up to this point. "Listen to me, you little shit," he says, his voice low and menacing. "I'm cutting you some slack because of your loss, but you're starting to try my patience. I took a lot of crap from Hailey, but I'm not going to take it from a punk like you. I love Russ, but like it or not, I've got a wife and another son to think about, and Russ comes with a lot of trouble that they don't need. You don't know shit about my life, you just got here, and I'll be damned if I'm going to let you sit there in judgment of me. You're not a member of this family, you're just part of the debris, a loose end who's still hanging around because he hasn't figured out where the hell else to go yet."

We stare across the table at each other, and I can see the naked hatred like a caged animal pacing frantically behind his eyes. I lived for two years with the woman he loved and the child he fathered, in the house he paid for. He traded his family for sex, and then traded that sex in for another family that I sometimes suspect he doesn't like very much, and while Hailey was still alive Jim was arrogant enough to believe that the only thing that kept him from taking back his first, better life was the man that had somehow supplanted him there. This isn't a guess on my part; I know it from the long, drunken messages he would occasionally leave on our answering machine in the middle of the night, crying to Hailey, begging her to call him.

"I'm not judging you, Jim."

"The hell you're not."

"This isn't about you and me," I say. "I'm just thinking about what's best for Russ."

Jim looks at me for a long moment. "You think it's so easy, why don't you keep him?"

"What?"

Jim shrugs. "He can live with you. Problem solved."

"He's not my kid."

"He may as well be." He sits back and finishes off his beer, instantly refilling it from the pitcher. "What do you think Hailey would want?"

"That's not the point."

"Isn't it?"

"I'm not in the equation. Like you said, I'm just part of the debris."

"And like you said, we're talking about what's best for Russ here," Jim says with a smug grin. "I guess we're both just babbling brooks of bullshit, aren't we?"

"He's your son, for Christ's sake! You can't just give him away."

Jim leans back in his chair, folding his hands behind his head and flexing his biceps for the ladies. "Angie is unhappy, and Russ is unhappy," he says. "It's my job to make them both happy, and the way I see it, there's only one way to do that, and the answer is you. And I know I'll just be confirming everyone's notion of what a shitty father I am, but in the end, doing what's right for your son is more important than looking good, right?"

"So you're saying giving up your son is the noble thing to do?"

"I'm not giving him up. I'm giving him his freedom."

I look at Jim, sweating through his polo shirt, so certain he's got the upper hand, and I think about Hailey, about how big her eyes would get when she talked to me about Russ, about how hard she was on herself about being a good mother. And I think about Russ crying into the unyielding granite of Hailey's grave, and lying in the humid dankness of Jim's basement listening to him and Angie fuck. And I think about how alone I am, how the desolation is like a cancer spreading through my gut, and I hear Claire's voice in my head, but I'm pretty sure that it's my own voice coming out of my mouth, saying, "Yes."

"What do you mean, yes?"

Just say yes.

"I mean okay. He can stay with me. I'll take him."

And if Jim is surprised, he doesn't let on. He just says, "Okay," and reaches across the table to shake my hand, like he's just sold me a car, and for reasons that elude me, I shake his back, smiling like an idiot. "He can come down to Boca to see us on holidays," he says.

"He'll be thrilled to hear it."

"Great," Jim says, getting to his feet. "He'll live with us until January, when we move. Maybe, once he knows he's not being forced to come, he'll be able to calm down and enjoy himself, get to know Angie and his brother a little bit better."

"Sounds good," I say.

"Okay," Jim says, reaching down to pat my shoulder. "Good talk." And then he's gone, weaving his way through the crowd to rush home and tell Angie the good news, no doubt figuring it will get him some extra loving tonight.

I sit there for a long time after he leaves, staring into space, oblivious to the crowd around me, running my tongue over the smooth lip of my beer mug. They're playing an old Billy Joel song on the jukebox, and I'm fifteen again, and I've just crashed a stolen Mercedes. My tongue is cut and I can taste the blood in my throat, my head is spinning as I watch the cops running in slow motion toward me, and I'm wondering, as I so often do, how I manage to get myself into these messes?

21

LONG AFTER THE COMING ICE AGE HAS BURIED this civilization, when archaeologists dig up downtown New Radford, the first thing their shovels will hit is the giant fiberglass Starbucks coffee cup suspended over the strip mall on Broadway like a Thanksgiving Day parade balloon. It's far and away the highest structure on the street, second in height only to the clock tower above the elementary school two miles away. Studying the way the town spreads out in concentric circles from Broadway, they might deduce that Starbucks was our temple, and coffee our God. And, much like God, I don't believe in coffee. I don't care how they flavor it, steam it, caramelize it, whip cream it, or foam it, it will still score your stomach lining like acid, ruin your breath, and strip the coating on your nerves, leaving them raw and exposed. Studies have not yet shown that Starbucks causes cancer, but the lawsuits are coming. I'm sure of it.

The problem with New Radford's downtown is that there's just not very much of it. Because of the municipality's maniacal determination to preserve the rustic feel of the town, the nearest true business district is three and a half miles down, where

Broadway becomes South Broadway and New Radford becomes just plain old Radford. But where Broadway runs through New Radford, there's just the one block of stores: Antonelli's Pizza, CVS, a few surprisingly mediocre restaurants, a mom-and-pop stationery store, the adjacent offices of the town's two competing real estate brokers, the Riviera Hair Salon, the Pink Petals Nail Salon, Mom's Homemade Ice Cream Shoppe, and, of course, Starbucks. Around the corner, on Roaring Creek Road, is the Super Stop and Shop and Blockbuster Video. A handful of investors tried to buy a piece of the Stop and Shop parking lot to put up an arcade, but the zoning board shot them down, just like they stopped Ikea, Bed Bath & Beyond, and the expansion of a local synagogue. Like all fairly affluent suburbs, preservation is the priority, not growth.

Consequently, it's next to impossible to venture into downtown New Radford without running into someone you know. Because one way or another you'll have to pass Starbucks, and there's always someone you know coming in or out of Starbucks. I never really thought about it until Hailey died, at which point simple trips to buy soap and razors turned into a grueling obstacle course of pity and gross fascination, friends and neighbors all eager to squeeze my arm, or hug me and ask me how I'm doing, or slowing down in their cars to point me out, rubbernecking in the parking lot like I was a disabled tractor trailer pulled over to the shoulder of the highway.

But it's morning and Claire wants her Venti Nonfat Mocha Latte or whatever, so in we go. We've missed the work crowd and now the place is filled with women, coming from the gym, headed to the gym, young mothers sitting in groups, mommy-thongs rising up over their low-rise jeans and designer sweat-pants as they bend over their toddlers. I nod awkward hellos to a number of people I know tangentially, who all smile and nod and they're probably averting their gazes almost immediately, although I can't be sure since I've already averted mine.

"I don't belong here," I mutter through clenched teeth to Claire. "I don't even drink coffee."

"Like a vegetarian at a steakhouse," she says.

"Like an atheist in church."

"Good one," she says approvingly. "Much better subtext."

"Thanks."

And here comes Mandy Seaver, one of New Radford's many housewives turned real estate brokers, a pleasant-faced, chubby woman who served on the PTA with Hailey, and used to bring me lasagna, garden salad, and inhumanly large wedges of her Harvey Wallbanger cake on Thursdays. Mandy, who would confide tearfully to Hailey that her husband had stopped touching her ever since her C-section, and who cried so loudly and consistently at the funeral you would have thought it was her wife they were burying. "Doug!" she yells across the shop, creating a small commotion as she charges noisily across the tiled floor. She grabs both of my elbows and then realizes that there's just not much to do with someone's elbows once you've gotten ahold of them, so she lets them go, her hands falling awkwardly to her sides. "It's so nice to see you out and about."

"Hi, Mandy."

"You look good," she says, her eyes crinkling up with concern.

"He looks like shit," Claire says, turning to the counter to order what sounds like six drinks but turns out to just be a coffee.

Mandy frowns at Claire, looking her up and down, worriedly speculating on the nature of our relationship. I sometimes forget how Claire looks to other women, stunning and too aggressively sexy for the suburbs.

"Don't worry," Claire says. "If I wasn't his sister, I'd be out of his league."

"Oh," Mandy says, and, in spite of myself, I'm annoyed by the expression of relief that briefly crosses her face. "I can see the resemblance."

"Bite your tongue."

"Claire, Mandy; Mandy, Claire," I say.

"Nice to meet you," Mandy says, shaking Claire's hand. "Do you live in the area?"

"Greenwich," Claire says. "Just visiting for a little while, to get Doug's ass in gear."

"That's nice."

"Okay," I say, trying to nudge Claire away. "That's enough."

"I mean, it's been a year already," Claire says, easily sidestepping me.

"Has it been that long?" Mandy says, surprised. "My God. It feels like so much less than that. I still have Hailey on my speed dial." And then, out of nowhere, her eyes are brimming with tears. It always strikes me as bad form to exhibit more grief than the bereaved, like showing off your new Lexus to a guy who drives a Ferrari. You think that's horsepower? You don't know shit about horsepower.

"Anyway," Claire says disapprovingly, turning on Mandy. "It's been a bit longer, actually. And I think it's high time Doug got back out there. Don't you agree, Mandy?" Claire is one of the only people I know who can bully you into liking her.

"I suppose, if he feels ready," Mandy says hesitantly, terrified of Claire.

"Claire's ready," I say wryly.

"He's not even thirty," Claire says. "What's he supposed to do, spend the best years of his life alone?"

"Of course not," Mandy says.

"I'm sure you know that it's been well documented that happily married people are quicker to remarry."

"I've heard that," Mandy says, nodding like a dashboard bobble-head.

"So, Mandy," Claire says, bringing it home. "You know any single women in these parts?"

Mandy grins widely, happily vanquished. "I'm a realtor. I've shown the houses of every divorced woman in town."

"Mandy," Claire says with a smile, looping her arm through Mandy's elbow. "We are going to get along famously."

And that's when Mike arrives, panting slightly as he comes through the door. "Hey, Doug," he says, coming right up to me and shaking my hand. "Sorry I'm late. I had to file a brief first thing in the morning."

"Late for what?" I say, taking an extra beat to figure it out. I turn to Claire, who winks at me. "Just say yes," she says, flashing her brightest smile.

"Wait a minute," Mike says. "She told me you wanted to meet me here."

"She lied. She does that."

"It's true," Claire says with a happy grin, leading Mandy to a vacant table. "I do."

Mike nods, looking uncomfortable. "Well, as long as we're both here, can we at least have a cup of coffee?"

"I don't drink coffee."

"Jesus, Doug," he says, shaking his head forlornly. "There are only so many times I can apologize before the words just lose their meaning."

I exhale slowly and nod my head. "Water's fine."

Mike smiles, not triumphant, just glad, quickly looking away before the moment turns awkward, and I feel a surge of tenderness toward him.

Marrying Hailey and moving out to New Radford had meant becoming friendly with a different sort of man than my younger, drunker, wilder single friends back in Manhattan. The men I met in Hailey's circle were all husbands and fathers either on the cusp or already descending into the tide pool of middle age. These men were all adrift in an alien landscape of mortgages and second mortgages, marriages and second marriages, children, child support, affairs, alimony, tuition, tutors, and an endless barrage of social functions. And all of their living had to be squeezed into those few hours on the weekends that they weren't working their asses off to pay for the whole mess. I'd always assumed that the people who lived in those fancy houses in the suburbs were financially better off than I was, and only once I'd joined them did I come to understand that it's all just a much more sophisticated and elaborate way of being broke. There's the jumbo mortgage, the home equity loan to renovate the kitchen and bathrooms, the two or three monthly luxury car payments; before you know it, you've spent a hundred grand of post-tax income before you've put the first piece of bread on your table. Curse of the middle class, my ass. They do it to themselves, all because they've got this Hollywood Christmas movie notion of what their life is supposed to look like. It's a tenuous existence built precariously on a foundation of colossal debt, and one miscalculation, one meager bonus or bad investment or unforeseen expense, can bring the whole thing crashing to the ground. In time, I came to understand that the idyllic streets of New Radford were to a large extent an illusion, and, charged with the responsibility of maintaining this illusion, it was understandable that even the most well-preserved men would start to show some stress fractures. And so they lost their hair and gained some weight and their complexions grew pallid, their eyelids heavier, their wit sour. And while some of them were smart, worldly, and even surprisingly likable, men with whom you could spend an evening knocking back a few more than you should and setting the world to right, they still scared the shit out of me, because now that I was theoretically one of them, albeit a bastard version, it seemed that all that was left was for me to become like them. I didn't want to get fat and bald and start indebting myself in the name of German cars and radiant heating under hardwood floors. And the greatest evidence of my love for Hailey is the fact that I didn't pack it in and bolt for the safety and comfort of my old life and young friends back in the city.

Instead I joined the gym and started playing racquetball with Mike Sandleman, who I met at a bar mitzvah of all places. He was only a few years older than me, in good shape, and actually understood when I was being ironic. We got drunk at the open bar and then made fun of all the fat old men doing the Electric Slide. He was a lawyer, but he had a sloppy, irresponsible streak that made me feel at home, and because he was single he could ogle the younger women and flirt with the waitresses without seeming lecherous. Hanging out with him, I felt my own age, which it had never occurred to me could be an important factor in a friendship, but there it was. So while I still socialized with the husbands of Hailey's many friends, somehow finding the fun between talk of the stock market and mind-numbing descriptions of the world's best Scotches, golf courses, and tropical resorts, when it came to seeing all the sci-fi and action movies that Hailey didn't want to see, or getting drunk and talking about all that existential shit that matters when you're drunk, Mike was my guy. And when Hailey died, it was Mike who came right over to sit with me and Claire and help deal with the airline and the funeral arrangements, and to run interference for me with everyone else who showed up afterwards. He'd proven himself to be a good and loyal friend, and under normal circumstances I'd have been thrilled to welcome him to the family.

But circumstances have not been normal for some time now. Circumstances have, in point of fact, been fucked-up beyond all recognition. Still, it occurs to me that there's probably more to getting back out there than watching Claire hunt down random single women that I will never date, and this is one area where just saying yes won't seem like a betrayal of Hailey. And maybe at some future point in time, I'll feel like having a friend to go to the movies with again, instead of going alone, like I do now. Of course, by then Mike will be married and Debbie will have him instantly whipped and won't let him go. But we could in theory.

So we sit down and Mike drinks his coffee—skim milk, decaf, like that makes a bit of difference—and I sip at my two-and-a-half-dollar bottle of water. The reason men almost never hold long-term grudges against each other is that we're so damn bad at making up. We don't offer heartfelt apologies, and then hug each other tightly the way women do, laughing and crying into each other's hair until the last remnants of hostility and resentment are gone. We just sit around, nodding inelegantly without making eye contact, shrugging and saying things like "Forget about it" or "Let's just call it even" or other meaningless clichés that save us from actually having to speak directly to each other about hurt feelings and anger. In most cases, we'd just as soon find a new friend as submit to the awkward process of reclaiming an existing one. But in this case, Mike's going to be family, and all the dinners and holidays headed our way leave us no choice. At least we're united in wanting the conversation to be over before it begins, so while it never gets quite comfortable, it doesn't take very long, and ten minutes later, I've agreed, against all my better instincts, to be one of his groomsmen. There will be a tuxedo fitting followed by a bachelor party in a few days. His younger brother Max will call me with all the details.

Mike has to get back to the office, so he gives me a warm handshake, happily punching my shoulder, and I head across the shop to Claire, who is actually taking notes on a napkin as she interrogates Mandy. "How many kids?"

"Two."

"What does she weigh?"

"I don't know."

"Ballpark it."

Mandy closes her eyes for a moment. "One thirty-five, maybe? One forty?"

"How tall?"

"Five foot three or so."

"Who is she kidding? She doesn't need a date, she needs Weight Watchers. Next."

"Are you done?" I say.

"No. Go away." She turns back to Mandy. "Tell me more about the dancer."

"You mean the aerobics instructor?"

"Whatever."

Starbucks has filled up by now, and I can feel the dread growing inside me, being heated to a quick boil. I still can't handle crowds, familiar faces nodding and smiling at me, aiming their good intentions and sympathy like darts at my head. I don't want their pity; don't want to once again put my sorrow on display for them. But I don't want to seem too fine, either, because in my mind that would somehow be a slight to Hailey's memory, belittling all that she was to me, and that leaves me no way to be at all, which makes me feel claustrophobic and panicked, and I want to throw down a pellet and disappear like a magician under the cover of a thick smoke cloud. I wonder where they get those pellets, and make a mental note to search online when I get home. There are definitely applications for the grief industry.

"I need to leave," I tell Claire.

"So leave. I'm sure Mandy can drive me home."

"Certainly," says Mandy, beaming like a Stepford Wife at her new best friend.

I flee Starbucks like a vampire caught out at sunrise, running like hell toward the safety of a hidden coffin in a windowless basement. In my case, the local multiplex will have to do.

22

SITTING IN A DARKENED MOVIE THEATER SMACK
in the middle of the workday makes you feel like life is a class
that you're cutting. The sea of empty seats reminds you that all
the normal, responsible people are not here but out doing normal, responsible things, which by implication means you are
neither responsible nor normal. Usually it's just you and the odd
assortment of senior citizens: helmet-haired ladies in their wrin-
kled, flesh-tone knee-highs and snub-nosed orthopedic shoes,
walking in little stooped clusters of two and three, their enor-
mous handbags crinkling and weighed down with snacks and
soda cans bought at the drugstore to avoid squandering their
fixed incomes on overpriced theater snacks; the lone, bowlegged
men sitting next to their worn overcoats with large tubs of popcorn on their laps, looking decrepit and sad, making you wonder if you look decrepit and sad too. When Hailey was alive I
would occasionally sneak off to the movies by myself in the middle of the day, but after she died it became something of an
addiction, a weekly craving for the soothing, air-conditioned
oblivion of the multiplex.

Today I choose an action film involving stolen nuclear warheads and the embittered commando, dishonored for question-able crimes, now reinstated and charged with shaving his beard and re-forming his elite unit to track and thwart the terrorists before they blow up Chicago. I'm early, and the theater is almost empty when I walk in, except for one woman sitting in the center toward the back. As I come up the aisle, I see that it's Brooke Hayes, Russ's guidance counselor, and she sees me before I can retreat. "Oh my God," she says, flustered. "Doug."

"Hey, Brooke."

Sheepish grins all around. Going to the movies alone only works in the insular company of strangers. Knowing someone, however peripherally, exposes you, like running into a friend in your shrink's waiting room. Now what am I supposed to do, sit with her? Like me, she undoubtedly came to sit alone in the dark and escape. But she might be insulted if I move to the other side of the theater, might think me rude, and then neither of us would enjoy ourselves anyway, knowing the other was sitting there. Our anonymity has been lost, and there's no graceful way in or out of the situation.

"This is so embarrassing," Brooke says, blushing.

"I know," I say. "But I think we can handle it."

"You found me alone at the movies. You busted me for being pathetic."

"If you're pathetic, what does that make me?" I say. "I do this once a week."

"Once a week? Really?"

"I'm on a first-name basis with the snack girl."

"What's her name?"

"Carmen."

"You made that up."

"I did. But she looks like a Carmen." I shuffle my feet. "Shouldn't you be over at the school right now, tending to our troubled youth?"

"Today I'm the troubled youth," she says breezily, throwing her legs over the seat in front of her. Her flared sweatpants ride up, exposing the curves of her smooth, pale calves. Hailey had nice calves too. I've always been a leg man. "I hope you won't rat me out."

"Your secret's safe with me."

"Thanks. And you don't even know my secret."

"Are you going to tell me?"

"That depends. Are you going to sit down? You're making me nervous, standing there like that."

"I thought maybe you wanted to be alone."

"I did." The light flecks of glitter on her eyelids sparkle in the dim lighting as she pats the seat next to her. "Now I don't." Then she looks up at me, instantly chagrined. "Unless you wanted to be alone. I mean, that's why you came, right? I would totally understand."

"I did," I say, moving into her row. "Now I don't."

Up close, she's somehow smaller, petite almost, and her skin is flawless, her eyes wide and unyielding. The fear of saying something stupid is a palpable tremor in my chest.

She indicates my tub of popcorn. "Buttered?"

"Yup."

"Excellent."

We sit in the soft, weighted silence unique to large empty spaces while on the screen they flash ads and the scrambled names of movie stars. "So," Brooke says, munching on some popcorn.

"So."

"So, after we met at the school that day, I kind of thought you were going to ask me out."

I don't actually spit out my mouthful of soda, or even choke on it, the way they do in the movies, but it's definitely a spit-your-soda kind of moment. "Did you?" I say. "I'm sorry."

"I shouldn't have said that," she says, mortified. "I always do that, say what I'm thinking, as if the pure shock value will excuse my saying it. I'm sorry. You don't have to answer me."

"You didn't ask a question."

"You're right." She nods thoughtfully, reaching for some more popcorn. "Fill in the blank," she says, after a minute. "When I first met you..."

"Excuse me?"

"It's a prompt, something I do to get the kids to talk about their feelings. Sometimes answering a question is hard, but finishing a sentence works for them."

"So you're treating me like a screwed-up kid?"

She smiles, keeping her eyes on the screen. "Should I not?"

"Fair enough. What was the question again?"

"It wasn't a question, it was a prompt."

"Right. Can you please repeat the prompt?"

"When I first met you..."

"When I first met you I thought about asking you out."

"So why didn't you?"

"It's complicated."

"People always say that, but it never really is."

"That's probably true."

"So," she says with a smile. "Fill in the blank. I did not ask you out because..."

Turns out that Brooke has little or no conversational filter, but neither do I these days, and the combination is kind of like bare-knuckle boxing. "I've never been very adept at approaching women," I say. "I'm a great responder. If you show up crying in my office, I'm golden. But starting has always been harder for me. Because no matter what I'm saying, you know I'm just saying it to break the ice, so that I can ask you out, so that we can go out, and if that goes well, so that we can have sex. So basically, I go from being this nice guy with no agenda to the sleazy asshole who's trying to sleep with you before he even knows you."

"You think maybe you're over-thinking the whole thing a little?"

"That's what I do," I say. "And the sad irony is that I thought I was done with all of that. I thought I had broken the ice for the last time and had earned myself a lifetime of never having to feel like that anymore. So then I resent the hell out of my dead wife for reneging on her part of the deal and stranding me here to fend for myself again, and then, of course, I feel guilty for resenting her, because it's not like she died on purpose."

"Okay," Brooke says. "You're still messed up about your wife's death. It's all very understandable. Textbook, even. But to be honest, not very complicated."

"I'm just getting warmed up," I say. "Then there's the whole mindfuck of Hailey's death being this great enabler."

"What do you mean?"

"My little sister is about to marry a friend of mine that she met at my shiva. So her husband, her unborn children, basically her entire future, comes courtesy of Hailey dying, and I just can't get my brain wrapped around that. That column I write is making a name for me, opening doors. I used to pitch books nobody wanted, now publishers are coming after me. My professional dreams can start to come true, and all because Hailey died. I'm famous for being sad. And then there's the airline settlement. I'm going to be paid handsomely for being sad too. So I'm going to be rich and successful, but if I could go back in time and somehow save her, stop her from getting on that flight, I would. In a heartbeat."

"Of course you would," Brooke says.

"But someday I'll fall in love again, right? I'll start over with someone, and maybe we'll buy a big old house with all this new money I have, and we'll have kids, and I'll be a professional writer, maybe even write some books. I'll have this whole great life, and it will all be thanks to Hailey dying in a plane crash. And I don't know exactly at what point it will happen, but the time will come when I'll have crossed this line to where maybe I wouldn't go back to save her, because I'll know that if it weren't for her dying, I wouldn't have this family I love, and this life I'm living. And the thought of that, of becoming this person who wouldn't go back to save her . . ."

I mean to say more, but there seems to be a malfunction with my voice, and even though my lips keep moving for a bit, no sound comes out, and goddamn if I don't feel tears running down my cheeks. Brooke nods and puts her hand on my arm.

"So," she says, "you're having a problem with causality."

"I'm obsessed with it," I say, wiping my damp face with my

hand. "I'm sorry. I don't usually cry until much later in the movie."

She squeezes my arm softly, looking ahead as I get myself back under control. "In a way, it's actually kind of appropriate, don't you think?" she says. "I mean, look at it this way: that's how she stays with you forever, by making sure you're okay after she's gone. It's like emotional life insurance."

"Emotional life insurance," I repeat, mulling it over. "They teach you that in psych school?"

"I just made it up on the spot," she says with a grin. "You've just borne witness to my twisted brilliance."

"It's pretty good," I say. "I'll have to think about that for a while. Thanks."

"Don't mention it." She gives me a friendly pat before removing her hand, and I can still feel the warm spot on my arm where it had been. "Well, you were right," she says.

"That it's complicated?"

"No," she says with a warm smile. "You're a great responder."

I nod. "So, what about you? What's your sad story?"

"What makes you think mine is sad?"

"You've already hinted at it more than once. And you have sad eyes."

"My fiancé always said they were beautiful."

"Your fiancé."

"Yup."

"And what happened to him?"

"It's complicated."

"Come on. Fill in the blank. I once had a fiancé but…"

But then the lights go down and the previews start, and I can see her gleefully triumphant smile in the glow of the screen. "But we're out of time," she says. "I have a strict no-talking policy during the feature. Ask me next week."

"How do you know I'll see you next week?"

She plucks a single kernel of popcorn from my tub. "Call it a hunch."

And we sit there, in an empty movie theater smack in the middle of the workday, elbows bumping lightly on our shared armrest, two people temporarily missing from the world, bathed in the flickering glow of the screen, lost in our own private sorrows as we watch Nicolas Cage save the world.

23

WHEN I GET HOME, STEPHEN IVES IS ON THE PORCH, trying like hell to break down my front door. He backs up all the way to the porch steps and then charges forward, hitting the door with his shoulder. Judging from his labored breathing and the dark pit stains on his Egyptian cotton dress shirt, he's been at if for a while already. "Claire!" he yells. "You're going to talk to me!"

"Go home, Stephen," Claire calls from an upstairs window. "You're going to hurt yourself."

I look up to see Claire and Russ perched comfortably on the window ledge outside Russ's old room.

"Hey, Doug," Russ says, grinning at me. He's drinking a Coke and clearly enjoying the show.

Claire waves tiredly, raising her eyebrows apologetically at me. "He won't leave."

I turn back to Stephen, who is now trying to kick down the door like a cop, but cops don't wear flimsy three-hundred-dollar dress shoes, which leave nasty crescent-shaped skid marks on my door, but don't really give much in the way of tactical support.

"Hey, Stephen," I say. "What's new and exciting?"

"Stay out of this, Doug. I'm warning you," he snarls, flashing me a menacing frown before throwing another running kick at the door. The usually immaculate Stephen, who dresses like a Hugo Boss ad and generally perspires only in the quilted tennis bubbles and steam rooms of his country club, is a sight to behold. His sweaty hair, thick with gel, hangs in descending spikes over his forehead, making him look like Elvis, not fat Vegas Elvis but skinny movie Elvis after he beats up the bullies in the diner who forced him to sing along to the jukebox.

"You're going to hurt yourself," I say.

"I'm going to hurt you if you take one step onto this porch."

"It's my house, Stephen."

He turns to face me, his handsome jaw trembling with rage, eyes wide and crazed. "Do I look like I give a shit?"

He does not, and I know he doesn't need a particularly compelling excuse to kick my ass. Stephen has hated me for pretty much as long as he's known me, and not just because I trashed him in his wedding toast. At Claire's prodding, he gave me a job at his company, which I could have told him would end badly. I screwed it up in a matter of months, by sleeping with one of the administrative assistants. As it turned out, he'd been planning to fire her, but now that I'd slept with her, he was scared of the legal ramifications, although he had no such concerns when it came to firing me. I used to fuck stuff up like that all the time. I didn't see the big deal. I do now, but you don't go and apologize to someone five years after the events in question. And even if I did, the fact would still be etched into my permanent record as far as he's concerned. He reached out to me and I crapped on his hand. A short while after that I got drunk at Thanksgiving dinner and punched him in the nose. They broke it up before he could hit me back, and nothing festers in a man more than an unanswered sucker punch. So I owe him an apology and he owes me a punch in the face and it's just not a good recipe for a friendly conversation. So I stay where I am at the foot of the porch stairs and say, "Knock yourself out," and Stephen goes back to hurling himself at my door and calling out to Claire.

"Get the fuck out of here, Stephen. I mean it!" Claire shouts.

"I just want to talk to you!" he shouts.

"Then you should have called me!"

"You won't take my calls!"

"Then you wait until I'm ready to take them. I don't work for you, Stephen. You can't schedule me like a meeting."

"Just get down here and open this fucking door!"

He hits the door again and this time I can hear the wood groan, the faintest sound of preliminary splintering, but then his legs crumple under him and he drops to his knees, letting out an agonized sob as he clutches his shoulder. "Is he okay?" Claire calls down to me.

"He's looked better," I say. "Why don't you come down and talk to him?"

"Butt out, Doug."

"Right. Sorry."

Stephen struggles to his feet, still clutching his battered shoulder, and staggers out from under the porch roof and down the steps, lurching past me to look up at Claire from the lawn, his eyeballs throbbing with desperation. "Please, Claire," he says, his voice ragged and hoarse. "Don't do this."

"I have to," she says softly.

"I love you."

"No. You love having me. I could be anyone, really. Now go home!"

"Is there someone else? Is that what this is about?"

"Okay. I'm going to start throwing things now," Claire says, tossing up her hands exasperatedly before disappearing from the window.

Stephen looks at me. "That's it, isn't it? She's having an affair."

"That's not it," I say, shaking my head.

I register a dark blur in the upper corner of my eye and then we both jump as a pair of Rollerblades lands with a hard thud on the grass between us. "Jesus Christ, Claire!"

"No, Stephen," she shouts down at him. "There's no one else. There has to be someone to begin with for there to then be someone else. And for me, there is no one at all, and that's why I'm leaving you."

"You're not making any sense!" he cries, approaching the window. Claire drives him back by throwing down the Louisville Slugger baseball bat that Russ has dutifully handed to her. The bat lands on its handle, carving out a fist-sized divot in the lawn.

"Fuck!" Stephen shouts, throwing himself against the wall of the house. "Will you just calm down for a minute!"

"Go home, Stephen. I swear to God I'll call the cops."

By now I suspect that at least one of the many neighbors standing on their porches watching the spectacle with growing consternation has beaten her to it. Things like this don't generally happen on our block.

Meanwhile, Stephen mutters something unintelligible, pushes himself off the wall, and steps under the window again. "I love you, Claire," he calls up to her. "I may not be the most exciting guy in the world, but I've always been good to you, and I've always tried to make you happy. I can't make you stay if you're going to leave me, but I think, after six years, that I deserve the courtesy of an explanation. You can throw anything down on me that you want." He drops to his knees like a dazed fighter in the later rounds, and looks up at her, panting as the tears run unchecked down his dirty, sweat-soaked face. "I'm not going to move from this spot until you come down to talk to me, face-to-face. I'm through ducking."

There's a moment of dead silence as Claire looks down at him, and then she hurls the desk chair out the window. Luckily for Stephen, it turns out he has one more duck left in him after all. I dive left and he lets out a yelp and rolls to his right as the chair lands with a heavy metallic crunch exactly where he'd been, the wheels and casters flying off in all directions like shrapnel. Rabbits run for their lives, and I wonder why I never thought of an aerial assault before. Stephen lands on his back and lets out an anguished scream that seems to go on until next week, while upstairs, Claire bursts into tears and disappears into the house.

I pull myself to my feet and walk over to Stephen, who is still lying on his back and staring up at the sky in a catatonic haze, the way you do when you're stoned and the clouds start looking like cartoon characters and old girlfriends. I bend down to pick up a chair wheel assembly and then sit down on the grass next to him, idly spinning it in my hands.

"I'm sorry about your door," he says after a while.

"Don't worry about it, man. You had your reasons. I'm sorry about my sister. That was uncalled-for. Really."

"She's really leaving me, isn't she?"

"It seems that way, yeah."

He turns his head and looks at me, his lips quivering with emotion. "Why?"

I rub the cool metal of the chair wheel against my palm and let out a deep sigh. "Because she's Claire," I say. "And that's what Claire does."

He considers that for a minute, and then looks back up at the sky, nodding to himself. "I really do love her, you know?"

"I know."

He gets up slowly, groaning with the effort. His right arm hangs limp, like something vital has been disconnected inside, and he starts limping toward his black Porsche, parked at the curb.

"You sure you're okay to drive a manual?" I say.

He stops and turns around. "No."

"You want me to take you home?"

"If you wouldn't mind."

I don't know how to drive a stick, so I take him in my Saab. He'll send someone for the Porsche. When you're as rich as Stephen, there's always someone to send in these types of situations. He sits with his eyes closed in the passenger seat, his head pressed against the window, a low, steady hum coming from inside his closed mouth, like he's singing a duet with the engine. The streets give way to boulevards and then to the highway, and soon we're wordlessly speeding north toward the gilded forests of Greenwich in the loneliest part of the afternoon, just before the light starts to fade. Stephen doesn't wear a seat belt, and I don't remind him to. He looks like he'd prefer to fly through the windshield if we crash, and I know that feeling, I'm one of the founding fathers of that particular feeling. And seeing him like this, so limp and beaten, I feel an unexpected stab of empathy for him. He married the woman he loved, was as good to her as he knew how to be, and still he lost her. It's incomprehensibly unfair, and I know that feeling too. Stephen's only mistake was in thinking that Claire would keep on loving him. It was an understandable mistake, since she'd made it too.

"I feel like I'm dying," he says hoarsely as I pull through the gates and into the driveway of his Mediterranean-style mansion. Stephen is rich, handsome, and athletic, and it occurs to me that this may very well be the first time he's ever lost the girl. There are tears in his eyes, and as much as I feel for him, I'm the last person he should be talking to about this. Later, he'll regret having let me see him in this vulnerable state, and because he can't take it back, he'll just hate me more for it.

"Look," I say, throwing the car into park. "I know right now it seems overwhelmingly bad, but you're in shock. I mean, between Claire leaving you and then the baby, it's just a lot to absorb. You need to take your time with this."

He turns slowly in his seat until he's facing me, and fixes me with a hard stare. "What baby?"

I nod slowly, lowering my head until it's resting on the steering wheel, and all I can think, over and over again, is *Oh fuck*.

24

LATER, AS THE DAY DIES, RUSS AND I STAND OUT IN the front yard, tossing a baseball back and forth in the lingering daylight while Claire screams into the phone at Stephen, who's been calling pretty much every hour on the hour to demand an audience. The block is filled with the muted sounds of suburban evening: crickets chirping, the musical jangle of dog leashes, the muted thrum of central air compressors, and the resounding slap of leather on leather as the baseball hits the woven pockets of our worn mitts. This is usually my witching hour, the time of day when the utter futility of it all threatens to overwhelm me, and by now I'm usually sitting on the porch, three or four swallows into the Jack Daniel's.

I just need a little time to figure this all out! Claire's disembodied voice, half crying, half shouting, comes floating through the windows and across the yard to us.

"Sounds pretty bad," Russ says, throwing me the ball. It lands in my glove with a resounding smack.

"It is," I say, winding up and throwing it back. I overthrow a little, but Russ extends and easily makes the catch.

"Does anyone actually stay married anymore?"

Throw...smack.

"I don't know." Throw...smack. "It does seem like an epidemic."

Stop trying to make deals with me, Stephen. This isn't the Middle Ages. You can't negotiate a marriage!

"Do you think you and my mom would have made it?"

Throw...smack.

"I'd like to think so. We had a pretty good thing going."

"That's true. But then again, you were still in the honeymoon phase."

Throw...smack.

I stop to think about it for a moment. "It wasn't perfect. I mean, we fought sometimes. Your mom liked to have everything organized, and I was a total slob. And sometimes she got self-conscious about being so much older than me, and I wasn't always as reassuring as I should have been. Sometimes I even teased her about it."

"Why?"

"Because I'm an asshole." I shrug. "I don't know. I guess I liked the idea that someone like her would worry about losing me."

Throw...smack.

"That must have pissed her off."

"I think it just made her sad."

Throw...smack.

"So who knows what would have happened down the road?" Russ says.

You think I like doing this? You think I woke up one morning and said to myself, Today would be a great day to fuck up Stephen's life?

"I think we had a shot," I say, throwing him the ball. "Your mom had been through a bad marriage already, and it was like she knew where the trapdoors were. There was only one way it would have ended, and that's if I screwed it up."

Throw...smack.

"And what were the odds of that, right?" Russ says with a light smirk.

"Exactly," I say, feeling suddenly deflated. I don't tell Russ that I can sometimes recall looking at Hailey and shamefully wondering how I'd feel when she was fifty and I was thirty-nine, wondering if I'd have it in me to stay with an older woman once she was actually old. I don't tell him that there are times, even now, that I experience a dark sense of relief that I will never get the opportunity to fuck things up, that Hailey died before the inevitability of my ruining us, because sometimes it seems inconceivable to me that I wouldn't have. Fucking things up, after all, was what I did. I don't tell him that I am still trying like hell to forget the way she sometimes looked at me, like she was seeing me for the first time and wondering how she'd so grossly overestimated my character. How in those moments I didn't think—I knew—that at some point she was going to get rid of me. There are some things you can never say out loud, even to yourself, sins of the mind that you can only file away in the hopes of absolution at some later date.

For now, all I can do is shake off the desolation that threatens to descend like a sudden downpour, and punch the pocket of my baseball mitt invitingly. Russ grins and throws me a pop fly, and for the next little while the only sounds are the emerging crickets, the ball hitting our gloves, and Claire's intermittent screams. There's something nice about throwing the ball with Russ, and now I understand the cliché about fathers and sons playing catch. We're together and engaged, but far enough away to say personal things without feeling exposed, and for the things we can't bring ourselves to say out loud, we have this ball to throw, and we can hear the neat smack of hard leather on soft and know the message has been delivered.

I'm hanging up now, Stephen! No! I'm hanging up!

"Thanks for talking to Jim," Russ says. "It's much better now, knowing that I'll be moving back here soon."

"You're welcome."

"It's the first time I've felt remotely okay since . . . you know."

"I'm glad."

"So I guess you're my stepfather again."

"I guess so."

"How does it feel?"

I think about it for a moment. "It feels okay," I say.

"Good."

Throw . . . smack.

25

LANEY POTTER WANTS ME TO TALK ABOUT HER vagina. *Tell me how much you love my wet pussy*. She really says this, depositing her tongue in my ear as we roll around naked on the guest room bed. When it comes to sex talk, I always run into a problem with the vagina. You're not going to actually call it a vagina, but every other name sounds crude or just plain juvenile and makes me feel like I'm doing cheesy porn. As a result, I never refer to it directly, but kind of talk my way around it, the way I used to talk my way around my mother-in-law. "Mom" was out of the question, but "Charlotte" sounded so ridiculously formal, so I just nodded and said "Hey," as in "Hey, can I get you another glass of tea?" And now I'm thinking about my former mother-in-law while I'm having sex, and there exists no more effective softener of erections, so I just banish the thought from my mind and try to focus on the task at hand, which has become slightly more complicated now that Laney has gotten comfortable enough with me to talk dirty during sex, which is just this side of too comfortable, if you ask me.

And Laney likes to talk. *Yes!* she says. *I missed you so much!* she says. *Oh my God, you're so hard!* she says. *I want you in me right now!* she says. And then, as she starts circling the runway of her orgasm, she breaks into a detailed play-by-play, complete with color commentary. *Oh my God, I'm going to come! Not yet, not yet. Oooooooh! You feel so good in me, oh my God, oh my God, my pussy is so wet, I'm dripping. Yes, yes, don't stop, never stop! Keep your fingers right there, oh my God, yes! I'm coming! I'm coming! I'm coming!*

Having sex narrated by your partner is not something I'm used to, and I find the effect somewhat distancing, making me wonder if it's actually me that's lying between her legs, because if it is, why does she find it necessary to report everything to me? Why can't she just grunt, moan, and shriek like a mature adult?

When we're done, she wraps her legs around me, kneading my ass with her fingers, and takes the flesh of my neck between her teeth. "Ummmm," she purrs, licking my chin like an ice cream cone. "I missed you so much."

"I missed you too," I say.

She smiles and looks up at me. "That's a lie," she says, "but it comes from a sweet place." She kisses my nose and rolls me over, so we're facing each other sideways. "I know this is strange for you, Doug. Whatever this is we're doing, we're each getting something different out of it. But you're a beautiful man, and a stellar lover, and I just don't want you to ever think you have to lie to me. I'm a big girl, and I'm going to try really hard not to fall in love with you, okay?"

"Okay," I say, kissing her eyelid.

"But in the meantime," she says, "I just can't stop wanting you. It's all I think about."

"I want you too," I say.

She leans forward to kiss my mouth. "That one I believe."

We lie in silence for a little while and then I surprise us both by saying, "I was thinking about starting to date again."

"Oh!" she says, unable to hide the look of consternation that spreads across her face. "Do you think you're ready for that?"

"I'm not sure," I say. "I don't know what I'm ready for."

She licks her fingers and then moves them to my crotch, grabbing me in her wet fist. "Well, I know one thing you seem to be ready for," she says, propping herself up and kissing her way down my belly. "And you know what they say?"

"No," I say, rolling onto my back. "What do they say?"

Her voice is muffled from under the comforter, and I can feel her breasts on my thighs, her lips vibrating against my spanking-new erection. "Why pay for the cow, when you can get milked for free?" And then she's on me in earnest, and I close my eyes, surrendering to the hot wetness of her mouth as Laney does her best to swallow me whole.

Later, we come upstairs and find Claire and Russ in the kitchen, quietly eating Laney's meatloaf right out of the tin. "Hey," I say awkwardly. "I didn't know you guys were home."

"We were being quiet," Russ says. "Unlike some people I could name."

"I'm Claire," Claire says, waving from her seat. "The screwed-up twin sister. I'm sure he's told you all about me."

"Nice to meet you," Laney says, blushing intensely the way redheads do, looking like she might spontaneously combust. "Hello, Russ."

"Hey, Mrs. Potter," Russ says. "Great meatloaf."

"I'm glad you like it."

"You want to stay for dinner?" Claire says.

"No," Laney says, louder than she probably meant to. "I think I'd better be leaving. I've got to...leave. So, thanks anyway."

"Okay. Well, thanks for being such a good friend to my brother," Claire says without a trace of irony.

"Don't mention it," Laney says, practically bolting from the kitchen.

"I'm sorry about that," I say at the front door.

"I'm still shaking."

"Kind of bursts the bubble a little, doesn't it?"

She gives me a quick hug, putting her lips on my ear. "I'll just blow another one," she says. And then she's out the front door, running across the lawn like she's being chased by wild dogs.

When I get back to the kitchen there's a place set for me, and Claire and Russ are quietly eating their meatloaf. "Okay," I say. "She's gone."

They continue to eat and feign disinterest until Claire points her fork at me. "That's it," she says. "From now on, I'm sleeping in Russ's room." And then the two of them lose it, beating the table and laughing until there are tears in their eyes, until I have no choice but to join them.

"Listen, Russ," I say after a bit. "I wish you hadn't seen that."

"Thankfully, I didn't," he says, wiping his eyes. "I just heard some of it."

"My ears are still bleeding," Claire says.

"I don't want you to get the wrong impression."

"My impression is that you were banging Mrs. Potter, who I've always thought is hands down the hottest housewife in New Radford. Which part of that is wrong?"

I collapse into a chair across from him. "All of it," I say wearily. "It's all wrong."

"If you feel that bad about it, send her my way, dude. I'm grieving too, you know. I would tap that in a heartbeat."

"Right or wrong, if she can screw like she can cook, then I'll sleep with her myself," Claire says, sliding me a plate. "This meatloaf is delicious."

"You certainly earned it," Russ says, and they burst into another paroxysm of laughter.

"Listen," Claire says after a while. "There's nothing wrong with some misdirected sex every now and then, but Russ and I feel that it's time for you to start looking for more suitable partners."

"You're in on this too now?" I say to Russ.

"What she said," Russ says with a smirk, cutting himself another slab of meatloaf.

"Now, according to my extensive research, your best bet is someone named Sabrina Barclay. Do you know her?" Claire says.

"No."

"Good. Then it will be a blind date."

"No, thanks."

"No choice, Dougie. You agreed to put yourself in my hands, and this is happening. Just say yes."

"Does your extensive research include anything aside from your single conversation with Mandy Seaver?"

"The woman's a realtor. She has an eye for detail."

"How do you know this Sabrina will even want to go out with me?"

"You don't have an ex-wife or kids to deal with. You've been forged by tragedy, touched by an act of God, not stained by a bad divorce. And you have a full head of hair. You're young, slim, and sad. Trust me," she says, chewing on some bread. "You're beautiful."

"Young, slim, and sad," I repeat. "Who knew?"

"Also, I already spoke to her."

"You made a date for me?"

Claire takes a bite of meatloaf. "I'm taking care of business, Dougie."

"Claire."

"Don't Claire me. You have no downside. Worst-case scenario, you hate her and drop her off after a quick dinner. Best-case scenario, you get laid by someone who isn't married, which I think we can all agree is a step in the right direction, don't you think?"

I sigh. "What do you know about her?"

"She's an aerobics instructor, she's built like a centerfold, and she's independently wealthy from her divorce settlement."

"So, nothing really."

"It's just a date, Doug. A few hours that I think you can spare from your crammed schedule of napping, drinking, and staring into space. Plus, thanks to you, Stephen knows about the baby and I will never know a moment's peace now, so you owe me one."

"That was inevitable, don't you think?"

"So is this."

I sigh and look over at Russ. "And you're really okay with all of this?"

He chews thoughtfully for a moment, and then brings his hand down decisively on the table. "You saved me from Jimbo, man. In my eyes, you can do no wrong."

"Seriously, though," I say. "I want to know how you really feel about me starting to date."

Russ sits back down and looks at me, blushing slightly. "My mom was the real deal, you know? It's going to take you a long time to find someone even remotely good enough to take her place, so the way I see it, you'd better get started."

"You're sure?"

He nods. "Yeah."

"Okay, then," I say to Claire. "When?"

"Friday night."

"Friday night it is."

Claire smiles and raises her glass in a toast. "To Sabrina Barclay. May she be of open mind, heart, and legs, and partial to sad, skinny men."

Russ raises his Coke can and smiles. "Sabrina Barclay," he says.

"Sabrina Barclay," I say, raising my own glass to bang their drinks. And so we toast Sabrina Barclay while eating Laney Potter's meatloaf and all the while I'm thinking about Brooke Hayes, and this heady stew of women either means that I'm not remotely ready to get back out there, or else I'm as ready as I'll ever be.

26

"...AND I SWORE TO GOD THAT I WAS THROUGH with blind dates, but your sister was so convincing, you know? You're lucky to have her. I wish I had someone like that looking out for me. The truth is, when you're divorced and living out here, you really have to be open-minded and willing to meet people. I mean, I tried the internet dating thing, but it's just a big headache, you know? You spend hours at the computer just trying to screen out the freaks, and then, when you think you've finally found someone who seems to be worth an actual date, you find out that he used a picture from ten years ago, before he lost his hair and gained thirty pounds, or that he lives in his mother's basement, or else he's a married guy just looking for something on the side—you wouldn't believe how many married guys try to date on the internet. Why don't they just call a hooker? Anyway, what was my point? Oh yeah, just that you have to be open to meeting quality people when the opportunities come up, because there are just so many nut jobs out there— Oh, excuse me, yes, please. Can I get the salmon special, but broiled and without the sauce, and can I have steamed vegetables instead of the mashed potatoes, I'm off carbs right now. Thank you—

Anyway, your sister told me that you haven't really gone out much since your wife died—is it okay to mention your wife? I'm sorry, I swore to myself that I wouldn't, I can't stand when I go out with a guy and all he wants to talk about is his ex. It's just boring already, right? I mean, everyone's got their spin, everyone wants you to know that the divorce was totally not their fault, that they were the wronged party and blah, blah, blah. I had my own divorce, and I've seen enough to know that in most cases, no one is ever really innocent, and if you try to tell me you are, I'm just not going to trust you anyway, so save your breath. Maybe you're not the one who cheated, but there's plenty of ways to ruin a marriage without cheating, right? It just happens, and as long as you feel you've learned from your experiences, I don't really care if you think it was your fault or not. I'm not interested in the past or the future, I only care about the here and now, who you are today and what you're looking for now, you know? I didn't cheat on Gary, although God knows I had my opportunities. When you work in a gym and you wear tight clothing, you get plenty of opportunities. And Gary didn't cheat on me, at least, that's his story and he's sticking to it, although he did get into another relationship pretty darn quick if you ask me. All of my friends think it was going on before we got divorced, but you know what? I'm so beyond that now. If it was, more power to him. We were done so long before that. I think after we had Jason, that's my baby, he's seven now ... What? I know. No one can believe I have a kid. It's called sit-ups, although I think I'm just a genetically thin person. My mother was very thin, and I have her body, except that I have boobs, thank God. She's completely flat. Anyway, what was I saying?

Oh yes, after we had Jason, Gary and I just went in different directions. We just wanted different things, you know? He wanted to keep having kids and just, you know, stay home and become middle-aged, and I wanted to be out there living again—oh, great, thanks. It looks delicious. Is that the fat-free balsamic dressing? Perfect.—So, what was I talking about? I'm talking too much. Let's talk about you a little. I love that column you write. I'm always in awe of people who can write. I get blocked writing thank-you notes after Jason's birthday parties. Did you always want to be a writer?...What did your wife do, if you don't mind my asking? Crap! I did it again. I swore to God I wouldn't mention her if you didn't, there's nothing worse than spending a first date talking about each other's first marriages. I guess it's just that you're the first widower I've dated, so it's a whole different dynamic. You don't have all this baggage that we divorced people come with, you know?...Oh, I'm sure there's baggage to go along with that too, I mean, everyone's got baggage, right? But there's just something about a guy who's been married before and isn't filled with hate and anger... Really. At whom, God?...Oh! Really? I don't think I know any atheists. I mean, I could certainly understand it, after what you've been through...Look, I have my doubts like everyone else, but I just find it impossible to believe that he isn't there in some form, you know, that everything doesn't happen for a reason. I mean, I have to believe that, or else it's all just chaos. I'm not a fan of organized religion, I mean, I went to Catholic school, but that was just because my parents thought I'd get a better education there. To me it's all the same, really. Jesus, God, Allah, Buddha, whatever. Somebody's got to be driving the spaceship, that's all. Otherwise what's the whole point?... Yeah, I suppose there doesn't have to be a point, but I'm much happier believing there is one. Wow. Religion, exes, we're breaking all the first-date rules, aren't we? I hope I'm not coming off like a complete asshole. I'm really not, it's just hard when you sit with someone you don't know at all, you know?... Thanks. And you're much cuter than I expected, although you do have the benefit of comparison to a lot of really bad dates. So tell me, am I the first real date you've had since, you know, your wife passed away? Really? Oh my God. I don't feel too much pressure now! Kidding. I'm kidding. Still, I do feel somewhat responsible to make sure you have a positive experience. I mean, you never forget your first date, right? The first guy I dated after I got divorced was this guy Charlie I knew from the gym and it was an absolute disaster. He spent the whole night giving me a detailed account of his entire sexual history, from the first time he masturbated to the girl he'd slept with the week before, and then he was actually shocked when I didn't want to sleep with him. And now I'm your first date. What will you say about me?... What? Ha ha! You're really very funny, you know that?—Oh, no dessert for me, thanks. I'm fine. But you feel free to get some for yourself.

"That was nice, thanks. Oh, I love this song, can you turn it up? I love Beyoncé. It's left over here, on Blackstone. Right. I mean, correct, not a right turn. And this is it. Thanks. I know it's big for just the two of us, but I'm really attached to it. Also, if I sell it I have to give half to Gary, and I'm sure as hell not going to pay for his fiancée's new Mercedes...Hey, would you like to come in for a while? Jason is at Gary's this weekend...Listen, I like you, Doug. You're sweet and handsome, and I can already tell you've got a big heart. I don't mind admitting that I'm very attracted to you, and I think we would have a very good time together. I know you're just getting back out there, and I don't want you to think it would be any kind of commitment. And it's not like I'm some whore who jumps into bed with any guy who buys me dinner. I can't go there if I don't feel a connection, and I really do feel a connection to you. It's fine if you don't want to, I'll understand, but I just wanted to extend the invitation, you know? No strings attached, and I mean that. If we only become friends, that's fine too. Also, I'm a very sexual person, very passionate, and I've been told that I'm great in bed, so, there's that too... You sure? Okay, I understand. No, it's fine. That's why God invented vibrators, right? I'm kidding, I'm kidding! Listen, I hope you don't think I'm this horrible slut, because it's not like that, it really isn't. It's just that decent guys are few and far between, trust me, so when one comes along, I try not to play any games... Okay. It's fine. Believe me, I totally understand. Let me give you a kiss... Mmmm. Sure you won't change your mind? Okay. Well, it was great to meet you, it really was. Call me, okay? I'd love to do it again... Me too. Okay. Have a good night. Can you just wait and make sure I get in okay? I hate coming into an empty house. Thanks. Okay, bye. Give me one more kiss... Mmmm. Oh my God, you have amazing lips. Okay. I'm going now. Say hi to your sister..."

27

THE TOWN OF NEW RADFORD HAS ONE OF THE best public school districts in the country. We have well-funded libraries, beautiful parks, clean streets, an exemplary police force, and great shopping. What we don't have anywhere in the vicinity is a single decent strip club. Someone tried to open one a few years ago, but nothing galvanizes an upper-middle-class bedroom community faster than the threat of tits and ass. Local lawyers offered their services pro bono to file all the legal motions, the wealthier financial professionals funded the opposition, the minivan set picketed the proposed site, and the local family associations and religious institutions united and mobilized to cram the zoning board hearings with raucous crowds to make sure the application and all subsequent appeals were shot down. Ironically, these same men who gave of their time and money to keep the strippers out are now forced to drive the forty minutes into Manhattan when they want to be grinded on by topless dancers in G-strings.

Even before I was married, I never liked going to strip clubs. Not for any grand moral reason, or because it objectifies women—I believe in a woman's right to choose to be objectified—but because I can't help seeing myself through the eyes of the dancers; a dumb, sexless mark too pathetic to achieve female contact on his own terms. But after Hailey died, the married guys saw me as the perfect excuse to make these trips. Going to a strip club might be a seedy and wretched act of misogyny, but bringing me along transformed it into a humanitarian mission, a noble act of friendship and compassion, the men gathering to buck up the sad, lonely widower in their midst. It was the flimsiest of justifications, but when naked women are involved, that's generally all a man needs. And so, with this rationale tucked neatly away as ammunition for the imaginary defense they would never present to their wives, they would call me, advising me that it would do me some good to come out and party with them. I knew that sitting with a group of middle-aged married men and watching them chat up the young, naked dancers writhing on their laps would only make me feel shittier, but sometimes it was easier to grin and bear it than to explain that to them. And so the night finally came that I found myself being dragged along on one of these little outings like a team mascot; not one of the players, but there to foster team spirit.

At first I figured I would just sit at the bar, or on the couch, get drunk on the watered-down drinks, tap my foot in time to the eighties hard rock, and take a mental nap until it was over, but then I learned yet another incontrovertible truth about being young and bereaved: everyone wants to buy the widower a lap dance. Like waving a pair of powdered tits in my face will somehow ease my pain. And suddenly I found myself shouting down the men in my party, who were throwing money at the girls and telling them to show me a good time, and then fending off the aggressive advances of the strippers themselves, who had sensed the dynamic and were ready to work the situation for all it was worth. And so I followed the dancer they'd selected for me down the dimly lit hall to the VIP room, but as soon as I was out of view, I ducked out of the club and used the batch of twenties my well-meaning friends had shoved into my hands for the dances to take a cab back to New Radford. And that was the last time anyone asked me to go to a strip club.

"We're going to a titty bar," Max says. "As soon as we finish here."

Max is Mike's younger brother, a good-looking guy in his mid-twenties, the kind of guy who still says things like "sweet" and "dude" and, of course, "titty bar," and who earlier informed me, apropos of nothing and without the slightest trace of self-consciousness, that one of his fraternity brothers "has this banging house in the Hamptons, and on weekends it's wall-to-wall models, man. You should totally come, dude. I'll hook you up." Whenever he speaks, I can picture him in his fraternity T-shirt, chugging beer through a hose, paddling the naked asses of freshman pledges, and date-raping semiconscious sorority girls.

It's Monday afternoon, and the members of Mike's wedding party have all gathered in the dressing room of Gellers Tuxedo Studio in lower Manhattan, to be fitted for our gray waistcoats and tails. I had hoped that Mike would have better sense than to dress his groomsmen, but I forgot that Mike is not calling the shots, and Debbie wants all the ushers dressed up as Kennedys. In addition to Max and myself, Mike's wedding party contains Paul, a hedge fund guy, and Rich, an investment banker, both from the neighborhood, who never stop taking cell phone calls and urgently checking their BlackBerries. And then, awkwardly enough, there's Dave Potter, Laney's husband, who is Mike's partner and whom I should have anticipated but somehow didn't, maybe because I've trained myself to forget he exists.

Since Paul and Rich are too busy being important, jabbering into their cell phones and frantically shaking and pounding on their BlackBerries like they're about to beat the high score, Dave gravitates over to me, talking while we get dressed. "I've been reading your column," he says. "It's amazing to me how you can write something so honest and raw, but still make it funny. You've really got a knack for it."

"Thanks."

"Sure. I hope Laney's not driving you crazy, bringing over food all the time."

It's strange, hearing her name spoken so casually by him. "No," I say. "It's really very nice of her."

"Sometimes she can go a little overboard."

I think of Laney straddling me, her auburn hair falling wildly around her face, eyes closed, mouth open, as she bucks and shrieks her way to orgasm. "It's fine," I say. "She's a good friend."

He pulls off his try-on shirt, and there's something about seeing the love handles and sagging pectorals of the man who doesn't know I'm sleeping with his wife that makes me feel even worse than I already do. Dave's not a bad-looking guy for forty-five, but he married a young sexpot and then let himself go, and I just want to grab him and haul him in front of the tailor's mirror and say, "Look at yourself, you dumb fuck. What did you expect?!" And for one crazy instant, I find myself stepping forward and opening my mouth to tell him, because in the long term I think there would be an upside for both of us, but then Max makes his announcement about the titty bar and Dave nods his head and says, "Now you're talking," flashing me a conspiratorial, titty-bar grin, and in that instant I feel a little less bad for him, and the impulse to reveal myself is gone before I can get myself into more trouble than I'm already in.

Max herds us to a high-end gentleman's club a few blocks away, the kind with crimson velvet ropes and stanchions out front, and the Armani-clad heavies working the door greet him by name. I consider a variety of ways to make my apologies and leave, but Mike and I have only just buried the hatchet and I don't want to do anything that might lead to a new misunderstanding. So pretty soon I'm sitting on a long, L-shaped couch in the dimly lit club with the other guys. Max heads over to the bar to put down a card, stopping to admire the two ladies currently dancing on the poles, while a handful of the other dancers working the room start circling us like birds of prey in their high heels and negligible lace outfits. Within minutes Rich has pulled out a wad of cash and bought Mike his first lap dance. A small-breasted brunette with a crown of teased hair and a sequined G-string is leaning her nude torso across him, moving slowly to the music, running her hand down his thigh as she whispers in his ear. Word of a bachelor party in the club spreads quickly, and soon we're surrounded by more dancers than we can handle. Paul grabs himself a tall blonde and heads for the champagne room, still talking on his cell phone, while Mike, Max, Rich, and Dave are content to have basic lap dances right there on the couch.

I miss my wife.

"Hey!" Mike says, looking out from behind his stripper, who is now sitting on his lap with her back to him, grinding herself against his crotch in a circular motion. "Someone take care of Doug."

"I'm fine," I say, holding up my drink. "Today is about you, not me."

"Bullshit," Mike says. "Max. Find this man a girl."

"I'm a little busy right now, man," says Max, who is almost fully reclined on the couch, looking lasciviously at the petite redhead bouncing on his lap.

"You're my best man, Max," Mike says. "Do your job."

"Stay where you are, Max," I say, quickly getting to my feet. "I can take care of myself." I head over to the bar on the far side of the room, and order myself a Jack and Coke. The trick is to keep moving, so as to avoid becoming a stationary target for any of the roving dancers. While I wait for my drink, I watch Mike and the guys in the mirror behind the bar, whispering and flirting with the girls on their laps, cracking jokes and high-fiving each other. Dave, in particular, seems enamored of his dancer, an Asian girl with disproportionately large breasts, and his hands keep snaking around to cradle her ass, a flagrant violation of strip-club etiquette, but he must be tipping well because she doesn't seem to mind.

"Hi," says a plain-faced brunette with long coltish legs and a sheer halter top, rubbing my shoulder as she sidles up to the chair next to me. "I'm Shawnie."

"Hi, Shawnie," I say.

"What's your name?"

"Jack." She lied first.

"You want to come with me to the Champagne Room, Jack?"

"No, thanks."

"How about a lap dance?"

I pull a twenty out of my wallet. "Here," I say. "You see that guy over there with the brunette on his lap?"

"Yeah."

"His name is Mike. Go give him a lap dance and tell him it's from me."

"Mike," she repeats.

"Right," I say. "But tell him your name is Debbie, okay?"

"Who's Debbie?"

"Who's Shawnie?"

She grins. "Debbie it is."

I drain my drink and order another, turning to watch as she pulls off her top and climbs onto his lap. He leans over to look past her at me, and I raise my glass in his direction. He flashes me a quizzical look, but then a new song starts, something by the Black Eyed Peas, and Mike disappears behind Shawnie's arching back.

Twenty minutes later, I'm still at the bar, realizing with disgust that while trying to stay just long enough to leave, I've drunk too much to drive, when Mike comes over to get me. "Doug," he says drunkenly. "I want to tell you something."

"Okay," I say. I'm pretty buzzed myself at this point.

"I feel funny, being in this place with you," he says, sitting down on the bar stool beside me. "I mean, I'm marrying your sister and all, and here I am, in a strip club."

"Don't worry about it," I say. "It's just some harmless fun."

"That's right," he says. "I just want you to know that I love Debbie very much, and I would never do anything to disrespect her."

"I'm sure you wouldn't."

"This is just some stupid male-bonding shit."

"I know, Mike. Don't worry about it."

"Debbie's way hotter than any of these chicks anyway," he says proudly, making a grand sweeping gesture with his arm.

"So is Laney Potter, but that's not stopping Dave," I say. We turn to look at Dave, whose face is buried between the giant breasts of his lap dancer, rocking her up and down with his legs to the beat of the music. "If only your clients could see him now."

"You think Laney Potter is good-looking?" Mike says.

I look down at my drink, wondering why I brought her up at all. "I don't know," I say. "That wasn't the point, really."

"No," Mike says, steering me away from the bar. "The point is, you're my buddy and you've been through a lot and the guys and I want to buy you some lap dances."

"That's okay, really," I say.

"Just sit down and enjoy yourself," Mike says, shoving me onto the couch, and the other guys call out their own intoxicated bellows of encouragement. Max leans forward and gravely whispers to me, like he's sharing state secrets, that for an extra hundred some of the girls will blow you in the Champagne Room, and before I know it, there's a naked girl on my lap with bleached blond hair and a metal stud in her tongue. She smells of gin, lavender body lotion, and baby powder, and her high gum line makes me wonder briefly about strip clubs and dental plans. "Hi," she says. "I'm Vanessa."

"Jack," I say, avoiding eye contact. She can't be older than twenty, and her body lotion makes her taut belly sparkle like a sidewalk, which makes me think for a sad instant of Brooke's eye shadow. And then the song starts, and it's an old Van Halen song that reminds me of Julie Baskin, my first high school girlfriend. Vanessa starts to sway and grind on my thighs, and I close my eyes and remember a party in someone's house, and how Julie and I stood outside in the shadow of the house, pressed up against each other kissing and petting, while inside this same song was playing on the stereo. She smelled clean, like scented soap, and tasted like Juicy Fruit gum; and I can still feel how in love I was, how pure and exciting and perfect it was to stand outside on a cool spring night kissing a pretty girl, and how whole we still were, as yet untouched in any way by life, and how easy everything was, because it was never meant to last. We never even broke up, just kind of dissolved peacefully, and a few weeks later we were each making out with someone else at another party, in love all over again.

"Hey," Vanessa says softly, still moving her hips unconsciously against me.

"Yeah," I say, opening my eyes.

"You're crying."

"Allergies," I say, wiping my face with the back of my hand.

Vanessa moves her face to within an inch of mine, and I can see a thin, raised scar that follows the line of her eyebrow. It's faded enough to have come from her childhood, and I wonder how she cut herself. I imagine a young, sweet-faced mother who pressed a wet cloth to her head and rushed her to the doctor and held her hand while they stitched up the wound and felt the pain like it was her own. And then I wonder what made that pretty little girl with the loving mother turn down the road that brought her to this dark club, and my sad, unresponsive lap.

"I'm sorry," I say, for more than she knows.

"You're not into it," she says. "What's wrong?"

And before I even know that I'm doing it, I tell her. "I miss my wife," I blurt out, so violently that our heads knock. "I miss her so much that it's like this cinder block in my chest, crushing my lungs so that I can't breathe." I point to Dave, still lost in the Asian girl's mountainous cleavage. "And you see that guy over there? I'm fucking his wife, and I never thought I'd be the kind of guy who fucks someone else's wife. And paying a pretty girl to grind on me would be sad under the best of circumstances, but now it's sad because, compared to everything else in my life, a pair of tits in my face is not terribly sad, which of course just makes it that much sadder, and I just want it to stop hurting already, you know? I just want to be able to breathe again. I'm tired of going to sleep every night terrified of waking up, but I'm scared for it to stop hurting, because that will mean I've moved on, and then she'll be gone forever."

And throughout this entire rant, she never ceases the slow, gentle rocking of her hips, and when I'm done, she runs her hand softly down the side of my face, the flesh of her fingers soft against my angry stubble, and pulls my forehead gently against hers. We sit like that for a moment, as the last bars of the song fade. "Jack," she says softly.

"Yeah," I say, looking into her wide green eyes. And in the instant before she speaks, I realize that I already know what she's going to say.

"You want to come with me to the Champagne Room for a private dance?"

28

THERE ARE FOUR VOICE MAILS ON MY CELL PHONE, all from Laney. I call her back as I'm driving home from the strip club, where I made good my escape soon after my aborted lap dance. She picks up on the first ring.

"Are you still with Mike and the other guys?" she says.

"I just left."

"Well, Dave just called and he says he's going to be out pretty late."

I'll bet. "Probably," I say.

"So."

"So."

"I want you in my bed."

Laney opens the door in a red satin teddy, her long auburn hair cascading wildly around her, and I know I should end this, but she's just so goddamn beautiful and after the strippers this feels positively wholesome, and it suddenly feels like I've been through a war today so I practically fall into her arms. Her bedroom flickers in the light of scented candles, and she sits me down at the edge of the high four-poster bed and undresses me slowly, kissing my chest and stomach, and then my thighs as she pulls off my pants. Once I'm naked she climbs onto my lap, wrapping her legs around me as she opens my mouth with hers, and I try hard not to think about the lap dance I had just an hour ago. Then, without taking her eyes off of me, she shimmies out of the spaghetti straps of her negligee and pulls it down so that her breasts are sudden, twin explosions of flesh in my face as she pulls my head into them. And as my hands reach around to find her ass, I can't help but think of Dave's hands on the stripper's ass, his face hungrily planted between her breasts, and this should feel like justice, but instead it just feels sad, because we're all the same. Dave, the stripper, Laney, and me; all trapped in the same pose, all wanting something other than what we're getting.

When we're done, Laney nods off and I quietly retrieve my clothing from the floor to get dressed. I'm making my way down the carpeted hallway when I hear a toilet flush and I freeze as Laney's daughter, Rebecca, four years old with her mother's red hair, steps out of the bathroom, small and cherubic in her pink pajamas. She looks at me through sleep-fogged eyes and then steps over to me and, inexplicably, lifts her arms to be picked up. "Tuck me back in," she says sleepily.

When I pick her up, she wraps her arms tightly around me and buries her face in the crook of my neck, her chubby cheek smooth against my jaw. In the dim glow of her Tinkerbell nightlight I can see the pink walls, the plush white comforter with a pattern of pink hearts, the assembly of stuffed animals protectively crowding the perimeter of her bed. I lie her back in the bed and wrap the comforter snugly around her. Then, just before I straighten up, she raises her head, eyes still closed, and kisses the bottom of my chin. "I love you," she says, before rolling back against the wall, and the hot tremor in my chest rises to my throat. I tiptoe out of the room and down the hall, and hit the first floor running.

I get home around midnight to find my mother's car parked in the driveway, and I'm sixteen again, busted coming home after curfew, having been up to no good and wondering how much they know. She's on the living room couch, dozing in front of Leno, cradling a sleeping Claire's head in her lap. Her hair is splayed and flattened against the back of the couch, her makeup smudged in a way that makes her look out of focus. Her left hand is buried in Claire's hair, and in her right is a half-filled wineglass, held miraculously upright against her chest, like she had fallen asleep with the glass on its way to her mouth. There's an empty bottle of Merlot on the table, and no other glasses in evidence, which is good, because it means Claire is being responsible about her pregnancy, but a little sad because it means my mother has polished off the entire bottle herself.

I'm quietly wrapping my fingers around the stem of the wineglass to take it from her when she pulls it away from me. "Get your own," she murmurs, barely stirring.

"Hey, Ma."

She opens her eyes. "You smell like sex."

"What are you doing here?"

She finishes off the wine in her glass and then hands it to me. "But if you were having sex," she says through a long yawn, "why wouldn't you stay the night?"

"Mom."

"A few theories come to mind, and none of them bode terribly well for you."

"I'm fine," I say, collapsing into an armchair.

"You look fine," she says sardonically, fixing me with a dour stare. "Come on, Douglas, we have no secrets in this family."

I laugh. "We have a truckload of secrets in this family."

"No, we have lies. Families need lies. Otherwise we wouldn't be able to look at each other anymore. But trust me, there are no secrets."

On the television, a hopped-up Leno whines through his monologue like he's been sucking helium.

"I thought you hated Leno," I say.

"I'm sitting on the clicker."

I reach over and turn off the television. "So," I say. "What brings you here?"

She gently brushes some of Claire's hair off her face. "Claire needed to talk."

"She called you?"

"Is that really so hard to believe?" she snaps, offended. "She's going through a lot right now, and she wanted her mother."

"No. I'm sure she did."

She looks down fondly at Claire. "The poor girl hasn't slept in days. She's always internalized her stress like that, ever since she was a little girl. And when it gets really bad, this is the only way she can fall asleep. I used to come to her apartment in the city, and then to her and Stephen's house. I know how to talk her down."

"I never knew that."

"Well, then, it's official. You don't know everything."

I lean back in my chair and close my eyes, feeling sad and guilty about too many things to quantify. "I'm sorry, Mom. I don't mean to be like this."

She looks back up at me. "You don't have to apologize to me. You're my little boy. Just be a little kinder. You don't have the market cornered on heartbreak, you know."

"I know."

"Good. Now be an angel and freshen my drink."

I lift up the empty bottle and turn it over. "I think you've had enough."

"And I think I just told you to be kinder."

"Are you spending the night?"

"I'll go home at dawn. If your father doesn't see me first thing in the morning, he becomes disoriented."

"You'll be exhausted."

"I'll nap in the afternoon. It's good practice for the nursing home."

She closes her eyes. In the darkened room, her wrinkles are gone, and she looks like my mother again, the woman who would lie in my bed at night and tell me stories that always began, "When I was young and beautiful..." And I would always interrupt on cue and say, "You still are," and she would kiss my nose and say, "So just imagine what I looked like back then." And then, after the stories she would sing me to sleep with show tunes. Sometimes I still hear her singing "Don't Cry for Me Argentina" as I'm drifting off to sleep. And now she's dozing on the couch of her widower son after rocking her divorcing daughter to sleep, before running home to make sure her demented husband doesn't trash the house in a panic.

"Mom," I say hoarsely, shaking my head.

She opens her eyes. "It's okay, Douglas."

"It's not okay."

"It's life, that's all. There are no happy endings, just happy days, happy moments. The only real ending is death, and trust me, no one dies happy. And the price of not dying is that things change all the time, and the only thing you can count on is that there's not a thing you can do about it."

"I'm sorry we all turned out like this," I say. "It must hurt you."

She shrugs. "If it were all so easy, no one would ever need me, and then what would I do for attention?"

"It's always about you, isn't it?"

"Life's a stage, and I'm the star of the show."

"You want me to make you up a bed?"

"Just bring me a blanket, I'm going to stay right here," she says, looking back down at Claire with so much tenderness that I have to look away. "And, Douglas?"

"Yeah?"

"Don't forget about my wine."

29

WORD THAT THE TOWN WIDOWER HAS BEGUN TO date spreads like a virus, and soon my machine is filled with messages from friends and neighbors calling to tell me about divorced and widowed women I simply have to meet, single sisters and cousins I would just love. Claire ruthlessly narrows down the field by first deleting any messages that don't meet her criteria, and then by making terse follow-up phone calls asking for ludicrously elaborate physical descriptions, accompanying photos, and detailed relationship histories.

"I'm just trying to avoid any hurt feelings down the road. Now you've got my e-mail address. We'll talk after I see the pictures."

"You've already told me about what a pretty face she has. I'm asking you about her ass. It's a yes/no question. Listen, put your husband on the phone."

"And was that by C-section or vaginal delivery? Okay. Find out and get back to me."

"It's got nothing to do with trusting you. All due respect, Rabbi, but your profession is in no way a guarantee of your aesthetic sensibilities."

Ultimately, she settles on Suzanne Jasper, a divorcée in her early thirties who is being championed by Mike. She is his next-door neighbor, and he would have dated her himself if he weren't madly in love with Debbie. I'm fast learning that attached men want to set me up with the women they secretly lust after, to date vicariously through me. They would if they could, but they can't so I should. According to Mike, Suzanne's life fell apart a few years ago when the fourteen-year-old girl her husband had met in a chat room and arranged to meet at a motel in Connecticut turned out to be an FBI agent trolling for sexual predators. Judging from her nervous demeanor over dinner at Mineo's Italian Bistro, Suzanne is still getting over the shock of it all. Her smile looks strained, like she's lifting weights under the table, and her laugh, which comes too quickly, is jagged and high-pitched. But she's got piles of long blond hair, smoky blue eyes, and a sharp, self-deprecating wit. And she likes me instantly because I have all my hair, and no ex-wife or competing kids. I have been touched by an act of God. I am appealingly damaged: young, slim, sad, and beautiful.

The problem with dates is that you invariably have to talk about what you do, and for me that will mean talking about my column, which will mean talking about Hailey, which is not something I want to do. So instead we talk about our childhoods and siblings—I can usually get some good mileage out of being a twin—and then we talk about movies, which is fine with me because I've seen everything, then the colleges we attended, and then, scraping the bottom of the conversation barrel, bad date stories.

And things are going fine, or as fine as things can go between two shaky, broken people whose previous lives were shattered overnight, and she's undeniably sexy, in a muted, bug-eyed sort of way, and I'm actually starting to wonder what it would be like to kiss her, and what kind of underwear she wears, when her cell phone rings. "Oh crap," she says, flipping the phone closed. "Sam's sick."

Suzanne has two young boys, Sam and Mason, and they seemed cute enough when I came to pick her up at her house an hour ago. But when we walk in now, Sam, the five-year-old, is standing on a chair and puking violently into the kitchen sink, and Mason, the three-year-old, is perched on the kitchen table, crying his head off. The babysitter, a chubby high school girl with a mouthful of braces and dime-sized chin zits, looks panicked and practically throws herself at Suzanne's feet when we walk through the door.

"Oh my God! How could he throw up so much?" Suzanne says, eyeing a large puddle of puke on the hallway floor.

"That was me," the girl says, embarrassed. "The smell of vomit makes me sick."

"Perfect," Suzanne says grimly. She grabs a twenty from her bag. "Go home, Dana."

"Are you sure?" Dana says, but she's already pocketing the money and heading for the door.

Suzanne runs into the kitchen and puts her hands on Sam's shoulders. "It's okay, baby. Mommy's here." Sam looks up at her, his face and shirt caked with dried puke, and emits a sad whimper before turning back to the sink to puke. "Oh my God," Suzanne says, feeling his neck. "He's burning up."

Meanwhile, Mason's cries are unrelenting, so I take a step

toward him, looking to calm him down, but he backs away from me and falls off the table, banging his head on the edge as he goes, and I'd have thought he couldn't get any louder, but Mason's got range, and now he digs deep and lets loose with a bloodcurdling scream that makes the small hairs on my neck stand up. He keeps it going for so long, that I worry he'll stop breathing and pass out, or have some sort of kiddy stroke. Suzanne scoops him up in her arms and says, "Breathe, baby," while Sam continues to heave over the sink. "It's okay, Mason, the man was just trying to help you."

"Ice!" Mason cries.

"Could you get him some ice from the freezer?" Suzanne says.

"Sure," I say. "Although it really wasn't much of a bang."

"Ice!" Mason screams, glowering at me over his mother's shoulder.

"He likes ice," Suzanne says, combing his hair back with her fingers.

In the freezer I find a hard blue ice pack, the kind you throw into coolers, and the instant it touches Mason's forehead, he stops crying like someone flipped a switch. Suzanne hands him to me, and, to my surprise, he comes willingly, nestling against my chest, holding the ice pack to his head with solemn urgency. Then she wets a dishtowel and starts rubbing Sam's neck and back with one hand, pulling off his vomit-crusted shirt with the other, whispering and cooing to him as she goes. This display of maternal competency, the effortless blending of compassion and efficiency, is something that I of all people should find attractive, having been married to a single mother myself, but it leaves me cold, although the cloying stench of vomit in the air might have something to do with that.

Sam's running a fever of a hundred and four, and after paging the pediatrician, Suzanne decides to take him to the emergency room. Having prematurely dismissed her nauseated sitter, she's now faced with the unenviable choice of bringing Mason along, or asking me to babysit. "I hate to ask you," she says, slipping a fresh T-shirt over Sam's head. "But I don't know what else to do."

"Don't worry about it," I say. "I'm great with kids."

"It's way past his bedtime. I'll put him to bed upstairs and you can just hang out in the living room and watch TV. You won't even know he's there."

"It's fine. I'm happy to help. Just tell me where you keep the mop."

"The mop?"

"I normally don't mop vomit until the third date, but it just feels like we're clicking."

She smiles. "I'm sorry about our date. I'll make it up to you, I promise," she says, and then blanches at what might have been perceived as a sexual innuendo.

"It's fine."

"You really don't have to clean up."

"Trust me. I really do."

She carries Mason back to his bedroom, leaving me in the hallway with Sam, who looks like the world's youngest hangover victim, leaning up against the wall for support, dazedly rubbing his eyes. "I know how you feel," I say sympathetically. Suzanne emerges a few minutes later, hurriedly throwing a coat on Sam as she hustles him to the door. "Make yourself at home," she says to me. "Help yourself to anything you want." And then she's gone.

It takes longer than you'd think to clean up vomit. The mop just seems to be spreading it around the floor, so I switch to paper towels, eventually going through three rolls. Then, after I've mopped again, I gather all the paper towels into a garbage bag and throw it in the garage, along with the mop, which is beyond saving at this point. But even after all of my cleaning and spraying the kitchen floor with Lysol, the smell of vomit seems to be following me, and that's when I discover the stiffened puke stain in the shape of Italy on my pants, just below the knee. I locate Suzanne's washer and dryer in an alcove off the kitchen, pull off my pants, and put them in with a little detergent. After setting the machine on permanent press, I walk around the house in my tighty-whities for a while, examining her pictures— all evidence of her ex-husband has been surgically expunged— and then poke around the pantry and the fridge, looking for a snack. In a cabinet above the fridge I discover a bottle of Johnnie Walker Black, and I hesitate for a moment, but I'm anticipating a long night and she did say I should help myself to anything I want, so I pull down the bottle, some Ritz crackers, and a Sesame Street juice box as my chaser, and settle down in the living room to watch some television. She's only got basic cable, which she was wise not to disclose earlier because it may very well have been a deal-breaker. Every channel seems to be showing a medical drama or a police procedural where the well-dressed cops spend half the show in a dim hi-tech lab that looks more like a nightclub, trying to mine drama out of running tests on a piece of clothing fiber, and Suzanne's DVD collection seems to be limited to animated Disney movies. I channel surf fruitlessly for a half hour or so, and before you know it, I'm a third of the way into the Johnnie Walker. When I stand up, the skin of my thighs separates audibly from the leather couch like peeling fruit leather.

Feeling a little woozy, I go to check on my pants. The wash cycle is over, so I throw them into the dryer and then look for the bathroom. There's a sheet of plastic taped over the doorway to the powder room, and through it I can see the stripped walls and exposed studs and wires of a renovation job in progress, so I head upstairs, my socks sinking into the plush carpeting, stirring up static electricity that zaps me through my fingers when I inadvertently touch the wallpaper. The hall bathroom is full of bath toys, and there's a strange, donut-shaped contraption on the toilet seat, ostensibly to keep the boys from falling in when they're crapping, and it doesn't look terribly sanitary so I decide to use Suzanne's bathroom. This means I'll have to go through her bedroom, which could be construed as an invasion of her privacy, but I've mopped the puke off her floors and I'm babysitting her son, so we've got to be past all of that, right? Besides, she specifically told me to make myself at home, and at home I don't crap on a plastic piss-stained hemorrhoid donut with Cookie Monster smiling creepily up at me like a puppet with a bathroom fetish.

Suzanne's bedroom is done in a dark gray, and her king-sized bed has a quilted leather headboard and is covered in a wine-colored satin duvet with matching throw pillows and sheets. It's a sexy bed that causes me to slightly revise my impression of her, as does the presence of not one but two identical vibrators in the drawer of her night table that I accidentally open, indicating that she is a woman who takes her orgasms seriously enough to have a backup plan for her backup plan. "Suzanne!" I say out loud, impressed. Still taking generous sips from the Johnnie Walker bottle, I head into the bathroom, which is a cluttered mess from her pre-date preparations: blow dryer, clips, brushes, eyeliners, lipsticks, and other implements of beauty strewn across every available surface. In my somewhat inebriated state, I'm disproportionately touched by all the trouble she went to just to have dinner with me.

When I come out of the bathroom, I lie down on the bed for a minute, sinking into the pillow mattress, enjoying the sensation of the cool satin against my bare legs. There's a framed picture on the night table, Suzanne and a girlfriend in their bikinis, holding up colorful umbrella drinks by the pool at some tropical resort. I prop the picture up on my chest and look at her for a little bit. I can't help but wonder, had our date gone on as planned, if we'd have ended up back here, in this soft, sexy bed. It hadn't really seemed like an option over dinner, but now that I'm here, I feel like we might have. I close my eyes and try to recall her face over dinner, looking for clues, trying to discern a hidden sensuality, imagining a credible sequence of events that would have led us from stilted dinner conversation to undressing each other and lying down on this crimson softness. Suzanne. There's an old Journey song by that name, I think. I hum a few bars, but can't quite remember the lyrics. Journey was such a long, long time ago.

"Oh my God!" Her voice yanks me out of sleep like a fishhook in the eye, and squinting through the blinding light, I can make out Suzanne standing in the doorway, turning Sam's face into her thighs, her eyes bulging in shock, mouth wide open, jaw trembling.

"Suzanne," I say, sitting up groggily, and in doing so I knock over the picture on my chest and spill the Johnnie Walker, wedged upright between my thighs in what I will later understand to be a somewhat phallic manner, onto the duvet.

"What the hell are you doing?" she shouts.

"Listen," I say, rubbing my eyes while the room spins around me like a carousel. "It's okay."

"You scumbag! Put on your goddamn pants right now and get the hell out of my house!"

Her face is twisted with rage and disgust, and as I roll off the bed and lurch toward her, she throws her hand up defensively, recoiling in revulsion against the wall. "Stay away from me!" Down the hall, Mason starts to cry. "Oh my God, Mason!" She darts out of the room dragging Sam behind her.

It feels like slow motion as I run downstairs in a dizzy haze, head pounding, thighs quaking, and yank open the dryer door. My pants come out heavy and soaked, and I realize that I never pushed the start button. I pull them on anyway, wet and frigid against my skin, and then run back upstairs. Through Mason's bedroom doorway, I can see Suzanne sitting on his bed, holding both crying children on her lap. "Suzanne," I say.

The withering look she shoots me carries a nuclear payload that makes every organ in my body contract like a sponge. "Just leave," she says, and I realize that there will be no fixing this, that there is no explanation she'll be willing to accept. I am now, and forever will be, the guy she found drunk and pantless in her bed. The next time she tells her bad date stories to another man, I will top the list, and as he shakes his head sympathetically, she'll shrug and make a self-deprecating comment about all the scumbags and perverts she seems to attract, and it doesn't seem fair that I should be included in that company, but it's not like I can file an appeal. And so, damage done, there's nothing left but to nod sadly, pull up the sagging waist of my cold, soaked pants, and beat the latest in my fast-growing collection of ignoble retreats.

Driving home, I'm laughing hysterically, or else I'm crying, I'm not exactly sure how to categorize the high, glottal barks erupting like gunfire from my throat, but either way, I can feel sharp, hot pricks on the inside of my chest, the floating jagged edges of all the things in me that are still broken.

In the weeks that follow, I have enough lousy first dates to merit a musical montage. Cue the pop song and watch Doug try on different outfits and pose in front of the full-length mirror as Claire directs him, laughing from the bed. Watch Doug escorting various attractive and semi-attractive women from central casting in and out of different restaurants and coffee shops. Fast cuts of different women seated across the table: speaking or not speaking, painstakingly scraping the dressing off a piece of Bibb lettuce, angrily underscoring some clearly salient talking point with a violent jab of her finger, weeping uncontrollably, and sucking up a seemingly endless piece of spaghetti. And then more fast cuts of Doug dropping each of these women off at their homes or apartments, shaking hands, or awkwardly jock-eying back and forth between handshakes and chaste good-night pecks, the camera lingering on them in the background to show on their faces the sad certainty of another man who won't be calling again, and then Doug coming into focus in the fore-ground as he heads back to his car, his expression bathed in the abject worthlessness of it all. The song choice is key here, some-thing slow, but with a beat, a gruff smoker's voice singing ro-mantic lyrics laced with irony to convey the utter futility of it all; the boredom, the wasted time, the awkward beginnings and endings, the instantly forgettable, canned-date conversation, the sad, damaged lives to which he is now unwittingly privy, a song that ends in fading minor piano chords as Doug drives home with the windows open, his face sadly vacant as he stares blankly at the empty road ahead.

Then one sleepless night, I dig out Brooke Hayes's business card from my wallet and dial her cell phone. She picks up on the fifth ring.

"It's Doug," I say. "Parker."

"Hi, Doug Parker," she says drowsily.

"I woke you up. I'm sorry."

"No. It's okay. What's up?"

"Nothing."

"What time is it?"

"It's one a.m."

"Oh."

"Look, this was stupid. I'm sorry. Go back to sleep."

"You sound funny."

"I'm a little drunk."

"Are you okay?"

"Yes."

"Okay."

"I lied. I'm not."

"What's going on?"

"I've started dating."

"Oh. That's a positive step, right?"

"I don't know. It just feels wrong and awkward and utterly hopeless."

"You're dating, all right."

There's a moment of silence during which I can hear her breathing, still heavy with sleep. "Hi," she says, after a bit.

"I just wanted to let you know that I'm going to the movies tomorrow, around noon. You know, just in case you were too."

"Oh. What are you going to see?"

"Whatever you want."

She laughs and says, "I'll see what I can do."

30

BROOKE SHOWS UP TO THE THEATER DRESSED IN a long, flowing bohemian skirt, and a baby T-shirt, her hair pinned up off her face by two bobby pins to reveal the multiple hoops and studs in her crowded earlobes. She looks effortlessly pretty, poised and relaxed, and I have to quell the urge to reach out and run my fingers down the side of her face.

"I was raped."

She tells me this with no preamble, in the middle of the movie, a zombie flick that is a remake of some other classic zombie flick, because, apparently, there are no new zombie stories to tell. Brooke picked it, and we're the only ones in the theater.

"What?" I say.

"You wanted to know my secret," she says nonchalantly, reaching over to take a sip from my soda. "I was raped. About two years ago."

I turn to look at her, but she's staring resolutely at the screen, where the zombies are pressed up against the glass doors of the mall where the last surviving humans are holed up.

"You want to get out of here?" I say. "Go somewhere and talk?"

"No," she says. "Here's fine."

"It's hard to hear you above the machine guns."

"I like it that way."

"What happened?"

"It was this guy from my yoga class. Benny. He was one of those big weight lifter types, you know? He used to walk me home after class if Greg couldn't pick me up."

"Greg?"

"My fiancé."

"Oh."

"Benny was always flirting with me, but in a harmless way. I thought he looked at me more like a kid sister, always looking out for me and being protective. I mean, he was practically twice my age. And he'd been doing yoga for years. Not that that matters, but you just don't think of people who practice yoga as closet rapists. Then one night he walked me home and asked if he could come up to my apartment to use the bathroom. I didn't think anything of it, but as soon as we walked through the door, he pushed me up against the wall and told me he loved me and he needed to show me. When I told him to stop he ignored me, and when I tried to push him off of me he smacked me, not too hard, but with the threat of hardness behind it, you know? Like the next one could take my head off. I mean, he was a big guy, bigger than most of the trainers. And then he looked me right in the eye and smacked me again, to let me know that the first one hadn't been an accident. And then he took my hand like a boyfriend and led me into my bedroom and raped me."

"Jesus," I say.

She nods. "You wanted to know."

"So, what happened to Greg? He couldn't handle it?"

"Oh, he was okay with me getting raped." She turns to look at me. "Not okay, but he was ready to deal with it. What he couldn't deal with was that I didn't fall apart over it."

"What do you mean?"

She sighs. "I guess I just wasn't a very good rape victim. I was supposed to have all these as-seen-on-TV symptoms of post-traumatic stress: nightmares, crying jags, weight loss, paranoia. But I got over all of that pretty quickly. I wasn't in denial. I knew what had happened to me. But I hadn't gotten hurt or pregnant, I had a lot of good friends, I was in love, and life was good, you know. I was sad for a few days, then I chalked it up to bad luck, like a car accident, and moved on. I thought that was a pretty healthy attitude—I still do—but Greg couldn't handle it. It was like he was being cheated out of his role as the supportive boyfriend. And then he became angry, and decided that I must have enjoyed it on some level, that maybe I'd even seduced Benny into raping me. And it became this big thing where he wouldn't sleep with me, acting like I'd somehow betrayed him, and after a while I actually found myself wondering if he might be right, which was like getting raped all over again. We just became trapped in this downward spiral of inescapable irony. The only way he could get over my being raped was if I couldn't get over it."

"So you broke up?"

She nods. "And of course, only after the fact did I figure out that I had, in fact, been traumatized, that I was furious with Greg for not being there to protect me, and my great attitude had actually been his punishment because I knew it would ultimately drive him insane. And once he was gone, the reality of what had happened to me kind of hit home, and that's when it all happened, the nightmares, the crying for days on end, all that good stuff. I had a little breakdown, I guess."

"So what brought you to New Radford?"

"He owned the apartment and I couldn't afford to rent my own. So I moved back home." She grins. "Twenty-seven and still living with my parents. Aren't I a great role model for the kids?"

"Has there been anyone since Greg?"

She shakes her head. "A few false starts. But at some point I always felt obligated to tell them about the rape, and then they either got weird about touching me, or else they got all macho and stupid. So I tried not telling a few, but then I felt distant, like I was hiding something."

"Damned if you do, and damned if you don't."

"I just need to be able to tell someone who will understand without it changing the way they look at me."

"You told me."

"But we're not dating."

"Couldn't this be a date?"

"A zombie matinee and popcorn?"

"I didn't say it was a good date."

She turns sideways in her seat and looks at me for a long moment. The explosions on the screen reflect like shooting stars across her dark eyes, and her knowing smile is warm enough to melt things in my chest. Something I didn't notice before: just at the edge of Brooke's upper lip, a bit to the left, is a small crater in her skin, an old acne scar that eats slightly into the meat of her upper lip, disrupting its curve, forming a small swirl of off-color scar tissue there. But that works just fine for me. Perfection is plastic, cold, and unyielding. Real beauty is a current that has to be grounded, and it's these little defects that do it. You need context, a reference point. Her scarred upper lip is the hook, the default nucleus from which everything else radiates. "No," she says. "I'm pretty sure this isn't a date, because if it was, we'd be holding hands."

She watches me as I slowly reach over, and then spreads her fingers to weave them through mine, running her thumb softly up and down the back of my hand as she leans her head on my shoulder. "Let's pick a different movie," she says.

"Which one?"

"Whichever one's the longest."

She never lets go of my hand, even in the harsh lighting of the multiplex hallway as we're switching theaters, and I take that to be a good sign.

31

I COME DOWNSTAIRS THE NEXT MORNING TO FIND
Claire already dressed in a blazer, skirt, and heels, hurriedly
checking her makeup in the hall mirror.

"Why are you all dressed up?" I say, sitting down on the bottom stair.

"This isn't dressed up," she says, still looking at her reflection.
"It's just well dressed. Not all of us can pull off your slept-
in-my-jeans-and-T-shirt look." She makes an imperceptible
adjustment to her hair, and then does that reverse pout that
women do after putting on lipstick, folding her lips in on each
other so that they disappear for a second. Sitting on the stairs in
my boxers, I feel like a kid again, watching my mother prepare
to go out on an audition. She would stay at the mirror long after
she'd finished her makeup, and I'd run lines with her, reading
from scripts I didn't understand, and she'd study her reflection
and tweak her expressions and head movements as she spoke.
Then she'd say, "Wish me luck," and I'd say, "Break a leg," and
she'd kiss the air near my cheek and head out the door, and I'd
offer up a little prayer that this would be the one she landed, and
it would make her a star, and we'd move to Hollywood, and I'd

be one of those cool Hollywood kids, dressing funky, going to premieres, and hanging out with beautiful troubled girls at night clubs. And now, watching Claire, I'm shocked to realize how much she looks like our mother, and I almost tell her, but although our mother's beauty is a matter of public record, I'm still not entirely sure she'd take it as a compliment.

"Where are you going?"

"I've got an appointment to see my obstetrician."

"Everything okay?"

"It's just a routine prenatal checkup and ultrasound."

"Why do you have to look so good for your doctor?"

"I get waxed for my doctor. I look good for me."

"You want me to come with?"

"Nah. I'm late already."

"I can be ready in five minutes."

She turns and runs her fingers through my grimy, sleep-sculpted hair. "You'll need ten minutes just to get your bed head under control."

"Seriously."

"I am serious," she says, flashing me a smile from the door. "Have you seen your hair?"

But after she's gone I replay the conversation and something in her tone bothers me, so I dial Debbie's cell phone number. "I'm walking into a meeting," she says in a low voice.

"Walk back out, I need to ask you something."

"Call me later."

"Should I have gone with Claire to her obstetrician appointment?"

"What?"

"She just left."

"Hold on a minute…" There's some muffled noise and the sound of a door slamming, and then Debbie comes on the phone again. "She went alone?"

"She said it was no big deal."

"Of course it's a big deal. How long ago did she leave?"

"Just now."

"Do you know who her doctor is?"

"No."

"I'll call Mom and find out. Then I'll meet you there."

"What about your meeting?"

"Doug," she says, sighing. "Claire is a mess, or haven't you noticed?"

I think of Claire curled up on the couch like a little girl, her head in my mother's lap as she slept, and it occurs to me that I may have missed a few things. "Crap," I say, feeling like a schmuck.

"Doug," Debbie says softly.

"I know," I say, cutting her off. "I'm trying."

"Try harder. She needs you."

"Yeah."

"And so do I."

"Pooh," I say, but she's already gone.

An hour later, Debbie and I are in a medical suite at Lenox Hill Hospital. The suite serves a practice of five doctors, whose names are screened onto the opaque glass door, and the waiting room is a crowded sanctum of hushed women with silent, patient smiles. I've never been to an OB/GYN office before, and you can almost see fractal bends in the air from all of the estrogen floating around in here. Like Claire, all of the women are well dressed and made up, and it strikes me as both sweet and odd that they feel the need to look good for anyone who's going to get into their pants, even under these clinical conditions. Many of the women are in various degrees of pregnancy, and seated awkwardly next to some of them are restless-looking men who fidget like children, checking their watches, reading newspapers, tapping aimlessly on wireless devices, or holding muted conversations with their wives, who flip calmly through women's health magazines, responding without looking up, humming along quietly to the soft rock being piped in through discreetly mounted speakers.

A little while later, we're still trying to talk our way past the bitchy receptionist, when my mother comes bustling through the door, flushed and slightly out of breath. "Mom," I say, surprised. "What are you doing here?"

"Where's Claire? Did I miss it?"

"We're working on it," Debbie says, turning back to the receptionist, a sullen-eyed girl with fake eyelashes, more lipstick than lip, a tiny diamond stud like a sparkling pimple in the pocket of her nostril curve, and hooked fingernails like painted claws.

"I'm not allowed to take anyone back there once the exam is in progress," the girl says firmly.

"I understand," Debbie says, matching her tone. "But we are her family and she wants us there. We're just a little late."

"She didn't say nothing to me about it. I can only take the father back."

"The father is out of the picture for now," Debbie says. "For all intents and purposes, she is a single mother, and I'm sure you can see how she might need our support right now."

"I'm sorry, but there's nothing I can do."

My mother steps over to the desk to look down at the girl. "I am Claire's mother."

The girl nods, unimpressed, and then picks up a ringing phone. "Doctor's office," she says, still meeting my mother's gaze.

My mother looks at her for a long moment, then she nods slowly, smiling sweetly, and, without breaking off eye contact, shouts "Claire!" at the top of her lungs and the girl practically falls back off her seat in shock. Rather than wait for her to recover, my mother turns and marches down the long hallway leading to the examination rooms.

Everyone in the waiting room looks up, and the receptionist jumps to her feet and calls after her, "Hey, lady, you can't do that!"

"Claire!" my mother shouts again, disappearing down the hall.

Debbie and I look at each other and quickly follow her, with the receptionist in hot pursuit. "You're not allowed back there!" she calls out, grabbing Debbie's elbow. Debbie turns on her like a whip, eyes blazing. "Are you absolutely positive you won't be needing that hand anymore?" she says.

The girl pulls her hand off and steps back with a defensive shrug. "Whatever," she says.

A guy about my age in scrubs and a badge that says "Medical Technician" steps out of one of the examination rooms and sees us. "Excuse me," he says, turning to face us. "Can I help you?"

"Claire!" my mother shouts in his face.

"Hey!" he shouts back at her.

And then, from behind one of the doors, comes Claire's voice. "Mom?"

"Claire, honey?"

"Mom!"

I step past the technician in the direction of Claire's voice and throw open a door. A half-naked woman in stirrups screams. The doctor working between her legs like a mechanic pokes his head up and slides back on his stool, granting me a cross-sectional view of the vagina that will from this day forward haunt my dreams like a demon spirit. "Wrong room," I say, slamming the door on her outraged cries as the technician pulls me back.

My mother opens the next door and there is Claire, lying supine on the table in a paper gown with her belly exposed, craning her head to stare at the monitor as the doctor, holding the transducer against her belly, turns to face us. "Hello," he says, bemusedly. "Can I help you?"

"They're my family," Claire says, and then, without prelude, bursts into tears.

"Baby!" my mother says, running over to hug her, getting blue gel all over her blouse.

"It's okay, Will," the doctor says, and the medical technician releases me. "Come on in."

We all gather around Claire as the doctor resumes the ultrasound. "So," he says. "I was just showing Claire her baby's heart." On the screen, there's a widening triangle of light, like someone opened a trapdoor into a basement. In the field of light are what appear to be two white threads crossing, and between them is a small throbbing bean. The doctor slides a second device over Claire's belly and the room fills with the rhythmic hiss of rushing water, followed by a fast, staccato tapping.

"Oh, Claire," my mother says, putting her hand on Claire's shoulder, her eyes welling up with tears.

"I know," Claire wails, still crying.

"Listen to the little guy go," Debbie says, taking Claire's hand.

The doctor adjusts the transducer and suddenly we can see the fetus in profile, the round, oversized head, the bud of a nose, the thin arms reaching forward, clasped in prayer.

"Oh my God," Debbie squeals.

"You're about twelve weeks in," the doctor says.

"I'm having a baby," Claire says, staring in wonder at the screen.

And looking at the screen, I'm suddenly overwhelmed by an uncharacteristic certainty that I could do this too. That I could conceive a baby and watch it grow in the womb, be there waiting for it when it entered the world perfect and untouched, and then devote myself to keeping it that way for as long as possible. That there are bigger, deeper things to feel than happy or sad, and I know that I'm a mess right now, but maybe, with time, all of this pain and uncertainty will add up to some small measure of wisdom that would make me a good father. And for the first time I can remember, it seems like a very viable option, and not a prospect that will make me break out in a clammy sweat even at the hypothetical stage.

"Is it a boy or a girl?" I say.

"I can't tell in this position," the doctor says.

"It's a girl," Claire says, looking up at me, smiling through her tears.

"How do you know?"

"Because I'm naming her Hailey, so if it's a boy, he'd better learn how to fight."

And then everything goes blurry as Claire reaches for me and pulls me toward her, and I close my eyes so that there's nothing but the sound of that brand-new, still-forming heart, filling the room with the relentless rhythm of its tiny, hungry life.

32

BROOKE'S PARENTS LIVE IN A MODEST, BOXY SPLIT-level that calls to mind the Brady Bunch house. It's on the southernmost side of New Radford, where the houses are closer together and not quite as set back from the street, just a few blocks from Jim and Angie's house. Her father is an engineer and her mother works for the Board of Jurors, and they're both still at work when I come to pick her up. She's wearing dark slacks and a white ribbed sweater, her hair tied up in a high ponytail, and when she steps back to let me in, she doesn't step very far. It would make sense for me to lean in and give her a peck on the cheek, but I freeze up and then the moment's gone, and to do it now will be awkward and contrived. I know there are men for whom this all happens effortlessly, just as sure as I know that I'm not one of them.

Instead, I say, "I can't remember the last time I picked a girl up at her parents' house."

"Don't rub it in."

"No, it's nice. I feel like I'm back in high school again."

"And my parents are out," she says, raising her eyebrows in

mock seduction. "We could go down to the basement and fool around."

I must be blushing because she quickly pats my shoulder and says, "That was a joke."

"I know," I say.

She steps forward and looks up at me. "What is it, Doug?" she says softly.

"It's nothing," I say, shaking it off. "You just look very pretty, that's all."

She reaches for my arm and then stands up on the balls of her feet to kiss my cheek. "Nice deflection, but I'll take it."

Below the surface, my skin throbs like a sunburn in the spot her lips touched.

Over dinner she tells me about her childhood, how her parents fought constantly, and still do, and how as a child she prayed every night that they would get divorced. How her father would hit her older brother, Ron, and then, when Ron got bigger, how he started to fight back, and then, to the sound track of her mother's futile screams, they would go at each other like cage fighters, breaking furniture and smashing dishes, leaving cracks and dents and fist-sized craters in the walls. How her mother ultimately grew tired of fixing the holes and would just hang pictures over them, so that eventually the walls were covered with random pictures in mismatched frames at odd intervals, rosy-cheeked childhood portraits of Brooke over scarred drywall, the pretty lies of the past used to hide the ugly truth. How as a child she learned to spot the warning signs and retreat upstairs to her bedroom, playing her records at top volume until the fighting stopped or the cops came. How every time her father and brother bounced off the walls downstairs, the records would scratch, and after a while the skips in her favorite songs became indelible parts of them, so that even now, when she sings along to certain songs on the radio, she's always somewhat surprised when the music doesn't skip where it's supposed to. In her mind, the damaged version is the true one. Even now, long after her brother has moved out, the brawls still occur every time he visits, and Thanksgiving and Christmas generally culminate with the neighbors calling the police.

"Jesus," I say. "How did you end up so normal?"

"I'm insane on the inside," she says. "I couldn't wait to finish college and get the hell out of there. And now here I am, right back where I started."

"I know the feeling," I say. "Once I got out, I never thought I'd leave the city, and now here I am, right back in Westchester."

"Are you from here originally?"

"Forest Heights. Two towns over."

"Oh. Rich kid."

"We were comfortable, I guess."

"You don't act like a trust fund baby."

"That's because I didn't have one. My dad was determined not to spoil us. He said kids with money have a harder time learning responsibility."

"I can understand that."

"I was still a fuckup."

"Maybe, but a fuckup with means is much more dangerous. Who knows what damage you might have done if price were no object? I see rich kids in my office at school every day, kids whose allowance puts them in a higher tax bracket than me, and their sense of unconditional entitlement is like a congenital birth defect. Your dad's a smart man."

"He was."

"Oh, is he gone?"

"No. But he's...different now."

"How's that?"

"He had a stroke that caused him some brain damage."

"I'm sorry."

"Thanks. Actually, we get along much better now."

Brooke sighs wistfully. "I wish my dad would have a stroke."

I laugh, and then I make her laugh, and we eat some more and we laugh some more, and people come and go, and somewhere behind us a waiter drops a tray, and a family sings "Happy Birthday," and outside the window pedestrians pass by, kids on skateboards, people walking dogs or pushing strollers or holding hands, enjoying the last few days of mild weather, and all the while something is growing between us like a magnetic field, invisible but palpable, surrounding us, cordoning us off from everyone else, until it feels like there's the rest of the world, and then there's Brooke and me, and I remember a greeting card that was popular back in high school, that had a picture of two yellow chicks in an egg, or two kittens in a cut-off milk carton, or two baby monkeys on a tree branch, and it said *Me and You Against the World,* and then on the inside it said, *Personally I Think We're Going to Get Creamed,* and looking at her now, with the candlelight dancing across her porcelain face, I wonder if she'd have been the kind of girl I would have wanted to give a card like that to back then, and if I would have been the kind of guy she'd have liked to receive a card like that from, and I suspect not, but that was then and this is now, and maybe only after she'd been raped and I'd lost my wife in a plane crash did we become the people we are at this very instant, and none of it should have happened, but it did, and so we eat and we laugh and the people come and go, and it's me and her against the world, and maybe we're going to get creamed, but we've both been creamed before, and there's something strangely comforting in that knowledge, and so I look up at her and I can feel the naked emotion, as yet undefined, embryonic, burning across my face, can see it reflected in the dark, twin universes of her eyes.

"I wanted to kiss you when I picked you up," I say.

"I wanted you to," she says.

It's suddenly very quiet, like the restaurant is filled with extras who have been instructed only to simulate conversation.

"I was nervous. I don't know exactly why."

"I know. It's okay."

"I'm not nervous anymore."

It's so quiet.

"I like the way you look at me," she says in a light whisper.

"Come closer," I say.

Her lips, soft and moist, collapse against mine, and I can feel the heat of the table candle on the underside of my jaw as our mouths open, just a little, to form a tighter seal, and she tastes of white wine and the basil from her salad, but underneath it all I can taste something else, an organic sweetness that is only her, the flavor that I know I will always taste whenever we kiss. It's a tender, unhurried kiss, more confirmation than exploration, and when it's over we stay close, our heads hovering over the little table like helium balloons, eyes wide, complexions flushed.

"That was nice," she says.

"Yeah," I say.

"I think you should ask for the bill."

"You charge for that?"

She laughs and kisses me again. And only then, as I scan the restaurant for our waiter, do I see Laney Potter, sitting with Dave and another couple at a corner table in the back, staring daggers at me even as she responds to the conversation going on around her. And I should have known, in a town with only three decent restaurants, that something like this was bound to happen, but that doesn't make the sudden chill in my belly any less icy. I try to focus on Brooke, but suddenly she sounds far away, and I can feel the moment we've just shared getting away from me. Laney's presence is making me squirm, like I have an indelicate itch I can't scratch in public, and I can feel her eyes on me like hot lasers, burning through my skin layer by layer, and it's only a matter of time before I burst into flames. I am trapped, like the sitcom kid out on a date when he's supposed to be home studying, and then his parents come into the restaurant and he has to hide behind his menu and assure his date that everything is fine even as he yanks her down to duck under the table.

I need a moment alone to regroup, so I excuse myself and head back to the restrooms, which are through an alcove and down a narrow hallway decorated with framed prints of pinup girls from the nineteen fifties. There's only one other diner in the men's room, a short, bald guy in a suit standing at the urinal and talking on his cell phone. "Wear that lace thong that I like," he says. "The black one." He is not talking to his wife, who is back at their table waiting for him to order dessert, and I'm no better than him, this multitasking man who can piss one-handed and have phone sex with his girlfriend and take his wife out to dinner all at the same time. "That's right, baby," he says, shimmying on his tiptoes as he shakes out his last drops.

I enter the far stall and lean against the wall, wiping the sweat off my neck with toilet paper, trying to achieve a Zen state of calm by taking deep breaths. I hear cell-phone guy leave, the bastard doesn't even wash his hands, the hands that will touch one woman intimately and then another. Then I hear the bathroom door open again, and the click of heels across the tiles. A woman's heels. They travel across the floor and come to a stop in front of my stall door. Through the crack, I can see a flash of red hair. "Am I coming in, or are you coming out?" she says.

"Laney," I say. "What are you doing?"

"I'm seizing the opportunity."

"Someone's going to come."

"Then you'd better let me in."

When I open the stall door she steps in, pulling it closed behind her and locking it. She turns to face me, her cheeks flushed, eyes blazing. "Why won't you return my calls?"

I look at her, wondering how to calm her down, terrified of setting her off. "I've been in a bad place," I say.

"I thought we were friends, Doug. Whatever else we were, I thought we were friends. I cared about you. You fucked me and left. You made me feel like a whore."

"I'm sorry. I didn't mean to."

"What happened? Is it that girl outside?"

"No. It has nothing to do with her."

"So what was it? You think I don't know that you're dating? The whole town knows that you're dating. I have to hear about it everywhere I go, everyone telling me who they think we should fix you up with. And I just smile and nod, like the thought of you with someone else doesn't kill me. Last week you were making love to me, and now you're having dinner with women you barely know and I have to chase you down in the men's bathroom. I hate that you're making me this person. Don't I mean anything to you?"

"Of course you do, but really, what the hell are we even doing? It can't lead anywhere."

She steps closer to me, so that we're practically touching in the narrow confines of the stall. "I love you," she says, and suddenly there are tears balanced precariously on the rims of her eyes, poised to fall. "I know I said I wouldn't, but I do."

"Laney," I say, reaching for her arm. "You're married."

"That didn't stop you before."

"It's stopping me now."

"I don't have to be married."

I shake my head. "Don't."

"I was going to leave him eventually anyway."

"That may be, but you can't do it for me. I'm not a good bet."

"So you can sleep with me but you can't have a relationship with me."

"I can't sleep with you or have a relationship with you."

"You used me."

"You used me too."

And now the tears hit critical mass and fall, streaming darkly down her face like twin exhaust lines, and there's nothing to do but catch them gently with my thumbs, a gesture she mistakes for an invitation, pressing herself against me and wrapping her arms around my waist, her fingers rubbing the small of my back. "Doug," she says, nuzzling me.

The bathroom door opens and we freeze in the stall like hiding children, holding our breaths as footsteps approach the urinals. Laney throws her arms around my shoulders, hoisting herself off the floor to rest her feet on the toilet seat, and we remain absolutely still, listening to the hissing splash of urine against the porcelain. And then Laney puts her tongue on the back of my earlobe and pulls it between her teeth. "Doug," she whispers, her breath hot and moist in my ear. I lean my head away from her, but it's a bathroom stall and there's really nowhere to go. She opens her mouth, running her lips slowly down my jaw, her hand sliding down my stomach and past my belt, rubbing and grabbing at my crotch. I grab her hand to pull it up and she struggles against me, smiling like it's a game, so I twist it and pull it behind her back, which has the unintended effect of pressing her body harder against mine, and she leans down and starts kissing my neck. "You know you want this," she whispers. The urinal flushes, and there's a quick spray of sink water, and then the bathroom door opens and shuts. I exhale and twist my body fiercely to get Laney off of me, and her foot slides off the seat and into the toilet with a splash. "Shit!" she cries, pulling her foot out, spraying my pant leg.

"Fuck!" I say, and we pour out of the stall.

"Oh my God!" Laney says, shaking her foot in the air, hobbling erratically across the bathroom. "My foot is soaked."

"I'm sorry."

She looks at me and then sighs deeply. "Serves me right, I guess." And just like that, the fight is out of her eyes, and she leans against the wall, looking sad and small and defeated, which of course, makes me feel like shit.

"Listen," I say.

"Please, don't. This is already humiliating enough." She pulls off her shoe, an expensive-looking sand-colored espadrille, and shuffles like a gimp over to the air dryer. "I really am going to leave him, you know."

"Laney." I take a step toward her, but she holds out her hand.

"Just go," she says, and then hits the silver button and the noise of the air dryer fills the room like a jet engine.

Later in my car with Brooke, in a random parking lot, a simple kiss has grown legs and turned into something more, something sweaty and breathless that fogs up the windows of my Saab. Mouths open hungrily, lips crush against lips, tongues dance and slide over each other, faces are stroked, hands slide easily under shirts to feel the skin baking underneath, sounds are made, soft gasps and moans, the universal dialogue of escalation.

We end up in the darkness of my front hallway, pressed up against the wall kissing and grinding against each other, and the heat from our friction will melt the clothes to our bodies if we don't undress soon. It's just that I'm not sure where to go. I don't want to bring her downstairs to the guest room like Laney, but I'm scared of what it will mean to bring her up to my bedroom, breaking the hermetic seal on Hailey's last remaining sanctuary, bringing the bulldozers in to the last untouched rain forest, killing off entire species to make way for hotels and strip malls.

Hailey, I think. *Hailey, Hailey, Hailey.* Just the sound of her name, two syllables, beating in me like a telltale heart.

But Brooke is sweet and sexy and somehow complete, and we had that moment back in the restaurant, that perfect kiss, where I felt loosely spinning things in me click into place, felt the planet stop rotating for just the tiniest fraction of a second to pay tribute,

Hailey, Hailey, Hailey...

and now her wet lips are shining in the ambient light from the kitchen, and her eyes are smoky, their lids half closed and fluttering under the weight of her desire,

Hailey, Hailey, Hailey...

and her skin glows like it's lit from within, and we're young and beautiful and we won't always be, but today we are, soft and hard in all the right places, and we owe it to the world to have sex the way it's meant to be had, and she tastes like cinnamon and sex and fuck it, this is what we're meant to do, what we're built for, and every molecule in our bodies is demanding it, and there's nowhere to be but here, nothing to do but this.

So I lead her up the stairs and into my bedroom, and shirts come off and the smooth skin of her belly is soft and hot against my lips, and her flesh against mine is electric, and I'm not thinking about Hailey, am not thinking about the last time we lay in this bed, the night before she got on that plane, how she finished on top, covering me like a blanket, her knees up beside my ribs, face flushed, smiling down at me through the hazy mist of our evaporating sex. How we were wrapped around and through each other, naked and sweating and thinking that it was just another beautiful day in happily ever after. *I had a wife. Her name was Hailey.*

"What's wrong?" Brooke says, pulling back breathlessly to look at me.

"Nothing," I say, but something has changed, some unknowable but vital element in our chemistry, and she can taste it.

"What is it?"

"I don't know."

"Do you not want to do this?"

"I do."

"Maybe it's too soon."

"It isn't."

"Are you sure?"

"I'm sure."

"Because we don't have to."

"I know."

And now it's officially arrived, the moment when you have discussed whether or not you are going to have sex too much to now go and have it, and I can feel levels falling, dials spinning furiously in reverse, molecules deflating as the air around us loses its charge.

"I'm sorry," I say, rolling off her.

"You don't have to apologize," she says.

We lie on our backs, side by side, staring into the darkness, and there's nothing but the sound of our breath slowing down as heart rates and hopes fall. The room still smells of sex and sweat, but those smells no longer belong to us and so they bother me.

"Just tell me if it's me," she says.

"It has nothing to do with you," I say. "I don't know why I'm being like this."

She turns on her side to face me and puts a hand on my chest. "Please talk to me, Doug."

But I don't want to talk, don't want to navigate my way through one of those painful postmortems that inevitably must follow aborted sex. I want everything to be okay between us, and I know it might be tomorrow, but nothing we say will make it okay tonight, so, that being the case, there doesn't seem to be a point to cutting ourselves more deeply. And since I'm not going to talk, there's nothing left to do but sort out the tangled heap of our clothing at the foot of the bed and drive in silence back to her Brady Bunch house.

She hugs me at her front door. "You'll call me?"

"Of course."

"And just to reiterate, this had nothing to do with my telling you that I'd been raped."

"Nothing at all."

"So why won't you look at me?"

I look at her. She looks back at me, and we stay like that for a moment, until I have to look away from the raw emotion in her eyes. I lean forward to kiss her good night, and she kisses me back, but there's no heat anymore, just the tender acknowledgment of separation.

Later, as I pull back up my driveway, two dark eyes like polished stones suddenly materialize in the glow of my headlights, then the frantic zigzag of white cotton, and before I can brake there's a sickening crunch under my wheel, felt more than heard. I step out of the car to find the rabbit, stretched and broken on the crumbling blacktop of the driveway. The rabbit is still alive, lying on its side, its white belly still rising and falling with labored breath, one mangled front paw lightly scraping the driveway, still reflexively trying to run. Its coffee bean eyes are wide open, staring off into nothingness, whiskers vibrating. I stand beside the dying animal at a loss, feeling sick to my stomach and utterly helpless. I should kill it, put it out of its misery, but I don't have a gun, and I don't have it in me to bring out a baseball bat and bash its brains in. All I can do is keep it company in its final moments, crouching beside the rabbit in the chilly night and looking into its eyes, apologizing repeatedly in soothing tones. The rabbit doesn't look terribly traumatized, does not writhe in terror and pain, but simply lies there, accepting and composed, as if dying is just one in a list of things it has to get done today. And there's nothing for me to do but sit there watching as its breaths become shorter, more like gasps, and then its body starts to tremble, and then its eyes close, and then it dies.

I grab a heavy gardening shovel from the garage and bury the rabbit in a shallow, unmarked grave at the edge of the backyard. I'm carrying the shovel back to the garage when, without warning, a spasm of sourness rises up in me and I fall to my knees, vomiting prolifically into the hedges, until there's nothing left in me, until I'm inside out, and then I perform a few wrenching dry heaves that threaten to dislocate vital organs, and then I'm done, feeling light-headed and tasting acid. Inside I rinse my mouth out with whiskey and then head upstairs. The strewn comforter and rumpled linens on my bed are more than I can take right now, so I head into Russ's room, where Claire lies under the covers reading one of Hailey's pink novels. Her eyes are bloodshot, either because she was sleeping earlier or because she's been crying. "Hey," she says, surprised to see me. "How was your date with Brooke? I've got a good feeling about that one."

I nod slowly. Sadly. "Oh, shit," Claire says.

"Yeah," I say wearily, pulling back her blanket. She slides over to the wall to make room for me, and I pull off my shoes and slide in beside her.

"You're shivering," she says, and I think of the rabbit in its death throes and wonder if I've been cursed, if I'll never stop shivering. But then Claire throws an arm over me and pulls me into a hug, and she's warm and smells of Noxzema and tears, and after a few seconds the shivering stops. Claire can be overbearing and intrusive and relentlessly superior, but when I've come apart, she's the only person who knows how to put me back together again.

"I screwed up," I say.

"Of course you did," she says, not unkindly. "But look at it this way: you actually had something to screw up. Baby steps, Doug. Baby steps."

"You look like you've been crying."

She shrugs. "Hormones."

"Yeah," I say. "Whatever."

We take turns crying in the dark and talking each other down, we talk until we're no longer making any sense, until our tongues are rubber and our mouths have run dry and we've emptied ourselves of words. Then we lie silent and still in opposing fetal positions, yin and yang, regrouping in our makeshift womb. I can feel heavy oblivion seeping into me like warm molasses, and the last thing I see before Claire's light breathing lulls me into a black, dreamless sleep are the first pink stains of dawn, fanning out across the night sky like groping fingers.

33

——————

"WHAT THE FUCK?" RUSS SAYS. I'M STILL MOSTLY sleeping, so he clears his throat and says it again. "What the fuck?"

It feels like all anyone ever does these days is wake me up. If only they would let me sleep, maybe I'd wake up refreshed, with a newer, healthier perspective, ready to take on my life and solve its myriad problems. Maybe the whole problem is not that I'm sad, or screwed up, or self-destructive, but just mired in a state of perennial exhaustion.

"Go away," Claire mutters, her voice barbed and frayed with sleep.

"I am trying to come up with an explanation for why the two of you would be sleeping here in my room like this, in the same bed," Russ says, still standing in the doorway. "I am trying, and I am failing."

"What time is it?" I say.

"It's just after eight a.m."

"Good. Come back tomorrow."

"Tomorrow will definitely be too late."

I roll over and open my eyes, trying to achieve some measure of focus. "What is it?"

"I hope you don't mind, but I'm going to be moving in ahead of schedule. Unless there's something twisted and wrong going on in here, in which case I'm going to have to leave town and join a cult and sell flowers at the bus station or something."

I lift up the covers to show him that I'm still in my clothing from last night. "Praise Jesus," Russ says.

"When are you moving in?" I say, rolling off the bed and onto the floor in a heap.

Russ looks at his watch. "Now's good."

"Too loud," Claire moans, rolling into the wall and banging her head.

"What happened?"

"Bit of a misunderstanding with the paterfamilias," Russ says, coming into the room to lean on the edge of his desk. I haven't gotten around to replacing his chair yet, which is still lying in pieces on the front lawn.

"How bad?"

"Scale of one to ten?"

"Sure."

He nods. "Fifty?"

"That sounds pretty bad."

"You have no idea."

"Well, I think you'd better tell me."

"I will. After."

"After what?"

Outside there's the sound of car doors slamming and then the doorbell being rung repeatedly. Claire groans and pulls a pillow over her head. Russ drops down in front of the window and peeks over the sill like a sniper. "After you get rid of Jimbo."

I walk over to the window. I can't see Jim but I can hear him under the eave below, pounding on the door. "Russ, you get your ass out here! I'm going to fucking kill you!"

At the curb, leaning against her car, Angie watches her husband with a bemused expression on her face. As usual, she's dressed like a teenager, in tight, low-riding sweats and a cut-off tank top, exposing her remarkable cleavage, toned abs, and sculpted arms, all tanned to her customary honey glaze. When she sees me in the window, she offers a sexy little smile and wiggles her French-manicured fingers at me, exactly as if her husband isn't trying to break down the door directly below.

"Russ!" Jim screams, and now I can see the neighbors in driveways and in windows, watching as yet another drama unfolds on their formerly quiet block. "Get out here!"

"Will somebody please just shoot that motherfucker?" Claire whines, her voice muffled under the covers.

"Jim!" I yell down from the window.

He steps off the porch to look up at me. He's unshaven, in jeans, slippers, and a dirty T-shirt, and it's clear that whatever happened this morning has superseded his usual ablutions.

"I know he's up there, Doug!"

From his spot below the window, Russ shakes his head and waves his arms at me frantically. "He's here," I say, and Russ throws his hands over his face in despair. "What's going on?"

"Just let me have him!" Jim shouts at me.

"I'm going to come down to talk to you," I say.

"It's none of your business."

"Suit yourself." I step away from the window.

"Doug!" Jim screams.

"What the hell did you do?" I say to Russ.

"I stole some discs from his porn collection."

I look at him. "He's mad because you stole some porn?"

"Well..."

"Russ."

"It was homemade."

Claire's head pops up from under the covers. "What was on it?"

"Pretty much what you'd expect."

"Do you have them here?"

"Claire!"

"I'm just asking."

"Please don't help me," I say. "So this disc—"

"Discs."

"Discs. They're of Jim and Angie?"

"Yep."

"You get off on watching your father have sex?" Claire says.

"Hell, no. Most of it is just Angie."

"Angie alone?" Claire says.

"She has toys."

"Where are the discs now?"

"The originals are back in his dresser."

Downstairs, Jim begins pounding on the door again. Between Russ and Claire, we are going to have to get a new door. Something stronger, steel reinforced.

"You made copies?"

"So he wouldn't miss them."

"Smart," Claire says approvingly.

"Shut up, Claire. How many copies?"

"Enough."

"Russ. I'm trying to help you out here."

Russ sighs and runs his hands through his hair. "I have this Web site."

"Oh . . . fuck."

He shrugs. "My friends are all obsessed with Angie. They begged me. And Jimbo never would have even known about it if he hadn't been snooping around in my hard drive. Serves him right for violating my privacy."

"You put naked videos of your father's wife on the internet and he invaded your privacy?"

"Two wrongs don't make a right."

I shake my head. "Okay, come with me."

"It's not safe for me out there."

"I know. I need you to lock the door behind me."

Outside, Jim is trying to climb up the drainpipe to Russ's room, which would be almost comical if it didn't look like he might actually make it. "Jim," I call up to him. "Get down from there."

"I'm going to kill that little shit," he gasps, sweating profusely as he pulls himself up a bit higher, his feet scraping furiously against the brick wall before finding awkward toeholds on protruding mortar and pipe brackets. The muscles in his arms flex and extend under his taut skin, threatening to burst through. I turn to Angie for some help, but her plan seems to consist solely of leaning languidly against the car and looking good. It occurs to me that the notion of horny teenaged boys pleasuring themselves to naked videos of her is not something she's terribly upset about.

"The neighbors have probably already called the police," I say to Jim's ass, which is now at eye level. "You really don't want to be breaking and entering when they get here."

"It's my house," he grunts, pulling himself up a little higher. Pretty soon he'll be in position to hoist himself up onto the lower roof over the front door, and from there it's an easy swing through Russ's open window.

"Angie," I say. "Will you help me out here?"

"Come down, Jim, you're making an ass out of yourself," she calls to him without conviction, then looks at me and shrugs. She has always adopted the attitude of an innocent bystander to the wreck of Jim's first family. Jim keeps shimmying his way up the pipe, sweating through his shirt, grunting as he goes, his ass crack smiling down at us from the back of his sagging jeans. He's about six feet off the ground now, and within striking distance of the roof.

"Get your ass down here, Jim," I shout. "I mean it."

He looks down scornfully at me. "Or what, Doug?"

"Or I'll bring you down."

Jim's face breaks into a contemptuous sneer. "I would pay good money to see that," he says. And I don't know where this bizarre situation was headed before he flashed me that you-and-what-army look, but the sneer pisses me off. The sneer leaves me no choice.

I climb up onto the porch railing, take a deep breath, and

then, before I can chicken out, I jump at him. My plan is to throw my arms over his shoulders, but I don't get as much hang time as I'd anticipated, and I end up with a fistful of his sweat-soaked T-shirt, which tears loudly as I slide down his back, and at the last instant I manage to wrap my other arm around his waist and grab on. His legs instantly lose their purchase and swing off the wall, his slippers coming loose and falling to the ground, and only his grip on the drainpipe keeps us from tumbling backward off of it. "Fucker!" he screams, trying to shake me off, and I can feel the pipe shaking, the brackets straining to support our weight. "Get the fuck off me!"

"You get the fuck off of my house!" I grunt at him. Then the molded elbow of drainpipe he's holding snaps like a wishbone and we both fly backward off the wall in a clean arc. Jim lands hard on top of me, sandwiching me between him and the ground like luncheon meat, and I can actually feel my lungs implode as every last bit of air is wrung from them. Before I can even roll over, Jim pulls me to my feet and throws me back down again. "You son of a bitch!" he bellows, and all I can see are his bare feet on the grass, heading toward me, and then I'm flying through the air again, and then back on the ground with my face in the grass, tasting dirt, and if only the yard would stop spinning like an amusement park ride, if only my mouth would remember how to suck the air down to my lungs, I could defend myself. I did, after all, study karate as a teenager with Sensei Goldberg at the Y. Upper block, reverse punch, side kick to the knee, knife hand strike to the neck. I can bring the pain. But the world keeps spinning and all I see are detached, fragmentary images at skewed angles that won't stand still, the house, the sky, Angie running forward with a panicked look on her face, Jim bleeding from his nose (did I do that?), advancing on me again. And somewhere above me I can hear Claire's screaming voice, *Get the hell off of him, you bastard!* And I stagger to my feet just in time for Jim to grab me by my neck and throw me up against the wall of the house, and I hadn't realized that we were so close to the house, maybe we weren't, maybe he carried me there by my neck, and over his shoulder I can see Angie's face, can see her mouth moving, and this shouldn't be happening to me, because I'm the good guy, I'm the widower, I'm not supposed to get the shit kicked out of me in my own front yard in full view of the neighbors, and my legs momentarily go out from under me, and I teeter to the side, which causes Jim's first punch to miss me, his massive fist whistling hotly against the skin of my nose without meaningful impact. And I can see the windup of the next shot like it's happening in slow motion, can see the punch being born, can plot the arc of its trajectory, and this is the hand on which he wears his obnoxiously large college ring, big enough to kneel and kiss, like he's the pope of Rockland Community College, and yet my hands are not coming up to block, my head is not ducking, and I understand the punch is coming, solid and pure of purpose, that it will be a mother of a punch, with Jim's full weight behind it, a face-altering, bone-crushing punch, and still my hands hang limply by my side. And then, from the periphery, a dark shape, air-borne, and then I'm on the ground again, and so is Jim, and so is Russ, who has jumped from the porch to tackle us, and now his fists are flying furiously, pummeling Jim, who rolls on the ground, arms wrapped around his head, and they are King Kong and

Godzilla and I'm the blond chick stuck in the middle, and when I try to pull Russ off, his swinging fist hits me square on the side of my face, an inch under my eye, and dark spots appear across my field of vision and I sit down hard. Russ jumps off of Jim, and runs over to me, cursing and apologizing, and Angie jumps onto Jim, and everyone's been hit, everyone's down, and somehow the fight is over as quickly as it began, like a broken spell, and I'm just trying to breathe, and I can feel the welt like a hot slug forming under my skin where Russ's fist connected, can taste the warm blood in my mouth, and Russ is crying, and Angie is crying, and Jim is shaking, and there are sirens in the distance, and I'm just trying to breathe, and the yard is slowing down, and if I could just breathe I could start to sort this out, if I could just get my mouth to open and my lungs to inflate, if I could just get some oxygen into my blood, I could begin to sort this out, and the sirens grow louder, and Claire is in the yard now, Claire is down on her knees in my face, Claire is saying something, but I can't hear her over the sound of blood rushing in my ears like a waterfall, and then I'm lying on my side again, seeing past Claire's knees, past Russ's legs, past the tangled forms of Jim and Angie, over to the other side of the yard, and there's a brown rabbit there, sitting in the shadow of the arborvitaes that line the property, and he's looking right at me, this rabbit, staring at me, thinking shit about me, silently judging me, and I'm just trying to breathe. I'm just trying to breathe.

Angie and Claire handle the cops. Their combined beauty is blinding and the young crew-cut cops don't know who to impress first. Apologies and explanations are made, flirtatious giggles are issued, smiles and nods are exchanged, breasts are stared at. The complex relationships that comprise our unblended family are laid out for the confused officers like blueprints. The father, the stepmother, the stepfather, the visiting sister, it takes a few go-rounds before it all makes sense. But ultimately, no charges will be pressed, no reports made. Hands touch shoulders, eyes are batted, wrists squeezed in gratitude. A family scuffle that got out of hand but now is most assuredly back in hand. The cops look over at Jim, Russ, and me, still sitting in the spots we landed in at the end of the melee, and we all nod, doing our best to look docile and penitent, but we are not beautiful so the cops don't talk to us. There was talk of an ambulance when I passed out, but I came to almost immediately, and Claire insisted there was no need. And then, casting last, longing glances at the united front of Claire and Angie, the cops reluctantly climb back into their patrol car and drive off. Then Angie packs Jim into the passenger seat of his BMW, and as soon as the door closes, he covers his face and starts to sob violently. Russ and I look away, the way men do instinctively when other men cry.

Then it's just the three of us, sitting on the porch, buzzed on the surplus endorphins and adrenaline still coursing through our veins, talking the way people do in the aftermath of a dramatic occurrence, weaving our three separate vantage points into a single, cohesive narrative that will become the official version, the source material for all future discussions of the event.

Claire goes inside and brings out ice in two ziplocked plastic bags for my face and Russ's fist.

"That's some shiner you've got there," Russ says to me.

"Try not to sound so proud of yourself."

"It was an accident. You walked into my swing."

"You were supposed to stay inside."

"I couldn't leave you out there to get your ass kicked. That's not how I roll, man."

"I was handling it."

"You're welcome. Jesus!"

"Okay. Thank you for pissing off Jim and then bringing your mess to my doorstep. And thank you for punching me in the face, and for giving me a shiner two days before my sister's wedding."

"And for saving your ass. We'd still be picking your teeth out of the grass."

I sigh through my bag of ice. "And for saving my ass."

"You're welcome."

And all around us, the quotidian sound track of suburban morning as the neighborhood comes to life, the rhythmic whisper of sprinklers, the whine of leaf blowers and mowers, the buzz of garage doors, the hydraulic hiss of braking school buses. And the people, these freshly shaved and shampooed people leaving their houses to start their days, these people who are moderately successful, who are upwardly mobile, who have things to do, places to go, and people to see. We watch these people going about the business of being alive like a choreographed dance number from our orchestra seats, we three entrenched on our asses, wondering where the hell they get the energy.

34

RUSS AND I SHOP FOR GROCERIES AT THE SUPER STOP
and Shop. We buy bottles of soda, bags of chips, boxes of pasta,
jars of tomato sauce, large quantities of white bread, sandwich
spreads, and frozen food. Everything we buy has the maximum
amount of chemicals and requires the minimum amount of
preparation to eat. We do not compare brands, do not look for
circulars and coupons, because we are slated to be millionaires
and price is no object. We do not consider nutritional factors,
because we are young and slim and sad and beautiful, we shine
in our grief, and we will eat what we want, when we want, with
utter impunity. We tear through the market like young royalty,
like elite fighter pilots, grabbing anything that catches our
fancy, intoxicated by the infinite possibilities of this new, alter-
native family we've become. We have been hammered by bad
fortune, cut off at the knees, and yet, here we are, rising above it
all, floating brilliantly among these suburban housewives who
can't help but flash us admiring glances as they fill their carts
with fresh vegetables and raw chickens. We are a sitcom family,
a Disney movie, a bold new social experiment. We buy sack-loads

of frozen chicken nuggets and french fries. We will need a second freezer.

The left side of my face has a wine-colored, kidney-shaped welt that throbs continuously, and I feel compelled to trace this new topography in my flesh every few minutes, like a tongue worrying a loose tooth. There's something undeniably satisfying about being marked by violence, some manly validation, even if it was an errant blow from the very boy I was supposedly defending. I've been blooded in a violent rite of passage and have earned a new standing in the tribe. It's been one day since our epic battle with Jim, and all parties, speaking through me, have agreed that it would be best if Russ moved in with me, effective immediately. I am now in charge of this sad, confused, angry boy, this long-haired, tattooed bundle of rage and grief. Me, a stepfather. It's a sick joke, an abomination, an accident waiting to happen. It's perfect. As we shop, we banter, a particular brand of softly ironic wit laced with affection that is entirely our own. We will perfect this repartee over time, until it becomes our trademark, like Hepburn and Tracy, and even though I've never actually seen Hepburn and Tracy, I'm sure we're infinitely funnier. I pull food items off the shelves and toss them like footballs to Russ, and our record is perfect until he misses the cellophane-wrapped watermelon half, which hits the floor with a juicy thud and the corner crumples.

"Fuck," Russ says.

"I can't believe you missed that."

"Dude. That was nowhere near me."

"I thought you were cutting left."

"I was faking left."

"Good job."

"Let's just take a different one."

"We can't put this back. Didn't you ever hear the expression, you break it you bought it?"

"Didn't you know that the customer is always right?"

"What would Jesus do?"

"Jesus wouldn't have thrown it like a little girl."

"Just put it in the cart."

And therein lies the tricky part. We can talk like buddies and live like roommates, be the brothers we never had, but at some point, my role as guardian has to kick in. If ever there was a kid in need of a decent male role model, it's Russ, and, qualified or not, I've landed the job. Granted, it was a battlefield promotion, but my shabby credentials notwithstanding, I'm hoping I'll surprise myself by divining a heretofore untapped well of maturity that's been accumulating somewhere inside of me like unspent interest, that will enable me to dispense a variety of wisdom and discipline that will in no way impede my overall coolness. And while I haven't yet figured out exactly how I'll navigate the more challenging terrain of issues like sex or drugs or truancy or internet porn, by God, I can do the right thing by this dented watermelon, and I allow myself a few seconds of warm and fuzzy for starting things off on the right foot, for passing our first ethical challenge with flying colors.

As Russ drives us home, we have our first official stepfather-stepson talk.

"Can I get a car?" he says.

"You don't have a license."

"I will soon."

"Let's deal with it then."

"It's not like money's going to be an issue," he says, looking away uncomfortably.

"Actually, I suspect money is going to be a huge issue."

We have never discussed the airline settlement, the unfathomable amount of money headed our way.

"Why's that?"

"Because you're a sad, angry kid who lost his mother and hates his father, and now you're going to be rich, and if there was ever a recipe for screwing up a kid, this is it. And it's my job to make sure you don't become one of those assholes who jet-set around with other rich assholes, dating skanky celebrities, investing in nightclubs, doing your first stint in rehab before you're twenty-five."

"It's heartwarming how much faith you have in me."

"You're a kid, Russ. It's a lot to deal with. You know, it wouldn't be a bad idea for you to start seeing a therapist. There are probably some who specialize in exactly this sort of thing."

"It's just a car, Doug. Jesus."

"Watch the road."

"I am."

We ride in silence for a few minutes, and gradually the panicked feeling in me starts to fade. "Then again," I say, "it's entirely possible that I'm overreacting. Let me think about it a little, okay?"

"Cool."

You swear you'll never become your parents. You listen to edgy music, you dress young and hip, you have sex standing up and on kitchen tables, you say "fuck" and "shit" a lot, and then one day, without warning, their words emerge from your mouth like long-dormant sleeper agents suddenly activated. You're still young enough to hear these words through the ears of the teenager sitting beside you, and you realize how pitiful and ultimately futile your efforts will be, a few measly sandbags against the tidal wave of genetic destiny.

Back at the house, Claire supervises the unloading of packages, the reorganization of fridge and pantry. Then Russ heads upstairs to finish moving back into his old room. Angie called this morning when the coast was clear, and Russ and I moved his stuff out while Jim was at work. My cell phone flashes with multiple messages from Brooke, from Laney, and from the irrepressible Kyle Evans, but I return no calls. I am becoming a stepfather now, and it requires all of my concentration.

"Let him get the car," Claire says. "You can't get laid in high school without a car."

"Do I want him to get laid?"

She points a rebuking finger at my chest. "Cock blocker."

"I'm trying to be responsible."

"You're still cock-blocking. Honestly, just because you didn't have any sex in high school..."

"I had sex in high school."

"My point exactly," Claire says. "Let him have a car, end of story. You can load the glove compartment with condoms and drunk-driving pamphlets if it will make you feel any better."

"Thanks. You've been a big help."

"It's what I do."

* * *

Russ, Claire, and I eat dinner together at the dining room table. It's the first time I've eaten there since Hailey died, the first time I've used place mats and real dishes, the first time I didn't just take something out of tinfoil, nuke it, and eat it on the couch in front of the television, washing it down with too much wine or bourbon. We talk between chews, teasing each other and cracking wise, acutely aware that this is more than just a meal, that it's an inauguration of sorts, the start of something new, and while not that much has changed, there is the unspoken sense that where there was once something and then nothing, there is now something again, something smaller and sadder than before, but warm and real and brimming with potential. If we don't fuck it up.

Please don't let us fuck it up.

35

IN THE SMALL WAITING AREA OUTSIDE BROOKE'S office at the high school, there is a girl sitting across from me, beautiful despite her painstaking efforts to not be. She wears black lipstick and dark, angry eyeliner, there is a metal hoop through her nostril and a ball stud nestled like a pearl in a shell in the cleavage of her plump bottom lip. But her eyes are wide and green, her cheekbones high, her complexion flawless. She is fooling no one, her beauty shines through like a fog light, and I wonder what compels her to try so hard. Two seats over is a boy with long, messy hair, a weak goatee, tattered jeans, and glazed stoner eyes. He slouches back in the chair, hands crossed across his chest, staring into the fluorescent lights, carefully, ostentatiously laid-back, cosmically unfazed. They take great pains not to acknowledge each other, these two kids, even though they are both troubled, both freaks, both resolutely hugging the outer walls of this hallway society. Their different slots on the food chain leave them no common ground in which to meet. And that's the genius of the system, really, pigeonholing the kids on the margins so that they can't even connect with each other, which would grow their numbers and threaten the ruling class.

We sit there, these two angry kids and me, three freaks, and it's amazing how powerful their silence is, how easily I am sucked into their rules. Every so often, their nervously roaming eyes cross paths with my own, quickly darting away before any intelligence can be exchanged, and I think it's a wonder anyone ever speaks to anyone else in high school.

"Doug," Brooke says from her office doorway. "What are you doing here?"

She has on gray slacks and a black silk blouse and she looks crisp and professional and not as thrilled to see me as I'd hoped. "I just needed to see you for a moment."

"Oh my God, what happened to your face?"

I rub my raised shiner possessively. "That's part of it."

"I'll be with you guys in a minute," she says to the two waiting kids, who are too busy trying not to exist to care very much one way or another.

"I'm sorry about the other night," I say, once we're seated in her office.

"There's no need to apologize for that," Brooke says.

"I feel bad."

"What you should feel bad about is not calling me these last few days."

"I do."

"And not returning my calls."

"I'm sorry about that too."

"And making me feel like an idiot."

"I didn't mean to. I'm sorry."

"What happened to your face?"

"I got into a fight with Jim."

"And he hit you?"

"Actually, Russ hit me."

"Russ hit you."

"But he meant to hit Jim."

"Are you speaking allegorically?"

"I stepped in the way of his punch."

"Ah."

"Long story short, Russ is now living with me."

Brooke smiles. "Well, that's good news at least. How do you feel about it?"

"Strangely okay," I say. "A little scared. Terrified, actually. But in a good way."

"You'll be fine."

"Thanks."

We look at each other for a moment. "So, is that what you came to tell me?"

"No. I came to see how you feel about weddings."

"You're a nice guy, Doug, but I don't think I'm ready for that kind of commitment."

"My sister's getting married this weekend."

"And you need a date."

"I don't need a date. I have Russ and Claire to keep me company. I just thought it would be nice if you came."

She sighs, a deep, melancholic, conflicted sigh. "Here's the thing, Doug. I like you. But I need to know if you're at that stage where every time we start to get close you'll panic and pull away, because if you are, that's fine, I'll understand. I just don't want to be a part of the process."

"I think I'm done with that," I say.

"Just like that?" she says skeptically.

"Just like that."

"Doug."

"I mean it."

"It's just way too early for this to be so complicated."

"I know."

She studies me for a long moment, chewing thoughtfully on her lower lip. And suddenly it seems vitally important that she say yes. There are alternate fates stretching out before us like a fork in the yellow brick road, and everything that will happen from here on out is predicated on what happens in the next five seconds. And I know I said that fate is a crock, but I've been wrong before, and if I believed in God I would offer up a quick little prayer, and say, *God, you have fucked with me enough, and I'm giving you this chance right here to begin making amends,* but I don't so I can't, and all there is to do is sit nervously and wait for the moment to end. And the moment is taking its sweet time, is expanding like a big red balloon, and all I can do is sit here and try to look appealing while I wait for it to burst.

"Doug."

"Brooke."

She lets out another loud, slow sigh and shakes her head. "I have nothing to wear."

36

DEBBIE'S WEDDING WILL BE A FULL-WEEKEND AFFAIR, taking place at the Norwalk Inn and Country Club in Connecticut. Friday night there will be a rehearsal dinner for close friends and family, and Saturday evening there will be a waterfront ceremony at sunset, followed by a lavish reception for five hundred in the main ballroom. It's the wedding my mother has been planning her entire life. Claire got married on the sprawling grounds of Stephen's parents' massive Chappaqua estate—referred to out of earshot by our family as the Golden Horseshit Estate—and Hailey and I decided on a small, informal gathering of friends and family at Tattinger's, our favorite Manhattan restaurant. My mother suffered these indignities with the perfectly nuanced silence of someone silently suffering an indignity. But for Debbie, her baby, there have been no such complications, and she has pulled out all the stops.

Friday afternoon, I'm in my bedroom getting dressed for the rehearsal dinner when I feel something in the jacket pocket of my suit and pull out a lipstick cylinder and crumpled receipt. The receipt is from the Hudson Tavern, the restaurant where Hailey and I ate on the last night we ever spent together. And it's these little things that set you back, that shouldn't but do, these last, lingering bits of her life lying dormant, waiting to be excavated like artifacts: the smell of her on a shirt, a scribbled shopping list seven pages into the memo pad by the phone, her lipstick tube and a receipt in my suit pocket, the residue of a vanished life. Against my better judgment, I peel open the receipt and there it is in smudged blue ink, the soups we had, her steak salad and my boneless rib eye, the bottle of Chianti, the Granny Smith apple cobbler we shared for dessert. And now that night comes flooding back to me in razor slashes of lucidity, Hailey's tight red dress, her hair pinned back behind her slender neck, the way she threw her head back to laugh, and more than anything, the sense memory of what it felt like to be whole and to be hers, what it used to feel like to be me. And that familiar, quivering ache returns to my belly, the heavy emptiness in my chest, but I will not cry. I close my eyes and I'm there again, sitting across from her, drinking her in like wine as the scabs in me come undone and the wounds reopen, and the searing pain of losing her is brand-new again, a red-hot poker stirring my guts. But I don't cry. *I had a wife, her name was Hailey. Now she's gone. And so am I.*

There's a red bra hanging on the bathroom doorknob, where Hailey left it a lifetime ago. I pull it off and throw it into a dresser drawer. Then I take everything off the top of her night table; books, catalogs, a perfume bottle, a ponytail holder, and drop them into the top drawer, along with the lipstick I found in my jacket. The strength goes out of my legs and I sit down on the corner of the bed—Hailey's side—and I can feel the tears forming, but I blink them away. Because even now I can hear the muted slide and bang of Russ's dresser drawers as he gets ready in his room, and Claire's high-heeled footsteps tap-dancing across the tiled kitchen floor, and they're like sounds from beyond the borders of your dream, luring you back to the waking life. So I allow myself just a few more quaking breaths, a few last moments of feeling lost without her, and then I pull myself up off the bed and head downstairs to get Claire to help me with my necktie.

The rehearsal dinner is taking place in one of the club's smaller banquet rooms, where the caterer has set up an elaborate buffet. There's a three-piece band up on the bandstand playing soft dinner music, the lights have been dimmed and large standing candelabra have been set up around the perimeter, bathing the room in a warm, gothic glow. In typical fashion, my mother has transformed an intimate dinner into a major event, and by the time we arrive, the room is already teeming with friends of my parents and relatives I'd prefer not to see. Claire points out the two manned bars set up on either side of the buffet, like a flight attendant indicating the emergency exits, and as she and Russ go to find our seats in the cluster of banquet tables set up in the center of the room, I make my way around the edges of the crowd, as inconspicuously as possible, until I'm standing at the bar. Two quick shots for courage, and when that doesn't work, another two for distance. Then I get a strong Jack and Coke to nurse, and wade reluctantly into the sea of guests.

This is the part I've been dreading, the unguarded scrutiny of people who have known me forever, the pointed looks, the wet-eyed hugs, the emotional arm squeezes, the suffocating pity of those who think they know, filling the air I breathe like anthrax. I am a celebrity of sorts, rendered larger than life by the dark things to which I've borne witness, and the trick is to keep moving, like a movie star leaving a nightclub, smiling for the cameras without breaking stride. I assume the look of someone on an urgent errand, moving quickly through the crowd, nodding hello without stopping to talk to anyone. All around me, relatives materialize like evil spirits: Uncle Freddy, my father's much younger brother, who we thought was so cool when we were kids because he wore motorcycle boots and did his hair like Jon Bon Jovi. Now he's bald and beer gutted, has three kids with two ex-wives, and bags under his eyes with the craggy texture of alligator skin. My cousin Nicole, the reformed lesbian, who came out after college and then came back in to marry Peter, her high school sweetheart. My cousin Nate, a few years older than me, who told me what a rim job was when I was eight, and gave me my first-ever puff of a cigarette at his brother Barry's bar mitzvah. Barry, who paid Claire twenty dollars to show him her boobs when we were fourteen. Aunt Abby, my mother's sister, who beat breast cancer and self-published a virtually unreadable memoir about it which she still gives as gifts on every possible occasion. Their gazes cut through the crowd like infrared security beams in a museum, and I am the wily art thief, spinning and dodging my way across the room without setting off any alarms. But of course, a handful of them do manage to stop me, hugging me and shaking their heads, aggressively sincere, telling me how wonderful I look, like I'm the fat guy who lost fifty pounds and suddenly has a neck again. They come at me from all sides, and I'm on the verge of panic, craning my neck to find safe passage, when I see my father pushing his way through the crowd toward me.

"Doug!" he says, coming over to hug me. He looks natty as ever in his midnight blue designer suit and lavender tie. "What are you doing here?"

"Hey, Dad," I say as he pulls me close, and I'm a little kid breathing in the familiar scents of his dandruff shampoo and aftershave. I just want to bury my head in the crook of his neck and wrap my legs around his torso as he picks me up and carries me upstairs to my bedroom to put me to bed.

"Come on," he says, leading me through the crowd. "Let's get you something to eat."

Debbie is positioned near the buffet speaking animatedly with some of her bridesmaids. She's dressed to the nines in a slinky black gown, her dark hair up in an intricate French braid. "Hey, Pooh," I say, leaning in to kiss her. "You look great."

"Look at your face!" she says.

"You look at it."

"What happened? Forget it, I don't want to know," she says, pressing an exploratory thumb against my shiner.

"Ouch! Jesus, Debbie!"

"It's going to be in all the pictures."

"They can Photoshop it out."

"Can they really do that? Because it looks terrible."

"That's funny, because everyone was just telling me how wonderful I look."

She shrugs and raises a cynical eyebrow at me. "Everyone is drunk."

Speaking of which, my own drink has mysteriously evaporated in the five minutes since it was poured, so I wander back toward the bar, where I bump into Russ walking off with a drink in hand. "Hey," I say. "Are we having fun yet?"

"Oodles."

"What do you have there?"

"Some tonic water."

"Uh huh."

"With just the tiniest splash of gin."

It occurs to me that I should not be allowing him to drink, and that this is something we should discuss.

"Russ. Can we be serious for a moment?"

"Doug, if we can't be serious for a moment, then the terrorists have already won."

"We don't have a lot of rules," I say.

"That's true."

"I can't control what happens when you're out with your friends. I just have to trust you to make the right decisions. But I don't want you drinking or doing drugs on my watch."

He regards me thoughtfully for a moment and then smiles and raises his glass. "Agreed. But surely one celebratory drink under your watchful eye…"

"Just go easy."

"Yes, sir."

"So," I say, throwing my arm around him. "Any women here catch your fancy?"

He looks over to where Debbie is laughing with her girl-friends and sighs. "Just one."

"I don't want to sound too negative here..." I say.

"I know," he says miserably. "Love sucks."

"Amen to that." We bang our glasses together.

The groomsmen congregate at the bar where Mike's brother Max is rowdily moderating a wide-ranging discussion on the S&P Five Hundred, sports teams, and which actresses they would currently be fucking if they weren't too busy being fat, bald, and married. I have nothing to contribute, but it's as good a place as any to hide for a few minutes.

"Doug," Max says, throwing his arm around me. "I think I'm in love. Three o'clock."

"What?"

"Over there," he says, pointing. "The girl in the black dress."

"She's very pretty."

"Are you kidding me? Look at the ass on her." He licks his lips. "I have got to get me some of that."

"Her name is Claire."

"You know her?"

"I do."

"Well, what's her deal, anyway?"

"She just left her husband," I say. "She's dying to get laid."

"You're shitting me."

"I'm telling you. It's a sure thing."

"Okay," he says, releasing me. "Wish me luck."

"Break a leg."

I watch him approach her, watch her eyes narrow as he makes his pitch, and then watch her take a deep breath and start to speak, and as much of an asshole as Max is, I actually feel a little sorry for him. He's back two minutes later, red faced and dejected. "You are such an asshole," he says.

"You lasted longer than most."

"That girl has got some major issues."

"Come on," I say, patting his back. "I'll buy you a drink."

"Doug," Mike says, coming up behind us. "You see Potter?"

"No."

"Neither have I and he's supposed to give the toast. I hope everything's okay."

Dave and Laney. Shit. I forgot they're going to be here. As if I didn't have enough to deal with, I'll have to pretend not to notice Laney staring balefully at me all weekend. "I'm sure they're fine."

"Well, I don't know what could be keeping him, but would you mind stepping in for him tonight if he's a no-show?"

There is irony, and then there's my life.

Once everyone has found their seats, and I'm safely sandwiched between Russ and Claire, my buzz having settled down to a nice, insulating hum, I am finally able to relax. My mother, looking radiant in her salmon-colored gown, sips at her wine and surveys the room with a satisfied smile. She leans against my father, who kisses her scalp every few minutes and taps his fingers along with the band, happily greeting all the well-wishers who stop by to greet him. "Stan!" they say. "Great to see you!" And he says, "Great to be seen, Phil, great to be seen."

They are positively beaming, my parents, vibrating together in their happiness, and I love them like never before. The rest of us talk about nothing in particular, cracking jokes and gossiping about our assembled relatives, and it's all moving along swimmingly until Mike starts tapping his water glass with a knife, and a hush falls over the room as he stands up to speak.

"Debbie and I are so happy that you could all be here to celebrate with us. All I can say is that I never believed someone this beautiful would ever be willing to marry someone like me."

"You and me both, buddy!" Max shouts out, and everybody laughs.

"Anyway, I just wanted to ask my good friend Doug, who, coincidentally happens to be the brother of the bride, to offer a toast."

I look up, horrified, as the room breaks into applause. I seem to recall Mike asking me to fill in for Dave, but I figured he'd give me some warning before I had to go on, and that's when I'd planned to worm my way out of it. So when the clapping dies down, I'm still slouched in my seat, wondering what the hell to do.

"Doug?" Debbie whispers across the table nervously.

"You're up, dude," Russ says.

I stand up slowly, turning to face the fifty or so expectant gazes, and it occurs to me that I'm somewhat drunker than I intended to be. They all seem far away, which is good, but so do I, which could be a problem. "You need a drink," Claire says.

"You have no idea," I say, and the room erupts into spontaneous laughter.

"I meant for the toast." She hands me somebody's wineglass.

Faces swim and merge kaleidoscopically in front of me, and a cold sweat breaks out on the back of my neck. "As many of you know, I'm not very good at this," I say. "In fact, I think the last time I did this was at Claire's wedding, and if you were there, you know how well that turned out." Strained laughter flutters around the room like a trapped bird looking for a window, and Claire shoots me a wide-eyed look of alarm. "I meant the toast, not the marriage. Oh . . . shit." Claire shakes her head and buries her face in her hands. "That toast didn't go over so well, is all I meant. And neither, apparently, will this one, so I think I'd better quit while I'm ahead."

"You're doing great, man!" Max shouts, laughing his ass off.

"Hey," Russ hisses up at me. "You're stinking up the room."

"Feel free to take over at any time," I snap back at him.

And to my utter amazement, Russ pushes his chair back and gets to his feet.

"What are you doing?" I say through clenched teeth.

"Just go with it," he says and then, clapping demonstratively, "Thank you, Doug," and there's nothing to do but collapse back into my chair.

"Excellent," Claire whispers to me, still shaking her head incredulously.

"I'm sorry," I say. "I'm just . . . sorry."

She nods up at Russ. "Our boy is wasted, by the way."

"He only had one drink."

"The waiters have been refilling his wineglass all night."

"Oh," I say. "Shit."

"Ladies and gentlemen, for those of you who don't know me, my name is Russ Klein. And I know you're all wondering what I could possibly have to say on this momentous occasion." Russ turns to face Debbie, who smiles nervously. "You see, I've only known Debbie for a few years, but from the first day I met her..." He stops to take a deep breath. "From the first day I met her I've been madly in love with her." Debbie's jaw falls open, and there's a small, collective gasp from the crowd. "I know I'm just a kid," Russ continues, "but I always imagined what I would say to you if I ever got the chance, and what I would say is that you are hands down the most beautiful girl I've ever known. You're kind and smart and funny and sexy, and so pretty, really, so perfectly pretty, and I would have happily given up the next ten years of my life to be old enough to be your boyfriend. And even though you're way out of my league, I know you're going to be the standard that I will measure every girl I ever meet against, and I already know they will all fall way short. But at least you've given me something to strive for, right? Anyway, now you're getting married and so I'll have to get over you, and I just figured I'd have an easier time doing that if I said these things out loud. So, Mike, I just want to say no disrespect intended, you're a solid guy and I just hope you never stop realizing how lucky you are. And, Debbie, I just want to wish you the best, you deserve it, and tell you that thinking about you got me through a very shitty time in my life—excuse me, everyone—and I will always, always love you for that." He looks around at the crowd, suddenly self-conscious, and raises his glass sheepishly. "Bottoms up, everybody."

There is a smattering of shocked applause and nervous laughter as Russ sits down, a commotion of fast conversation, and then Debbie stands up, red-eyed and blushing profusely, and the room falls silent again. "Russ, I don't even know what to say. That was the sweetest thing I ever . . ." She pauses for a moment, unsure of how to proceed. "Well, all I can say is that if things don't work out with Mike, you'll be the first to know." The crowd laughs and Russ looks like he's seriously considering slitting his wrists.

"Fuck me," he says.

"Don't worry about it," I say. "That took a lot of guts."

"I made a fool out of myself."

"You were very sweet," Claire says, leaning over to kiss him. "There isn't a woman in this room who didn't just fall in love with you."

Debbie clears her throat. "There's something I'd like to say," she says, and I don't like the way her eyes find mine and then quickly dart away. I don't like it at all. After a while, you develop a sixth sense about these things.

"This family has been through a lot over the last few years," Debbie says, and you can feel the room holding its breath, mesmerized, waiting for the next plot twist. "And I just want to take a moment to mention my sister-in-law, Hailey. She was my sister and my friend, and now, on the eve of my wedding day, it's just unimaginable to me that she isn't here. We love you, Hailey, and we will never stop missing you."

And now my mother is crying, and Claire is crying, and Russ is shaking, and people at other tables are wiping their eyes and blowing their noses, and the only one who isn't crying is my father, who looks singularly perturbed, like he's trying to work something out. Every eye in the room is on me, like the nominated actor who hasn't won the award, and I can feel them all looking, waiting for my reaction, and my skin is crawling and my heart is pounding like a war drum and it's like a sauna in here, I'm sweating through my shirt. And then Debbie's voice fades away, all sound fades away, the room is reduced to a narrow black corridor, and there is nothing except the soft whisper of my soles against the plush floral carpet, the slide of the fibers under my shoe with each hurried step. And I know they're coming after me, Claire or Russ or my mother, I can sense the movement behind me, but I can't look at anyone right now, so I barrel through the heavy fire doors and start moving quickly down the hallway, through the lobby and out the front doors into the cool night air. I stand in the driveway, underneath the fluorescent lighting of the club's awning, leaning against the wall, just breathing, in and out, waiting for my racing heart to slow down.

There are footsteps behind me, and then my father steps out into the driveway. "Doug," he says, walking over to stand in front of me.

"Hey, Dad."

He reaches out to my chin, to make me look up at him. He's still panting a little from chasing me out of the building, but his blue eyes are sharp and clear. Did I even know he had blue eyes? "Hailey," he says haltingly. "She's dead."

"Yeah, Dad. She's dead."

He nods. "How long?"

"Going on thirteen months now."

"Did I know?"

"Dad."

He shakes his head. "Did I know?"

"Sometimes you know. Most of the time you forget."

He shakes his head and his eyes fill with tears. "What you must have gone through. What you must be going through."

"It's okay, Dad."

"And I haven't been there for you."

"It's not your fault."

"I am so sorry, Doug."

I close my eyes, and when I open them he's reaching for me, and the tears fly out like bullets from between my soaked lashes as I let out a single, convulsive sob and fall into his embrace. He holds me like that for a while, rocking us gently back and forth, his chin resting on the crown of my head, his hand warm and dry against my neck. I think it's the first time since Hailey died that I've actually cried into someone, and it feels different, more complete, and I weep like a motherfucker, I empty myself of tears, as if all the other times I've cried were just dress rehearsals for this one perfect cry into my father's soft, sturdy chest. "You never cried when you were a kid," he says when I'm done, stepping back, his hands on my shoulders. "We always thought something was wrong with you."

"Something was."

He shakes his head. "Come on back inside, Doug."

"I will soon. I just need a minute."

"You sure you'll be okay?" he says, studying my face.

I nod, offering up a wan smile. "What choice do I have?"

"That's the spirit," he says, smiling warmly as he backs away.

A few minutes later I'm still standing there, staring up at the blue-black sky, still hiccupping from my recent outburst, when a figure steps out of the shadows of the parking lot. And I'm still a little light-headed and bleary-eyed from crying so hard, so it takes me an extra second to recognize that it's Dave Potter. He's dressed in suit pants and a T-shirt, and his hair looks like he stepped out of the shower and into a wind tunnel.

"Doug," he says.

"You're late," I say.

And that's when I notice that he's holding a gun.

37

THE GUN IS A SIX-SHOOTER, A .357 MAGNUM OR A .38 Special, I don't know, one of those revolvers that, after loading the barrel, you spin it like a wheel for effect before snapping it closed with a flick of your wrist. I picture Dave Potter standing over the rich mahogany desk in his study doing just that. Who the hell keeps a gun like that in the suburbs? The man's got children in his house. Hasn't he read the statistics?

He's not pointing the gun, just kind of dangling it at his side, and for a second I dare to hope that he's not going to raise the gun, that he's already changed his mind, having cogitated long and hard on the viability of shooting me on the drive over. I wonder if he played the radio while he was driving, if he hummed along to the music, if he signaled his turns. Then he lets out a small, strangled noise and points the gun directly at my chest.

I've never had a gun pointed at me before, but like most people I've imagined it. I've pictured the angles, considered various disarming techniques, from Chuck Norris–style spinning kicks, to the quick grab and twist, employing a jujitsu armlock that allows me to simultaneously discard the gun and bring my assailant to the floor. And Dave is older and slower than me, so I should be able to take him. Except that someone's been screwing around with my gravity, because suddenly I weigh a thousand pounds, and it feels like my shoes have been nailed to the floor, and my ass is clenched so hard I wonder if I'll have to have it surgically unclenched. And all I can do is stare down the dark barrel of Dave's gun, while pandemonium erupts in my stomach as my innards run for cover, diving headfirst behind counters, overturning tables, pressing themselves up against walls.

"Doug," he says, again.

"Dave," I say. "How's it going?"

"Not so good." His face breaks into a maniacal little grin that scares me more than the gun. "Pretty damn bad, actually, if you must know."

I nod, studying his flushed, sweaty face. I need to get him talking, to put as many words between that gun and my chest as possible. It's hard to kill someone in the middle of a sentence. That's how James Bond always buys those extra few minutes he needs until the commandos show up. He shoots the breeze.

"Are you going to shoot me, Dave?" I say. Maybe hearing the words out loud will bring the insanity home for him.

"You fucked her, Doug!" he screams at me, making me flinch. "You fucked my wife."

For one crazy minute, I consider the practicalities of a full-blown denial. *What?* I'll say, my eyes wide with shock and hurt. *I did what? Listen, I don't know what's going on between you and Laney, but I never touched her, Dave. Never!* And I'll do it loudly, with the utmost sincerity, just enough to give him pause, and that will be enough. Because you don't go shooting someone who just may have slept with your wife, do you? I mean, before you head down that road, you'd want to be pretty certain, I would think.

But I can see that he knows, that whatever Laney has said to him has left him with unshakable certainty, and my denial will only inflame him, will be just the push he needs to squeeze that trigger.

"Dave," I say. "I don't think you want to shoot me."

"Well, no one's ever fucked your wife, have they, so how the fuck would you know what I want?"

"You're right, I'm sorry."

"God damn you, Doug." He takes two steps closer—close enough now for me to see his jaw trembling with rage, to see the angry protrusion of thick veins running up the side of his neck—and aims the gun at my face. He is ten, maybe twelve feet away now. He won't miss. "You fucked her, Doug. Like she was just anybody. You turned the mother of my children into a whore."

"I messed up, Dave. I'm sorry. I was a mess and I was still crazy from everything and—"

"Well, cry me a fucking river!" he shouts hysterically, jabbing the gun in my direction. "What is that, like a new stage of grief? Denial, anger, bargaining, and fucking your friend's wife?"

"Calm down, Dave. Please."

"Shut up!"

"You have kids who need you."

"Don't you dare mention my kids."

"I'm sorry."

"Shut up!" he screams again, almost pleading.

I shut up. Dave stares at me, the sweat on his face glistening under the awning lights, and I stare at the barrel of his gun. His finger is tight on the trigger, flexing unconsciously, and with a heavy sense of dread, I realize that he's about to shoot me. I close my eyes and try to summon up an image of Hailey. If this is how it ends, then this is how it ends, but if I'm going to die it will be with her face on my mind, her name on my lips. "Hailey," I murmur to myself, like a prayer, and I can see her on the backs of my eyelids, smiling at me, loving me, and I'm ready, I think.

"What the hell is going on out here?" my father's voice jolts my eyes open. And then Claire screams. They are standing in the doorway, gaping in disbelief.

"It's okay," I say.

"It's okay?" Claire says. "You can't be serious."

"Put the gun down, son," my father says, slowly approaching Dave.

"Get away from me!" Dave swings the gun at him. My father raises his hands, but holds his ground.

"It's okay, son," my father says.

"He fucked my wife!" Dave says, and his voice cracks as he says it.

"Oh, fucking hell," Claire says.

"Is that true, Doug?" my father says, never taking his eyes off Dave.

"Yeah," I say.

"Okay," my father says, taking another step closer to Dave, who now has the gun trained on my head again. "You've been wronged. You're hurting. You want justice. It makes sense. But you know this isn't the way."

"I'm going to kill him."

"No, you're not," my father says softly. "You want to, and no one can blame you for wanting to, but you're too smart to think this is the answer. This is just your time, son, that's all. Your time to hurt and bleed and tear apart your notion of what makes you who you are. Life knocks us all on our ass at some point. And then we get back up, and we make some changes, because that's what men do. We adapt. And when we're done adapting, we're better equipped to survive."

"He doesn't deserve to live," Dave says, and now there are tears in his eyes, and the gun is starting to shake in his hand.

"That's not for you to decide," my father says. "You have much more important things to worry about. You have a family? Children?"

"Yes," Dave says, and now his whole body is shaking with tension. But the gun is still up there, still aimed at my face.

"Then you worry about them first," my father says firmly. "And then you worry about yourself, about the changes you're going to make to survive this. Because you will survive this. But you pull that trigger, and survival is no longer an option. The only move left after that is putting that gun in your own mouth. Are you prepared to do that?"

Dave stares at me, trembling and sweating, and at that moment I wish he would pull the trigger, just so I won't have to see the anguish distorting his face like a stocking mask, the pain I caused because I was too consumed with my own to care. "Doug," he says, and now his voice is more of a whimper.

"It's okay, Dave," I say, meeting his gaze. "I understand. I'm ready."

"Shut the fuck up, Doug! You are not!" Claire shouts at me, crying. "He is not!"

Dave looks at me for a long moment, and then, impossibly, his face relaxes into a sad little smile. "This is not how I pictured the day going when I woke up this morning."

"That makes two of us," I say.

And then, just as he's lowering the gun, Russ suddenly materializes from the darkness of the parking lot and hurls himself at Dave, his outstretched arms reaching for the gun, and in the instant before his momentum knocks them both over, there is a deafening roar that blows every other sound in the world out of existence, and a brief muzzle flash like a magnesium flare, and then Russ and Dave are rolling on the floor in a sailor's knot of limbs, and I can see the gun clattering across the cobblestone driveway, can see that Claire is shrieking, and my father is yelling and pointing, but there is no sound, everything has been silenced, and I'm wondering where the bullet went, and Russ is lying on the ground and he isn't moving, and Claire is still screaming and my father is looking around, bewildered, and Dave is climbing to his feet with a dazed look on his face, and Russ is not getting up, oh Jesus, he is not getting up, and I can feel the scream building in my throat, and he needs to move, he can't be shot, that can't be how this ends, and I can feel the brick wall against my back, tearing into my suit jacket, and please move, Russ, just get off the fucking floor and show me something, I will buy you a car, I will buy you a fucking Ferrari if you would just move, and then, incredibly, he does, he rolls onto his stomach and pushes himself up to his feet and looks at me, his eyes bulging with alarm, and I'm so relieved, so fucking happy, that for a moment nothing else matters, not a single other thing in the world matters, because Russ is okay, and then he starts to rise, floating up above me, and Claire and my father are rising too, like helium balloons, getting higher and higher, and it's the strangest, most magical thing I've ever seen, my family rising up and hovering high above me, and then, just as the sound comes back in a loud rush of confusion, I feel the hot wetness spreading out from my side, radiating across my belly and up my chest, and I realize that I'm lying on the cobblestone driveway, staring up at the metal skeleton of the club's white awning.

"Doug!" Claire screams, falling beside me, her hands on my shoulders, and I want to tell her to calm down, that I actually feel strangely fine, comfortably numb, that it feels okay, that it feels like two Vil Pills washed down with a bottle of wine and three puffs on a water bong all wrapped into one, that I can see her hair actually growing in its follicles, can see the sweat emerging and spilling out of my father's pores as he gets on his knees to lean over me, can see the vein in Russ's temple throbbing to the beat of his heart, and it's all okay.

I'm dimly aware of new people, of a crowd forming around us on the driveway. "Call nine-one-one," my father says to Russ, who is staring down at me, frozen in place. "Russ!" my father shouts at him, and this time Russ blinks and then reaches into his suit pocket for his cell phone.

"It's okay," I say, but no one seems to hear me, and I wonder if I actually said it, or just thought it.

Claire is crying and my father grabs her hands and pulls them off my shoulders, and then pushes back my jacket and opens my shirt. "Let's have a look," he says calmly. His hand on my bare skin is like fire, and I recoil so fiercely that I bang my head on the cobblestones, and his other hand, now covered in blood, comes down on my chest. "Hang in there, Doug," he says, holding me down firmly. He tears a piece of my shirt off and uses it to clear away some of the blood pooling on my belly. "Can you hear me?"

"Yeah," I say, my own voice sounding hollow in my ears.

"Good. Listen to me. You're going to be okay. I just need to roll you a little bit for a second—Claire, put your hands under his head so he doesn't bang it again— Claire! Pull yourself together and do what I say!"

I can feel his hands under my back and then he rolls me and the pain is every color of the rainbow, sudden and complete, and then he rolls me back, and Claire's tear-soaked face is hovering upside down above mine, her hands cradling the back of my head, and my father is gently pressing some cloth against me, just above my right hip. "It's a clean exit wound," he says, nodding. "Went right through you."

And then Russ is on the ground next to me, crying, and I want to tell him not to worry, that I'm fine, but I can't seem to find my voice anymore, and Claire won't stop crying, and I can hear my mother's voice, shrill and verging on hysterical, and then the paramedics are there, and my father is giving them instructions, speaking authoritatively in medical jargon that makes me proud, and the flashing lights from the ambulance spin and blink, bathing everything in their kinetic red glow, and even though I can't see them, I'm aware of everyone standing around me, Debbie, who is crying, and Mike, who is holding her, and Mike's asshole brother, and all of my relatives, and everyone I've ever known in my whole life, and this seems like as good a time as any to disappear, so the next time the red light spins past me, I catch hold of its edge and ride it like a wave into oblivion.

38

I WAKE UP AS THEY'RE WHEELING ME INTO THE EMER-
gency room, two paramedics, one on each end of the stretcher, and
my father, walking between them, his hand resting proprietarily
on my arm. A young female doctor in blue scrubs and a white
coat falls into step with us as soon as we clear the sliding doors.

"What happened?" she says to the paramedic closest to my
head.

"It's a single gunshot wound to the lower left stomach with
clearly visible entry and exit wounds," my father says. "Vitals
are stable, no signs of any internal bleeding. Start an IV, irrigate
with five hundred CCs of saline, and get me a CAT scan of the
stomach and pelvis to rule out solid organ damage."

"What he said," the paramedic says to her, rolling his eyes.

"I'm sorry," she says, confused. "Who are you?"

"Dr. Stanley Parker. I'm his father."

"Well, Dr. Parker, I need to call up for a surgical consult."

"What's your name, young lady?"

"Dr. Holden. Stephanie Holden."

"Well, Dr. Holden, you just had your surgical consult. Now,
who's the attending on call?"

"Dr. Morris."

"Sanford Morris?"

"Yes."

"Go wake him up and tell him that Stanley Parker's son is bleeding all over his ER."

I am supposed to lie still for the CAT scan, but my wound is throbbing now, hot and itchy, and I just can't seem to stop twitching. When it's over, Dr. Morris tells us that the radiologist has confirmed no solid organ injuries, but cannot rule out the bullet's possible entry into the peritoneum because I was moving too much. They'll keep me overnight and do a repeat CAT scan in the morning.

"Here's my pager number," Dr. Morris says, handing my father a card. "I'll be here all night. You page me if you need anything, okay?"

"Thanks a lot, Sandy."

"Anytime, Stan. It's great to see your face. We miss you around here."

"I miss it too."

When my father wheels me back into the room, my mother is waiting by the window, Claire and Debbie are lying on the bed, and Mike and Russ are on either arm of the large reclining chair in the corner. Russ is still looking pale and scared, and his fear touches me even as I feel a sharp pang of guilt for putting him through this.

"Hey!" my mother says, running over to me. She bends down to kiss me and then starts to cry.

"I'm okay, Mom."

"I was so scared!"

"He's fine, Evie," my father says, gently pulling her off of me.

"He could have been killed!"

He leads her over to the window, where she collapses against him, and he holds her tightly, murmuring quietly into her ear.

Debbie and Claire climb off the bed to help me into it, and then climb back on to lie next to me. "It always has to be about you, doesn't it?" Debbie says, kissing my cheek.

"I'm really sorry, Pooh. I ruined your dinner."

"I'm just glad you're okay," she says. "Anything to get out of coming to the wedding, right?"

"The police are downstairs," Mike says. "You need a lawyer?"

"Tell them it was an accident. He was showing me the gun and it went off."

"You sure?"

"Will that keep him out of trouble?"

"As long as he has a license for the gun, he should be okay."

"I'll be down in a minute," Debbie tells him as he leaves.

"You should have seen Dad," I say softly. "He still knows what he's doing."

"He was also pretty impressive saving your life back at the club," Claire says.

"I guess he's having one of his better days."

"Legendary."

"It's good to know he's still in there," Debbie says.

"He's there," I say.

"My stomach is killing me," Claire says.

"Is it the baby?" Debbie says, alarmed.

She shakes her head. "Twin telepathy."

"Really?" Russ says. "You guys feel each other's pain and all that?"

"We don't have twin telepathy," I say.

"Don't listen to him," Claire says. "He's just being negative."

"It's been that kind of day," I say. I can feel my eyes starting to close. "What time is it?"

"It's just after one a.m.," Debbie says. "Hey. I'm getting married today."

"Congratulations."

"We'd better go," she says, leaning over to kiss my forehead. "Thanks, Pooh."

"I was thinking that tonight would be the perfect time for you to stop calling me that."

I consider her thoughtfully for a moment. "I don't see the connection."

She shakes her head and smiles. "You get some rest."

"Pooh."

"Yeah."

"I love you."

"That's just the morphine talking."

My father leans over and kisses my forehead. "Good night, Doug," he says.

"Thanks for everything, Dad. You were amazing."

He looks me in the eye while he runs his fingers gently across my face, and I can feel the hotness forming at the base of my throat. "You'll be okay," he says.

"Don't eat the food here," my mother says. "The place is crawling with disease. We'll bring you breakfast in the morning."

Claire kisses me and says, "You're a mess."

"I know."

"But you're my mess, so please, I think we've had enough action for a while."

"It hasn't been dull."

"Dull is sounding pretty good right about now."

Russ closes the door behind all of them, and he's just turning to face me when the door opens again and Debbie steps in, slightly out of breath. "Russ," she says.

"Yeah."

"Your toast was incredible."

Then she throws her arms around him and gives him a long, soft, openmouthed kiss on the lips. When she's done, she gives him another, shorter one, and then a peck on his forehead. "I think you're beautiful too," she says. "Okay. Bye."

And he just stands there blushing after she leaves, looking utterly dumbfounded until, gradually, a wide smile spreads across his face.

"You okay there?" I say after a bit.

"Just give me a minute," he says.

Then he jumps up onto the chair and does a little dance, and then he runs across the room, opens the window, and lets out a long, triumphant scream. After he closes the window, he comes back across the room and climbs onto the bed next to me, panting from his exertions and still smiling. "Is today the best day ever, or what?" he says.

* * *

I wake up in the middle of the night, empty and confused. Russ is sleeping beside me, still in his suit and tie, snoring lightly, and I'm glad he's there, warming the bed for me. I am deeply exhausted, can feel the fatigue burning like embers in every muscle of my body. I am a man who was shot by a jealous husband. I am that guy. It will take some getting used to. My eyes roam the darkened hospital room, trying to identify the shapes of alien objects, but everywhere I look, I see the dark round barrel of Dave's gun staring back at me, all knowing. I looked up at him last night and told him that I was ready, but now, lying here, with Russ's low, steady breath in my ear, I realize that I was wrong. I am nowhere near ready to die. I've died enough. I still have some living to do. I've just got to start doing it a little more carefully.

39

I OPEN MY EYES TO FIND LANEY POTTER SITTING beside my bed, looking tired and frail, her eyes swollen from crying. "Hey," she says softly.

"Hey."

"Russ went to get you some breakfast."

"Oh. That's good."

She nods, and opens her mouth to say something, but nothing comes out.

"Laney," I say.

"I'm so sorry, Doug." She starts to cry. "I never imagined he would do something like this."

"I know."

"You might have been killed."

"It's okay."

She leans forward in her chair. "It's my fault, all of it. You were grieving and I took advantage of that. I was supposed to be your friend. And then, when you tried to move on, I couldn't handle it. If something had happened to you..."

Something did happen to me, I think, as she sobs into her

hands for a few moments, and then roots through her bag for a tissue.

"Listen," I say. "It was my fault as much as yours. I guess for the last year I've been treating Hailey's death like a free pass. It was selfish and stupid, and I've decided not to do it anymore."

She nods and sits back in her chair. "Mike came by last night to get our story straight for the police. Thank you for that."

"It really was an accident, Laney."

She looks at me for a while, nodding unconsciously. "How did we get here, Doug?"

I don't have an answer for that, so I just shake my head and close my eyes, and when I open them, Russ is sitting where Laney had been, chewing on a bagel. "And he's back!" Russ says.

There's been a multiple-vehicle accident in White Plains, and the CAT scan will be tied up all morning, so my discharge will be delayed. My mother comes for a quick visit and to drop off muffins before she has to disappear into the whirlwind of wedding preparations. "Where's Dad?" I say.

"He's having one of his bad mornings," my mother says, looking down at her hands.

"What do you mean?"

"What do you mean, what do I mean?" she says. "He woke up angry, won't say a word to me, and when I left the house he was throwing things at Rudy."

"Jesus," I say. "I guess I thought, you know, after last night..."

"You thought he'd snapped out of it."

"Yes."

She shakes her head, smiling sadly. "He's always going to be like this, Doug."

"How do you deal with it?" I say, instantly and deeply depressed.

She shrugs sadly. "It's like anything else," she says. "I just hope for more good days than bad."

"I'm sorry, Mom."

"Also," she says, "I self-medicate."

The CAT scan is still tied up at noon, and I'm starting to get a little antsy. Russ has set up a wastebasket on the windowsill and we're tossing crumpled magazine pages at it and keeping score. He's winning because I'm injured, and also because I suck. When we run out of paper, he goes and collects all of our crumpled balls and stockpiles them on the bed for a second round.

"Let's play Horse," he says.

"I can't leave the bed."

"So you'll lose."

"Okay, you go first."

He shoots lying down on the floor behind the bed. He shoots from the bathroom. He shoots standing with his back against the far wall. "Nothing but net," he says. He opens the door to shoot from the hallway, and Brooke is standing there, about to knock.

"Ms. Hayes," Russ says.

"Hi, Russ," she says, looking past him at me. "Is now a bad time?"

"No, it's a great time," I say. "Join the party."

She steps tentatively into the room, looking morning fresh in jeans and a long-sleeved black jersey under a gray T-shirt.

"I was just going on a soda run," Russ says. "You want anything?"

"No, thanks."

After he leaves, she sits down stiffly. "Are you okay?" she says.

"Yeah. Actually, I think I might be better than I've been in a long time. I guess it took something like this to help me figure a few things out."

"Are you going to make it to the wedding?"

"Nah," I say. "I'm sorry about that. I was looking forward to bringing you."

"I think it's probably for the best," she says, and her voice is laced with something: Regret? Sadness? Anger? I can't quite tell, but I know instinctively that it doesn't bode well for me.

"What's going on, Brooke?"

She meets my gaze for a moment and then she looks away. "Doug," she says quietly.

"That bad?"

"I think so, yeah."

I nod, absorbing the news. Somehow, in view of everything that's happened in the last twenty-four hours, this isn't a terribly surprising development. I remind myself that we've only been on a few dates, that this is not the end of something major, but underneath the dull blanket of the morphine, I can feel something shifting, like a pulled muscle that's going to hurt later. "I understand," I say.

"No, I don't think you do," she says. "When you wouldn't

sleep with me, I just figured you weren't ready for sex, but it turns out you'd been having plenty of sex. You just weren't ready for me."

"Because you mattered," I say. "I swear, that's the truth."

"I know," she says, with a sad smile. "I believe you. I'm not hurt. I mean, I am, but I'll get over it. The point is, you couldn't be intimate with me because I mattered, but you could give yourself to a married woman who didn't matter without any problem. And I'm not judging you, Doug. Please don't think that I am. You were grieving and alone, she was a compassionate friend. Things happen. But the fact is, it's just not the behavior of someone who is ready for a real relationship, and I like you too much to let you drag me through your shit with you."

Sometimes you walk past a pretty girl on the street and there's something beyond beauty in her face, something warm and smart and sensual and inviting, and in the three seconds you have to look at her, you actually fall in love, and in those moments, you can actually know the taste of her kiss, the feel of her skin against yours, the sound of her laugh, how she'll look at you and make you whole. And then she's gone, and in the five seconds afterwards, you mourn her loss with more sadness than you'll ever admit to. Brooke has one of those faces, but this time I didn't pass by and mourn her, this time I stopped and we actually found something, and now I'm going to lose her anyway.

"Can we at least be friends?"

"Like you and Laney Potter?"

"Jesus, Brooke."

"I'm sorry, that was bitchy. Just...this is hard for me."

"So don't do it."

"I have to." She stands up. "I just wanted to make sure you were okay."

"I was doing fine until you showed up."

She grins sadly and leans over to kiss me softly on the temple. "I'm sorry." She is heartbreakingly close, excruciatingly beautiful, and she was never mine to lose.

"You know what the tragic thing is?" I say, when she reaches the door.

"What's that?"

"That it was all changing. I was finally on track. Today, with you, was going to be the first day of the new me."

Her hand squeezes the doorknob and she briefly rests her forehead against the door. "Timing has never been my strong suit," she says, and then she smiles one last time, and then she's gone.

"Fuck it!" Russ says exasperatedly when he returns and sees my expression. "No more visitors."

But there is one more. Late in the afternoon, there's a knock on the door. "Don't open it," I say. "For the love of God!"

"Who's even left?" Russ says, looking up from his magazine. "Aren't all the hot, depressing women already accounted for?"

There's another knock, then the door swings open and in walks Stephen Ives, the horseshit heir. "Hey," he says, pulling a chair up to the bed.

"Hey," I say.

"I heard you got a little shot."

"Good news travels fast."

"I always knew that dick of yours would get you in trouble someday."

Over by the window, Russ suddenly spins and hurls the wastebasket at Stephen, who falls to his knees to duck it. "Hey!" Stephen yells, jumping to his feet.

"Now I recognize you," Russ says with an angry smirk. "Claire's husband."

"What the hell is wrong with you?" Stephen says, turning on Russ, eyes blazing.

"Doug is having a rough day," Russ says, standing his ground. "He doesn't need any more shit from anyone."

Stephen stares at him for a moment, and then turns back to me, nodding apologetically. "You're right, I'm sorry," he says. "That was uncalled-for."

"Damned straight," Russ says, itching for a fight. We've been holed up in this room all day, and he's pulsating with nervous energy.

"I'm sorry, Doug," Stephen says, sitting down next to me. "I'm an asshole."

"Forget it."

"Are you going to get out of here today?"

"I should have been out of here hours ago. Apparently there's been a run on CAT scans."

"Well, I'm glad to see you're okay. We've had our differences, but we're still family, right? At least for the time being."

"Thanks, Stephen," I say, touched in spite of myself. "I know I've been a schmuck to you in the past, but I've always suspected that deep down, you might not be a complete tool."

He nods and clears his throat, and we look in opposite directions for a few seconds.

"I remain unconvinced," Russ says, and we all share a light, tension-breaking chuckle.

"So I take it you're not going to the wedding?" Stephen says, and that's when it dawns on me that he's wearing a tux.

"What, you are?"

He nods, his face turning red, and runs his fingers through his hair. "I need to see her, Doug. I'll die if I don't."

In the harsh fluorescent lighting, I can see all the weight he's lost, the gauntness of his face and the stricken look in his bloodshot, tired eyes. He reminds me of me.

"Yeah," I say. "I guess you do."

"Where do you put my chances?"

"It's Claire," I say. "There are no odds. It's all wild card."

"Well," he says, getting to his feet. "I guess I've outstayed my welcome. Is there anything I can get you before I go?"

I look at Russ, standing against the wall in his sleep-rumpled suit. "I'm having a thought," I say.

He looks back at me. "Are you thinking what I think you're thinking?"

"My little sister is getting married," I say, rolling out of bed. It hurts, but not as bad as I thought it would.

"Yeah," Russ says, coming over to help me. "That's what I thought you were thinking." He goes to the closet and pulls out my bloodstained suit pants.

"You can't just leave," Stephen says.

"Watch me."

"What about your CAT scan?"

"The longer I wait for it, the less fun it sounds."

Waiting at the elevators, we are spotted by one of the nurses. "Where are you taking him?" she says, walking hurriedly toward us.

"Out," Russ says.

"You haven't been discharged!" she calls as we step into the elevator. "You can't just leave."

"Watch him," Stephen says as the doors slide shut.

Stephen's Porsche is built for two, with just a narrow leather plank for a backseat, but somehow, Russ manages to contort himself into it, with his long legs spilling into the front on either side of the stick shift, his feet braced against the dash. I sit in the passenger seat, using his leg as an armrest and grunting in pain every time we hit a bump in the road.

Bump.

"Oof."

"Sorry."

"It's okay."

Bump.

"Ugh."

"I'm so sorry."

"It's fine."

On the way, Stephen calls for a limo and driver that will meet us at my house. Once home, Russ showers and changes into a dark suit, while I do my best with a sponge bath and a quick shampoo, since I don't want to deal with changing my bandages. Then Russ helps me into the ridiculous gray tux and tails that

Mike chose for his wedding party, and we stand together in my bedroom, studying our reflections in the full-length mirror behind Hailey's closet door. We look like something out of a magazine. We are young, slim, sad, and beautiful. We are forty minutes late.

"We look killer," Russ says.

"We are not without a certain raffish charm," I say.

"So, let's do this thing."

"No drinking."

"No bleeding."

"No hitting on the bride, under any circumstances."

"No gunplay."

"Deal."

"Deal."

The limo is a stretch, of course. What else would Stephen have on speed dial? He is standing on the sidewalk, finishing a fat cigar when we step outside. "Finally," he says, putting out the cigar on the sole of his shoe. "I was about to send a search party." We descend into plush leather seats, and the limo pulls away from the curb like a yacht from its berth. We sit in silence, looking out the tinted windows, absorbed in our own nervous thoughts, and then Russ flips through the CD collection in a compartment next to the stereo and selects an old KISS anthology. And soon the bass drums are pounding and the guitars are riffing, and there's nothing to do but sing along to the crude lyrics, purging our collective nerves in the thunderous, throbbing music. *I want to rock and roll all night, and party every day! / I want to rock and roll all night, and party every day!* And even Stephen joins in, bouncing his knee and nodding to the beat as he does, and we're all singing, at full volume, rocking in our seats and banging on upholstery, trying to empty our bellies of every last bit of nerves. The song ends too soon, before anything transcendent can occur, before we can be saved by Rock and Roll. None of us knows the words to the next one, I mean, it's KISS after all, and who really knows more than one or two KISS songs? So Russ turns it down and we go back to looking out the windows as the limo cruises up the interstate, three lost, confused, well-dressed men, hurtling northward toward uncertain salvation while outside the last clinging tendrils of sunlight slowly disintegrate in the evening sky.

40

THE COCKTAIL HOUR HAS ENDED, AND THE GUESTS have all been herded outside, where five hundred folding chairs have been set up on a bluff overlooking the beach, facing a canopied platform through which you can see the sun setting over the ocean. Moths fly kamikaze missions into the bright standing lights that ring the area, and the sharp, recurring thwack of golf clubs hitting balls is faintly audible from the club's driving range about fifty yards over, behind the tall wooden fence. By the time we make it down, the quartet is finished playing, the processional is over, and Debbie and Mike are standing under the canopy, flanked by her bridesmaids in elegant black gowns and Mike's diminished pool of groomsmen. He should have chosen some alternates. I'm relieved to see that Dave Potter is not in attendance, because that would be somewhat awkward for all concerned, I think.

Rabbi Gross, the rabbi of my parents' temple and my mother's go-to guy for all religious occasions, is officiating, and he's just stepped up to the microphone and cleared his throat. Since there don't seem to be any empty seats, Russ, Stephen, and I stand at the back of the aisle, comfortably out of view.

"Friends," Rabbi Gross begins in his soft, gurgling voice. He's a tall, angular man with silver hair and a Vandyke that makes him look like Sigmund Freud. "We are all honored to be here on this joyous occasion, coming together with Deborah and Michael as they celebrate their love. And before I perform the ceremony, I'd like to just take a moment and read a passage from Psalms that I think encapsulates all that we wish for these two wonderful people."

The rabbi clears his throat again and starts to read, and I'm watching so intently that it takes me a minute to realize that Debbie has spotted me. Her eyes grow wide and she leans over to whisper urgently into Mike's ear. Mike turns to look back at me as well, and then Debbie grabs two fistfuls of her bridal gown, steps down off the bandstand, and starts running up the aisle. There is an audible gasp from the crowd, and the rabbi stops his reading in midsentence. And I have to admit, I feel a little self-conscious about being here. The brother of the bride has fucked another man's wife and everyone here has indubitably been brought up to speed on all the salacious details, weddings being much more entertaining when there's some juicy backstory. But my baby sister is getting married, so I mutter an impressively comprehensive slew of disjointed expletives under my breath to calm my jangling nerves, and start limping down the aisle to meet her halfway. When we collide softly, she's laughing and there are tears in her eyes as she throws her arms around me.

"You look great, Pooh."

"Thank you, thank you, thank you," she whispers into my ear. "I can't believe you came."

"I wouldn't have missed it," I say, suddenly finding myself short of breath.

She grabs my hand and leads me down the aisle, back to the raised canopy. I can't quite do the step up on my own, so Mike leans down to help me—"Hey, buddy, glad you could make it," he says—and there's a moment of excruciating pain as my torso stretches, I can feel the raw edges of my pierced tissue pulling and fraying, but then I'm up and Claire steps out of line to give me a hug. "I was summoning you all day," she whispers, tapping her temple as she steps back into place. "Twin telepathy."

"Is everything okay?" the rabbi wants to know, his palm covering the microphone.

"Perfect," Debbie says, stepping back into her spot beside Mike.

"I'm used to people walking out of my sermons, but when you start losing brides at their weddings, it's probably time to consider another line of work," Rabbi Gross jokes like an old pro, and the crowd laughs and we're back on track. I locate my parents' faces down in the front row smiling up at me, and I give them a small wave, feeling sweaty and exposed in the glare of the video crew's lights. But then Mike is slipping a ring on Debbie's finger, and she's putting one on him, and I just watch my sister's face as she stares up at Mike, and for the moment I am suffused in the warm glow of their unmitigated happiness. It feels like forever since I've felt something so simple and pure, and for the time being at least, everything else has faded to background noise.

The wrapped glass is summarily crushed under Mike's shoe, effectively ending the ceremony, and the guests applaud and catcall as the wedding party raucously follows the freshly minted couple up the aisle. Claire loops her arm through mine to walk slowly behind my parents, who are waving and nodding to friends as they go, and when we reach the back, Stephen is standing there, nervously wringing his hands as the crowd files past him.

"Stephen!" my father says, stepping forward to give him a hug. "What are you doing here?"

"Yeah, Stephen," Claire says in a thin, sharp voice. "What are you doing here?"

"Hi, Claire. I'm not here to bother you. Can we just go somewhere to talk for a minute?"

"Here's fine."

"I'll leave you two alone," I say, but Claire tightens her grip on my arm. "You stay right here." Then she looks at Stephen and says, "Go ahead."

"Okay." Stephen nervously clears his throat as the throngs meander past us, back toward the main house. "I love you, Claire," he says. "I never stopped loving you, never stopped feeling lucky as hell to have you, but somewhere along the way I failed you. To be completely honest, I'm not exactly sure how, and this would be a much better speech if I knew, but I do know, in my heart, that I failed you, and I am truly, truly sorry for that. I'm not here to ask you for another chance, because I know how you are when you've made up your mind. If you're going to divorce me, then that's what's going to happen, and I will make sure you're taken care of. That's our child you're carrying, and I want things to be good between us so that we can at least be good parents together. But if, on the off chance, you're having some second thoughts about all of this, then I just wanted to tell you that I want you back, and I swear to you, I swear to you, that I won't fail you again."

Claire looks at him for a long moment. "I'll just hurt you again," she says softly.

"It can't be any worse than this," he says.

"Trust me," she says. "It can."

He nods and clears his throat, and then nods some more. "Okay. Well, I said what I came to say. And, anyway, it was good to see your face again." He looks over at me and nods. "You feel better, Doug."

"Thanks."

"You want me to send the limo back for you?"

"Thanks anyway. My car is still here from last night."

"Okay, then." He steps forward and kisses Claire's cheek. "Good-bye, Claire. I'll wait to hear from you." Then he turns around and joins the crowd making their way up the lawn to the tall glass doors of the inn. Claire watches him leave, and I watch Claire.

"What limo?" she says. "You brought him?"

"More like he brought us."

"How does something like that happen?"

"Well, he just happened to be in the room when I decided to leave the hospital, so he offered us a lift."

"Why would he visit you?"

"I don't know," I say. "Because I'm family?"

She nods, looking up the lawn at his disappearing figure. Inside, the band has started to play "Celebration," by Kool and the Gang, and the familiar horn riffs come floating across the lawn. "Fucking hell," Claire says, shaking her head. "Fucking hell."

"Just go."

And then she's off, running up the hill in her high heels, calling his name. There's just enough time to see him turn around, to see her start yelling at him, and then they're swallowed up by the crowd.

It's amazing, really, how fast a wedding is over. With all the anticipation and planning that precedes it, all the tension and excitement, you kind of expect it to last a week instead of six hours. We dance, we eat, and we dance some more. Mike makes a nice little speech about Debbie, and Max brings the house down with a drunken, borderline pornographic toast that ends on a surprisingly emotional note. I sneak a few Vil Pills from my mother's clutch, strictly for medicinal purposes, and then Rudy, all decked out for the occasion in a dark blue tuxedo, takes a break from standing vigil over my father to change my bandages in a bathroom stall. My mother gets hammered, sings a few showstoppers with the band, and seems prepared to stay up there doing encores all night until Claire talks her down, and then we're eating dessert as the crowd begins to thin. Debbie and Mike make their farewells, hugging and kissing everyone in arm's reach, pocketing envelopes discreetly, and then they're off to their hotel. They'll leave for Antigua in the morning. Then the band plays "The Wee Small Hours" and it's just my parents, dancing alone to Sinatra, cheek to cheek in the center of the dance floor, while the caterers clean up and Russ, Claire, and I eat miniature chocolate truffle cakes with our fingers. Stephen is off to the side, trapped in a typically endless conversation with Uncle Freddy that will last until one of us gets off our ass to rescue him.

"Shit," Claire says. "I think I lost an earring in the limo."

"What were you doing in the limo? Oh. Oh!"

"I know," she says, shaking her head incredulously. "He knows I've got a thing about him in a monkey suit."

"Well, if it means anything, I like him a lot more than I used to."

"Thanks," she says. "It doesn't." She leans her head on my shoulder, squeezing the fleshy part of my hand between her thumb and forefinger.

"How does it feel to see him?" I say.

"I don't know. I'm too hormonally fucked to be sure of anything."

"It's okay to be unsure."

"Are you sure?"

"I'm serious. Maybe the thing is to just take it slow," I say. "Feel your way."

"I'm not exactly famous for my even keel," Claire says.

I lick some chocolate frosting off my finger. "People can change," I say.

Claire decides to come home with Russ and me, but arranges to meet Stephen for lunch tomorrow. Out in the parking lot, it's gotten chilly, and the steam comes off our warm bodies as we say our good-byes. My mother hugs me and presses her forehead against mine. "It's good that you came," she says.

"I'm glad I did."

"Are you going to be okay?"

"Yeah. A few days, and I'll be good as new."

"That's not what I meant," she says.

"I know, Mom. I'll be fine."

"Really?"

"Really."

She gives Russ a peck on the cheek. "You take care of my boy, you hear me?"

"You got it, Mrs. Parker."

"For God's sake, I think you can call me Eva by now."

"Okay, Eva."

My father looks tired, but happy. "Some party, huh?" he says.

"It was a blast," I say, stepping into his perfect hug.

"You give Hailey my best," he says, patting my back.

I hold on to him for an extra few seconds and then say, "I will, Dad."

Rudy takes the wheel, and my parents climb into the backseat of the Audi. My mother rests her head on my father's shoulder, and as they pull away, I see his tuxedo-clad arm emerge from the window, palm down, fingers spread to ride the wind as the car picks up speed and heads down the road, disappearing into the surrounding trees.

41

I HAD A WIFE. HER NAME WAS HAILEY. NOW SHE'S GONE. And so am I.

A few weeks after Debbie's wedding, on a soggy gray Monday, I sit down at my computer and type those words onto a blank screen. Kyle has negotiated a deal with a major house and, after a few days of soul-searching, I've decided that it's time I got back to work. I have no outline, no guide other than the four-page proposal Kyle wrote and signed my name to, and the twelve columns I wrote for *M* that were the basis of the deal. A few days ago, I sat in a conference room high above the city while Perry Manfield, the acquiring editor, brandished a rolled folio of my columns and called the by-product of my ruined life "great stuff."

I won't exactly be getting wealthy off the advance, but then again, I'm going to be wealthy anyway, and besides, that's not really the point. I've got Russ to think about now, and even though we don't need the money, I don't think it would be setting a particularly good example for him if I sat around scratching my balls all day. The book will be a memoir chronicling the mess I made of things after Hailey died. I'm not terribly eager to relive that time, but in the final analysis, it's the best way I can think of to keep her alive. Because I know now that the pain will inevitably fade, I can already feel it happening, like dying embers at the edge of a bonfire, turning a lifeless gray and disintegrating into the breeze. Knowing that there is a published record of us will go a long way toward helping me to let go, or that's the theory anyway.

So now I'm officially an author. I have a contract, an editor, a new laptop, a deadline, and no idea of how to write this thing. But it's a strange and not entirely unpleasant feeling, having something to do again. I sit at the desk in my bedroom, with the hard autumn rain pounding on the roof, clattering like applause on the metal top of the air compressor on the side of the house, and I look out the window and organize my thoughts.

I had a wife. Her name was Hailey. Now she's gone. And so am I.

That's all I've got so far. But I've got a year to write the rest, and it's not like I have any shortage of material. I'll come up with something.

To celebrate the book deal, Russ drives me to the tattoo parlor, where I commission a smaller version of Hailey's comet to be placed on the inside of my right wrist. This way, no matter where I am, I'll be able to flick my wrist and see it and remember that she's a part of me. I know that sounds corny as hell, but it just feels right to be marked by her. I explain my reasoning to Russ while the tattoo artist snaps on his latex gloves and starts scrubbing my arm with alcohol.

"Makes sense," Russ says.

"Which begs the question," I say. "Why did you put yours on your neck?"

"I don't know. It just seemed like a cool place for a tattoo."

"But you can only see it by twisting your neck in the mirror, and then you're bending it out of shape."

"Good point. I'll have to get another one like yours."

"The hell you will."

It's a very respectable tattoo parlor, sandwiched in a strip mall between a bakery and a dry cleaner, and the tattooist looks like your grandfather, with a ring of white hair around his bald, freckled dome of a head, a kind, thin-lipped smile, and a lumberjack shirt under his apron.

"You have no tattoos," I say, looking down at his pristine forearms.

"The cobbler's children go barefoot," he says, powering up the needle. "How are you with pain?"

Russ and I look at each other and smile.

The nights can be rough. They used to be the easiest part of the day for me, the only time the pain would fade to a dull throb. There was less of a sense of the world continuing outside your windows, of people going about their lives, of time marching on, of you being sidelined from everything by the immense load of your grief. Also, by nightfall I was usually drunk. I don't keep any booze in the house anymore. Pot, either, for the record. So now I'm a clean and sober stepfather with nothing to take the edge off the witching hour.

I walk into Russ's room and he quickly flips off his computer monitor. There is a girl now. I'm learning about her in small in-crements, but it's still on a need-to-know basis. He's not yet comfortable talking about her, and I don't want to pry. I'm happy for him, but it's little things like this, turning off his moni-tor when I walk into the room, that remind me that no matter how chummy we are, I'm still the guardian and he's still the kid, and as much as we may blur the lines, they are still immutably there. I know that's probably a good thing, but I'd be lying if I said it didn't hurt a little. I've only been his stepfather again for a few weeks, and I'm already sad about the little pieces of him that I'll inevitably lose.

"How's it going?" I say.

"Swell."

"Want to go to a movie?"

"Can't," he says. "Homework."

"Fine. Be that way."

"Why don't you call Ms. Hayes?"

"Yeah."

"Why not?"

"She made it pretty clear she doesn't want to hear from me."

"You're going to let a minor detail like that stop you?"

I think about Brooke from time to time, and by "from time to time" I mean pretty much all the time. I look for her when I drive Russ to school, I deliberately drive past her Brady Bunch house several times a day, and I sit in the movie theater by my-self, wondering if this will be the day she comes. I calculate the odds, days of the week, number of movies playing in the multi-plex. It's something of a long shot. I consider leaving her a mes-sage to let her know when I'm going and which movie I'll be at, but then I see her expression when she said good-bye to me, and I can't bring myself to dial her number.

"You know," Claire says to me over coffee and water at Starbucks a few days later, "a therapist would probably tell you that it's a marked improvement that you're pining over a living woman now, instead of a dead one."

"That's why I don't go to therapy. Too much useless information."

"What's that on your wrist?"

"I got a tattoo."

"You did not!"

I show her Hailey's comet, streaking across the inside of my wrist. "That's amazing," she says, running her fingers over it. "You're so counterculture."

"I'm edgy."

"You're dark and dangerous."

"Tell me about it."

"Now I'll have to get one."

"Why?"

"You can't be the only one. It upsets the whole balance."

"I don't know, Claire. A tattoo is a pretty big commitment."

"What are you saying?"

"Nothing. How are things with Stephen?"

"Okay, I guess," she says. "We have a lot of sex now. And then we talk about the sex. We rate it. We designate areas for improvement. But soon I'll be a fat horse, and then we won't have very much sex, and we'll have to come up with something else to talk about."

"Well, you will have a child," I say. "There might be something to talk about there."

"Could be."

"So, are you going to move back home?"

"I don't know," she says, looking sadly out the window. "I kind of like things the way they are now."

There has never been any helping Claire. For whatever reason, my beautiful, brilliant sister will always struggle against her own deeply ingrained compulsion to repeatedly slash and burn and rise from the ashes. She will always mistrust her own happiness, will feel compelled to subvert it, and realizing this makes me feel sad and old.

"Do you love him?"

"I think so."

"Well, that's good."

"You think I should move back in, right?"

"You'll know when the time is right."

"Bullshit."

"Okay. I'll tell you when the time is right."

"Thanks."

"The time is right."

"Oh, fuck off."

And so we go, back and forth, thrust and parry, pro and con, and none of it matters because I have no wisdom to impart and Claire is Claire and I'm me and we'll both always be defective to some degree. Maybe it's the price we have to pay for never having had to be whole on our own because we always had each other to fill in the gaps. Whatever it is, I don't like knowing that she'll never be truly happy, but all I can do is hope that maybe becoming a mother will wake something up in her, activate some long-dormant contentment gene. Or maybe it will be the thing that pushes her over the edge. I'd like to say I'm hopeful, but I'm still holding off turning the spare room into an office.

Late one chilly night, I drive over to Stop and Shop to stock up on groceries. The lot looks haunted, with only a handful of cars and abandoned shopping carts rattling back and forth across the pavement propelled by the strong autumn wind, like the ghosts of shoppers past. I'm about to step out of my car when I see Laney a few rows over, loading her bags into the back of her minivan. It was inevitable, I guess. I do my shopping at night to avoid people, and I guess she does too now. She's dressed in jeans, heels, and a clinging white sweater, and seeing her makes me inexplicably nervous. I slouch down in my seat, hoping she won't see me. Mike told me that she and Dave are in counseling, but they're sleeping in separate bedrooms and the prognosis is not good. I think of Laney's little girl, hugging me tightly as I carried her to her bed, and I know I'll always hate myself for this. I watch Laney wheel her cart over to the cart park, and I know I should just get out and say hello to her, I mean, we're going to run into each other at some point, but this lot is haunted and I'm paralyzed by a fear that makes no sense, and I don't stop shaking until I see her taillights light up and the minivan start to move. I've got a tattoo on my wrist to remind me of what I've lost, and I've got Laney Potter in parking lots to remind me of what I've done, and I'll just have to get used to it, but sometimes the absolute permanence of everything is like a tire iron to the skull.

I don't throw things at the rabbits anymore. After burying the one in my backyard, the least I can do is grant the rest of them full grazing rights, so his death will not have been in vain. They sit quivering on my lawn, sometimes alone, sometimes in groups of two or three, nibbling at grass, or just meditating on whatever it is that rabbits think about. The rabbits pay no attention to me, do not cast accusing glances in my direction as I feared they might, do not seem to connect me at all to the dark fate that befell their brother. The rabbits know that sometimes shit just happens, and there's nothing anyone can do about it. So they graze, and I watch them, and it would be nice to think that we're all maybe a little wiser than we were before.

And that's what I'm doing on Thursday afternoon, sitting by my open bedroom window in front of my laptop, watching a lone rabbit resting in the shadow of the giant ash tree and tinkering with my ever-changing outline, when the phone rings. "Doug? It's Brooke."

Her voice is an aria, and the little hairs on my arms perform a standing ovation. "Hey," I say. I stand up and pace the room nervously.

"I'm calling about Russ," she says quickly, heading me off at the pass.

"What about him?"

"He stole the driver's ed car."

"What?"

"He somehow pinched the keys out of Coach Warren's jacket and now he's gone."

"That's unbelievable."

"I don't want to involve the police yet, but it's been twenty minutes, and he's not a licensed driver. He could get hurt. Or hurt someone."

"I know," I say, my mind racing. "Where the hell is he going?"

"I was hoping you could tell me."

Outside, a car beeps loudly to the beat of "Shave and a Haircut." "Hold on a minute," I say. "Is it a white Corolla?"

"Yes."

"Don't call the police. I'll have it back to you in fifteen minutes."

When I get downstairs, Russ is leaning against the car, grinning from ear to ear. "My first solo flight," he says. "Am I good, or what?"

"Why the hell would you steal the driver's ed car?"

"It's a manifestation of my lingering grief?"

"You could have been arrested."

"It was an acceptable risk."

"You don't get it. You're in deep shit now."

"It was this, or get into another fight. And I've renounced violence, for the time being."

"But what were you trying to accomplish?" I say, exasperated.

"I don't know. I'm just a stupid kid."

"That you are. And we're going back there right now."

"I'll drive," he says, and I flash him my dirtiest look. He shrugs and tosses me the keys, which I snatch angrily out of the air. "Fine," he says, and then looks at me appraisingly. "You're not going to wear that, are you?"

"What?"

"That T-shirt has a big hole in the armpit. Go put a sweater on. And brush your hair, for fuck's sake, it looks like you slept in it." He leans in and sniffs me. "You know what, just take a quick shower. I'll wait."

"What the hell are you talking about?"

And then he smiles at me, my crazy, beautiful, fucked-up stepson, and understanding dawns. "She's looking very good today, Doug. I saw her in her office."

"You're insane."

"The course of true love is never straight."

"I can't believe you did this."

"Why not?" he says. "It's exactly like something I would do."

I stand there scratching my head like an idiot for a minute, and then I shake my head at him and smile. "Give me five minutes."

"Make it ten. And wear the blue cable crewneck. It matches your eyes."

"Okay, now you're just being weird."

"Sorry."

On the drive over to the school we sing along to The Clash at the top of our lungs with the windows open. We sing the guitar solos note for note, we bang out the drumbeats on the dashboard in perfect time, we harmonize on-key when it's called for. No one can do it like we do. Our instincts are impeccable, our chemistry sublime. Drivers at stoplights stare at us, awestruck, as we play and sing our hearts out.

I'm not expecting anything too dramatic. There will be no impassioned speeches, no falling into arms, no holding up of boom boxes in the rain outside her window, no long, seminal kisses in the hallway while the gathered students cheer. But maybe seeing me will remind her that there was something nice about what we were just starting to have, something easy and real, and seeing her will fill me with the fortitude to try to see her again. Maybe we'll exchange a look, or a laugh, something that will cause the ground beneath us to shift just enough to make me feel okay about leaving her a message the next time I go to the movies alone. And maybe something in my eyes, or in my voice, will let her know that it would be okay for her to come, that I'm a better bet now than I was then. At this point in my life, I'm not looking for any happy endings. I'm just looking to get things started.

The song ends, the DJ jabbers like a windup toy, and Russ flips off the radio. In the sudden quiet, I catch myself thinking that I'll tell Hailey about how funny it is when Russ and I sing in the car. It still happens like that sometimes, even now, like a conditioned reflex that can't be unlearned, and a wave of acute melancholy washes over me. Russ starts to say something but then stops, sensing my change in mood, and we ride in companionable silence the rest of the way. I guess that's how it's going to be now, long stretches of noise punctuated by occasional moments of silence, like the gap between songs. And there's something comforting in knowing that Hailey will be there, waiting for me in the silence, while I'm out here with Russ, living in the noise.

I turn into the school lot and throw the car into park. Then we just sit for a minute.

"You think I'll get suspended?"

"I know you will."

He shrugs. "It was for a good cause."

He needs a haircut, but I'm not going to be the one to tell him. Outside, the sky has gone completely gray and a strong wind whips around the car, sending crisp, brittle leaves and crushed cigarette boxes skittering animatedly across the asphalt. It's going to be getting cold soon.

"You know," I say, sitting back in my seat. "You're allowed to be happy."

Russ nods thoughtfully, looking straight ahead. "So are you."

"I know."

We look at each other for a long moment, and then back outside at the changing weather. The air between us suddenly feels charged, like the last instant of silence before the overture begins. We are young, slim, sad, and beautiful, and anything can happen.

"Okay," I say. "Let's do this."

We open our doors simultaneously and step out into the wind.